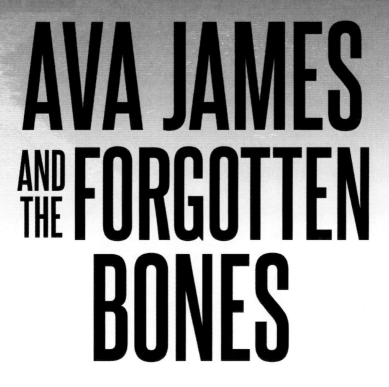

AVA JAMES

AND THE FORGOTTEN

BONES

A.J. RIVERS

PROLOGUE

5 Years Ago…

"**9**11, WHAT'S YOUR EMERGENCY?"
"Someone's broken into my house. Oh, my gosh! I just heard a shot!"
"What's your address?"
"509 Pleasant Hill Drive, Hidden Cove, Kentucky."
"Okay, ma'am, the police are on their way. Stay calm and lock the door to the room you're in, and please stay on the line with me until they arrive."

⌁

Two cruisers fired up the forest-bordered road into Hidden Cove. The red and blue lights painted the surroundings in great bold strokes as the sirens warbled and split the normal calm of the backcountry community.

Officers Tate and Milhorn were first on the scene. Weapons drawn, they moved toward the house. Dusk had fallen. The cruiser lights were the only source of illumination outside. Shadows jigged and danced in the strobe of the bar lights, making everything seem suspect.

Officers Upton and Gouge came to a skidding stop in the gravel just shy of the other cruiser. They joined the other two officers on the wrap-around porch.

Adrenaline pumped, nerves twanged, and senses were heightened as Milhorn shoved the partially opened door inward.

Tate announced, "Police!" and the others swung in behind them.

Amber lamplight glowed from the corners of the living room to their left. A man lay face-down in front of the fireplace. Blood pooled darkly around his shoulders and head.

Making quick work of it, they cleared the first floor, establishing that no one was there but them. At the top of the stairs, Tate and Milhorn turned right toward the master suite and another bedroom, both lit by overhead lights. Upton and Gouge turned left toward the bathroom and the adjacent room, the small nightlights at their entries giving them a haunted glow.

But there was nothing there.

Tate motioned to Milhorn as they approached the master bedroom doorway. A cordless phone lay on the floor just beyond the threshold.

Two minutes later, the entirety of the second floor had been cleared.

Tate spoke to emergency dispatch, confirming that the phone had dropped the call minutes before they arrived.

The four officers cordoned off the outside perimeter and waited for forensics to show up. Detective Rogers was already there.

"What happened?" he asked Tate.

"Homeowner's dead in front of the fireplace in the living room. ID'd as Dustin Johnson. His wife, Katherine, is missing. There was no sign of her or the perpetrator."

"You searched attic to basement and everything in between?"

Annoyed, Tate nodded. "Yes. Twice. There's nobody alive in there."

"Signs of forced entry?"

"Not that I saw."

Detective Rogers nodded, looking over Tate's shoulder toward the house. "Scene has been secure since you all came out, right?"

"Not a rookie here, detective. Everything by the book." Tate gritted his teeth and stared beyond the strobing cruiser lights toward the complete blackness of the woods.

"Good man, Tate. Why don't you and Milhorn run along and start on the paperwork now? I think I can handle this until forensics gets here."

∽

Four months later...

With a feeling of failure and emptiness, Detective Rogers watched as the last of the evidence bags was sealed and placed in the box with the rest of the items from the Johnson file. With no leads, barely anything in the evidence department, and Mrs. Johnson still missing, they had no choice but to label it as a cold case and move on.

Detective Rogers was kicking himself for it. He wanted more than anything to find Mrs. Johnson, but with the leads cold, there was simply nowhere else for him to go. He'd had no other choice but to ship it off to the FBI. No progress had been made in months of searching.

Detective Rogers wasn't consoled by the fact the case was still open and just considered cold, but he knew there were other cases on his desk that could be solved and closed. How long the Johnson file would languish in storage gathering dust, he did not know.

It was in the hands of the FBI, and he knew if any law enforcement entity could solve it, it would be them. That gave him some hope as he hung his head and walked away.

CHAPTER ONE

Now…

AVA JAMES DIALED HER FATHER'S NUMBER, LOOKED AT THE SCREEN, and back to the pile of cold cases she had been assigned to go through. Her father was expecting a call from her within the day, but she didn't know what to tell him.

"*Hi, Dad. I know Mom's missing and all, but the Bureau refuses to let me go to Africa to help look for her. Sorry. I know you hoped for better from your daughter, the useless FBI agent.*"

Yeah, she thought angrily. *Not happening. Not right now, anyway.*

She closed the app and shoved the phone back into her pocket. "Well, backlogs, what do you say we get good and acquainted? I might even let you spend the night if you're nice. Maybe we'll go out for coffee later. Who knows? Maybe we'll even celebrate New Year's Day together if we're both still here, which I highly suspect we will be."

With a groan, she picked up a stack of files and moved to her seat behind the desk. Her task was to narrow down the cases to a handful she thought she could successfully close out in a timely manner.

She had asked Supervisor Fullerton what exactly he'd meant by a 'timely manner'. He had shrugged and said, "Just so you can close them is the main part."

"I thought the Cold Case Initiative was only for cases that were thirty and forty years old, or older. Some of the ones I've looked at in these," she had motioned toward the pile on top of the filing cabinet, "are only a few years old. Like five and ten years."

Supervisor Fullerton, Max to his friends outside of work, and always Fullerton to Ava because she didn't think they would ever be on first name terms, had raised a hand and put his thumb on one temple, his middle finger on the other. She was annoying him.

Probably not a good idea since she had been yanked out of the field, reassigned out from Supervisor Martinez, and put on cold cases, but she couldn't seem to stop herself. She was angry. Her mother was missing, and she was plenty upset.

"Agent James, you have been given an assignment. Is there a reason, a *good* reason that you cannot fulfill your assignment? Are you in the hospital, knocking on death's door?"

Ava had looked to the floor. "No, sir."

Maybe annoying Fullerton hadn't been such a good idea.

"Are you currently active in the field on some mission of which I was unaware when I gave you this assignment?"

"No, sir." *Way to rub salt in the wound, thank you, sir,* she'd thought, but knew better than to say.

"No, sir is right. You were put in the Cold Case Initiative Unit to do a job. I would suggest that you do that job. Does it really matter if the cases are decades old or just a few years old? Justice needs to be served, families need closure, and you need to clear out as many of these as you can."

That had been several weeks ago.

The 'maybe solvable' pile had grown slowly to fifteen files. That meant fifteen or more boxes of evidence and other items she would have to go through.

Lifting from the cold stack again, she moved toward the desk. Sitting there, she stared at the coffee-stained manila folder on top without opening it.

Her coffee had gone cold, her stomach rumbled, and a small headache had come to life at the base of her skull.

The clock said it was still shy of lunchtime, much to her chagrin. At least lunch would be an excuse to get out of her tiny, windowless office for a while. So what if the December weather was miserably cold? So what if the ground, where not covered in snow, was mushy, muddy, and treacherous? Even that beat sitting in the office all day. The day had already seemed a year long.

Just one more, and then lunch, she told herself silently.

The words on the first page just wouldn't compute. Her attention was shot. Her mother was still missing, and that ate up all her mental faculties for such tasks as concentrating on anything else for more than a few minutes at a time. It had been that way ever since she learned her mother had disappeared on her UN trip to Africa.

She pulled out her phone for the second time, looked at the clock on the wall, and then dialed her father's number.

This time, she actually punched the little green button and put the phone to her ear.

"Hi, Dad," she said when he answered.

"Hello, sweetheart. I was waiting for you to call. I figured it would be later, though. Everything all right?"

Hank sounded strained. Her heart hurt, she wanted to erase that sound from his voice.

"Yeah, yeah, Dad. Everything's fine. Just finished up some work and had a few minutes before lunch. Thought I'd call and check in." Which wasn't all she had in mind. She just had to figure out how to start the barrage of questions without ramping up that terrible strained sound from him. "How are you feeling today? Did you eat breakfast? Did you sleep last night?"

"Whoa! Slow down with the interrogation, Agent James." He chuckled, but it sounded hollow and humorless, as if he were faking the amused sound for her benefit alone.

"Dad?"

"Yes, dear?"

"You didn't answer my question."

"There were so many. Which one, Aviva?"

She rolled her eyes at her father's counter. The prominent prosecutor was an expert at avoiding subjects he didn't want to discuss.

"Your choice."

"Okay, then. Um. Yes."

She laughed. He could be obstinate. And everyone wondered where she got that particular trait from. In her opinion, her family was chock full of it. "Yes, to which one?"

"Oh, I forgot you didn't take clairvoyance class at the Academy. Yes, I slept."

The banter continued for another eight minutes or so, and her father's mood seemed to have improved a bit. Ava decided to just jump in with the questions about her mother.

"So, Dad, can I ask you a few questions about Mom?"

There was a long sigh from his end. "Shoot. Just take it one at a time, though."

"Did you know ahead of time that Mom was going to Africa?"

"Ah, she gave me a two-day warning. You know this. We've been over all this, Aviva."

"I know. I'm just doing what I do, Dad. Bear with me, please."

"All right. I know you're as worried about her as I am. I just have to know something, though."

"Anything."

"Are you doing anything you've been told not to do? Are you planning on doing something crazy? You're a federal agent, Aviva. Your mother wouldn't want you to jeopardize your career, and maybe get into some serious trouble to boot."

"I'm not doing anything of the sort. I just..." she let her voice trail off. She just what? Had to drag her dad and herself through the same questions yet again? Had to wallow in the pain and frustration of nothing new ever coming up in these sessions?

"Honey, I know. Me, too. It's all I think about day in and day out. I've been over the weeks and days and hours leading up to her leaving the house. I've replayed the last conversation we had after she landed. She didn't give a hint of anything suspicious going on. If she had, you'd be the first person I would have told."

"I just want to go look for her. I know I could find *something* if they'd just send me in. Who knows her better than me? Who could get into her headspace and trace her likeliest steps if certain scenarios happened? Me. I understand why they won't send me, but then again, I don't understand when I could be so much of a help."

Tears stung the backs of her eyes. She squeezed them shut and leaned back in her chair. No time for crying. Not now.

In his usual calm manner, her father said, "Aviva, honey, you know exactly why they can't have you working on this case. You're too close. There's too much of a risk that you could jeopardize your safety, the safety of others, and the case. It happens. The rules are in place for a reason."

"I know, but that doesn't make it any easier to sit here and do nothing but read cold case files all day every day. They stuck me here to keep me out of the field. They think I can't handle being out there because Mom's missing. If they're not going to let me look for her officially, then I *need* to be in the field. I feel like I've already been in this cracker-box-sized office for a year this morning. A week is nearly unbearable to think about. I need to do something."

"Then do your job, Aviva."

It was the same thing Fullerton had said. But when her father said it, it made sense to her. She understood instead of becoming angered. He was right, of course. She just needed to do her job. Lose herself in her work.

"Thanks, Dad. You're right. That's what I need to do, and God knows I've got enough here to keep me busy for a while."

"That's my girl. I love you."

"Love you, too, Dad. Talk later."

They hung up, and Ava forgot about lunch. She forgot about getting out of the office and about Fullerton's attitude toward her. She forgot about everything for a while and read the case file in front of her.

Something niggled at her memory as she read over the documents. The names of the victims? She didn't think so. She picked up the paper and read it again, paying extra attention to the details.

"That's it! This house was in the news recently," she announced to the empty room. She pulled out her phone and did a quick search of the address, calling up a local news story.

"509 Pleasant Hill Drive," she murmured to herself, hoping that at least her own voice could fill the silence and make things pass a little easier.

The article itself was of little substance, mostly consisting of a direct transcript of what had been on the 30-second local news spot. But it was enough to jog her memory.

Recently, a young couple had been murdered in the house. Their three-year-old daughter had been found hidden under a stack of blankets in the master bathroom closet, crying. Her mother lay shot dead in the master bedroom, her father downstairs in the living room.

But that was not the case she was reading about. The cold case file in her hands had happened five years ago, when Dustin Johnson, and his wife, Katherine Johnson, lived in the house. They were roughly the same age as the recent couple, in their mid-twenties. Dustin had been found shot dead in front of the fireplace in the living room, and his wife had never been found. Neither had the murder weapon. Nor was there ever a good suspect. There wasn't a child involved in that case.

"Why would two young couples fall victim to murder in the same house five years apart?" She read the rest of the file, scribbling names and pertinent details in a small notepad.

With renewed interest in her current assignment, Ava put the file on top of the ones she would take on. She would run it by Fullerton. If he gave her the all-clear, she would pull up stakes and go to Kentucky for a while.

CHAPTER TWO

VA LUGGED THE BOXES FROM THE JOHNSON INVESTIGATION INTO her bedroom. She'd been told over and over again that it was a bad idea to work on cases in the same room she was supposed to use for sleeping, but she'd never listened. She was comfortable in there, and she could spread everything out on the bed around her where everything was within arm's reach. Files and evidence made for uncomfortable bedmates, but she didn't mind as much as she probably should.

She set the three boxes on the floor at the foot of the bed and decided to wait until the morning to really dig in. Fullerton had given permission for her to do whatever she needed to solve the case. Even he couldn't deny the strange similarities between the cold case and the new one.

Both were murdered in the same house, of course, but it went deeper than that. Both sets of victims were around the same age. Both male victims had been found in the living room near the fireplace.

It went even deeper than that. The first set of victims, and the recent ones, had the same initials. Dustin Johnson, Katherine Johnson. Derrick Jakobson, Krystal Jakobson. Maybe just a weird coincidence, but there it was on paper, in black-and-white, staring her in the face. She couldn't rightly ignore it.

It made Ava think of something her mentor, Agent Emma Griffin, had said to her long ago:

"There are no such things as coincidences."

Ava had called the Hidden Cove Police Department before making the long drive from her office through the dense woods. All the arrangements were in place for her visit on Monday. She would have two days to go over everything in the boxes with a fine-toothed comb before heading to the rural community for the boots-on-the-ground investigation.

Part of her figured that Fullerton had no faith she could really solve the case. He had been in charge when the FBI was called in years ago. That made her more determined. He was going to just send her in alone, but Ava bristled at that. It took some doing, but she was able to at least convince him to send one agent as backup. Said he couldn't afford to send anyone else. They were working extra hours as it was to solve as many of the cold cases, most of them much colder than five years, as was possible.

Politics and funding had always played, and always would play, a big part in any superior's decisions in such matters. Ava understood, but didn't like it. The pure detective in her railed against such insults.

After getting ready for bed, Ava flipped back the covers and lay on her back, hands behind her head, staring up into the darkness and listening to the snow peck at the windows as the wind whipped against the house.

Thoughts of her mother wouldn't leave her head. Where had she gone? Was she safe? Was she undercover for some reason or was she in danger? There was no way to know.

She knew her mother was a UN ambassador. She was more than capable of handling herself. But Ava couldn't help the way her mind reeled, throwing catastrophe after catastrophe into the realm of possibilities.

She was used to such panicked thoughts. Ever since that fateful day, just after turning 18, that she and her best friend Molly had been abducted by mysterious strangers off the streets in Prague. They'd locked her up in a room, ready to do God knows what to her. The memory still made her shudder. Somehow she'd managed to escape, but she'd never found her best friend. Even now, all these years later, she could only pray that Molly wasn't suffering.

She tossed and turned, trying in vain to relax completely. The fine muscles in her upper back spasmed. She took several deep breaths and forced her eyes closed. There was no insatiable need for sleep to claim her, she only wanted to relax her body. The hope that her mind would follow suit was there, but she had pinned no requirement on it.

Elizabeth James' disappearance might have something to do with the murders at her sister-in-law Kay's celebration gala. What had been meant as a beautiful showcase on an opulent island had turned into a bloody mess of betrayal and murder. In the process of the investigation, Ava had upturned a vast criminal network of international drug and human traffickers secretly using the charity Kay worked for as a front. Could it be possible that some member of the organization had escaped capture and was now orchestrating a revenge plot?

At least, that was one worry Ava had. One of about a hundred thousand. But her mind kept dredging the bottom of the bucket where all the worst fears lay, and that her mother had been taken as some form of revenge kept coming up.

She had copies of all the files and notes from that case. She kept them in a box in the front of her closet where they were easily accessible whenever she had the urge to look up something, which seemed to be often.

Ava rolled to her right side, facing away from the closet, and tucked her right arm under her pillow. Again, she forced her eyes to close and willed her body to relax.

It had been put forth to her, mostly from well-meaning friends outside the Bureau, that something totally mundane might have happened to her mother while she was in South Africa. Absolutely impossible in Ava's estimation. Mundane things don't just happen to UN officials and their families never hear from them again.

If there had been a car wreck, a health issue, a mugging, anything of the 'mundane' sort, for one, it would have made the headline news. Two, her colleagues and superiors would have been notified immediately, and then her family.

It had been too long for that to be a possibility.

Ava huffed and flipped onto her stomach, keeping her head turned from the closet and the temptation to get up and go through all the paperwork again. She had been through it at least a hundred times, and there was never anything new. Evidence wouldn't appear no matter how much she willed it to do so. Her wishes went unanswered in that department.

She could draw no new conclusions that made sense. Why her mother had simply vanished was beyond her, but it had to be something bad.

Very bad, indeed.

Elizabeth James was one of the most solid and dependable people Ava knew. She would never go so long without finding a way to get in contact with someone in her family. No matter what happened, Elizabeth would contact at least her husband or daughter. Unless something terrible had taken place and she wasn't able to get to a phone to make a call or a piece of paper to write a letter.

Or she wasn't able.

A tear slipped down the side of Ava's nose and dripped to the pillow. "Mom, where are you?"

In Prague, while Ava and Molly had been missing, Elizabeth and Hank had been relentless in their efforts to find the girls. Elizabeth had taken no guff from anyone involved. She had bravely set out on foot to the streets herself over the objections of her bosses, showing photos and questioning anyone she thought might have seen them. She threw herself in harm's way to find the girls, no matter how sketchy the people were, no matter how shady the place was. The police couldn't keep her from it. Hank couldn't have stopped her either. Her father was a formidable force when he needed to be, but even he would have been no match for her mother.

If the tables had been turned—and once upon a time, many years ago in Prague, they had been—Elizabeth would never take no for an answer from her superiors, or from anyone else, to get a message out to her family. She would beat the streets and use every resource available to her whether they were deemed strictly legal or not.

Although Ava wanted, perhaps needed, to break down, she refused. Instead, she threw back the covers, flipped to her side, and sat on the edge of the bed facing the closet.

She still considered that she could use the backing of the Bureau in finding her mother. If the time came that they would agree to let her help, she wanted to be in their good graces. Whoever had caused her mother's disappearance, no matter the outcome, would feel the full force of the United States Federal Bureau of Investigation.

The pull of the small cardboard box in the closet containing the Ivy Grove case was strong, but she knew where that road would lead. She would be sitting in the middle of her bed, papers flung all around her, frustrated to the point of tears when the sun came up.

But her newest assignment sat at the foot of the bed merely three feet away. She could delve in and not regret it if the sun rose and caught her red-handed with those files. After all, that was the case she was supposed to be investigating.

And that's just what she did.

She took out her little notepad, obsessively checking and double-checking all her information, and then ripped out the pages to reorganize her notes. She drew up every possible connection she could think of between the two cases, pored over the evidence, and read the files over and over again until she knew them back to front. Once satisfied, she stretched and slid off the side of the bed to stand in the warm shaft of morning light pouring through her window.

Rubbing her eyes, she assessed the mess on her bed. Papers were strewn about as if a child had thrown a tantrum in the center. The files radiated outward, forming a starburst design. The evidence bags lay in two concentric half-circles toward the foot. The empty boxes were tumbled on the floor, their lids helter-skelter a bit farther away.

"That's going to take a hot minute or two to clean up," she muttered wryly as she walked to the bathroom.

Her reflection showed a woman aged beyond her years with dark circles under her eyes and a sallow complexion. The lack of sleep had done her no favors mentally or physically. She took enough time to apply a bit of concealer under her eyes to hide the dark spots. Questions about her health were the last things she wanted to deal with.

As she replaced all the files and evidence bags, she held the flash drive with the emergency call on it. It was the recording from five years earlier. She had not taken the time to listen to it, but she would.

Hearing the woman's voice would make her seem all the more real to Ava. Not that she didn't think of the victims in such cases as real, but hearing a voice made it easier. She would no longer be just a name in a file or a picture on a newspaper article.

For the moment, she had other things to do.

CHAPTER THREE

AVA LOOKED OVER THE LIST OF PEOPLE INTERVIEWED IN THE COLD case. There were many. As a base list, she had written:

Dustin Johnson—victim, deceased, gunshot wound to chest and shoulder

Katherine (Ray) Johnson—Dustin Johnson's wife, missing

Jack Kearns—being sued by Dustin at time of murder, preventable injury, former friend of Dustin

Robert Mitchell—neighbor

Landscaper—Enrique Ponce

Greg Johnson—victim's brother

Cybil and Tom Ray—missing woman's parents (owned the house)

She sighed. It was pitifully short, but they were the people who would have the most information that might actually help her in piecing together what had happened.

The original list compiled by the responding detective was much longer and included friends and relatives of each of the ones she had listed on her paper. They had been interviewed as character witnesses in some instances, and in others, only to verify alibis. Every single person on the suspect list had been cleared as they had solid alibis.

Eventually, she had no doubt, she would interview everyone again. She would painstakingly recheck every alibi.

The contractor who had done some sort of renovations on the house during Dustin and Katherine Johnson's tenancy had been cleared first. Frank Lauter was a family man, sort of. He had a long-time girlfriend and they had a son together. Frank had said he was at home with his family the night of the murder, and his girlfriend Stephanie confirmed it. The agents had no reason to disbelieve his story. He was a known man in the area, and everyone seemed to have a good opinion of him, other than a few men thinking his work was less than stellar. For the price, apparently, he couldn't be beaten, though.

The neighbor, Robert Mitchell, had lived in his home for over twenty years. He had been married when he was twenty-five and divorced when he was twenty-seven. He never married again in all the years since. He was a private man who enjoyed his solitude. He had been night fishing on a lake three hours away the night of the murder.

Jack Kearns had been on vacation at the time of the murder. Although it sounded too convenient, the agents diligently checked his alibi. It had been noted that Jack Kearns was seen on CCTV footage in a Florida hotel bar the day before the murder.

Ava drew a small star by Jack's name. Before the murder, Dustin had been suing Jack for an injury that was Jack's fault. At least, according to Dustin. The injury left Dustin with permanent damage to his lower spine and his left leg, which caused him to walk with a limp, and he was in constant pain.

It hadn't been difficult to clear the family members of both victims. They all had families of their own, lives of their own, and had several witnesses to their whereabouts at the time.

Ava went back up the list and put a question mark beside Katherine Johnson's name. Was she a victim? A body had never been found. There was no blood or sign of a struggle. Nothing at the scene stuck out as her having definitively been the victim of any crime.

She could have been kidnapped, but just as easily, she could have been the murderer. She could have killed her own husband and then skipped town before anyone was the wiser. Ava wasn't discounting anything at this point.

Just because all of her family and her husband's family were adamant that she couldn't have done anything like that did not make it impossible. Improbable, but not impossible.

The last name on her list was Enrique Ponce, the landscaper. A note from the original case file said that Enrique owned a substantial landscaping company. He and his crew worked from daylight until dark all around Hidden Cove and the surrounding five counties all through the warm seasons. Their clientele included local banks, doctors' offices, retail stores, and residential homes. In the winters, they worked almost as much, clearing snow from driveways and parking lots, and even from rooftops.

Nobody had anything bad to say about Enrique, but Ava thought he might have seen or heard something suspicious in the days leading up to the murder. If someone had been watching the house to get a feel for the Johnsons' schedules, then perhaps Mr. Ponce would have noticed since he took care of the Johnsons' yard personally.

Ava's mind raced to find a likely suspect on the list, and she came up with nothing. If the detectives had done their jobs as proficiently as she hoped every detective did, everybody had alibis. And yet, the case remained unsolved.

Something was overlooked. It had to have been. There is no such thing as a perfect murder. There was always some small lead, inconsistency, or trace evidence that gave up the perpetrator.

It was up to her to find that missing piece, no matter how small, and solve the case.

She used her afternoon preparing for the extended trip to Kentucky. She packed light. There would be no need for many clothes, only the ones she wore for work and a few sleep outfits, but they needed to be warm. She knew mountain winters could be brutal.

After finishing her packing, she laughed at her one small suitcase with all her clothes and toiletries all crammed inside, making the soft-sided case bulge. Molly would have never believed how sparse it looked. When they had gone to Prague, both girls had taken trunks, bags, suitcases, makeup cases. Molly's mother had apologized profusely for the exorbitant amount of luggage her daughter was imposing on the James's.

Ava's dad had said, "That's mild compared to Elizabeth and Ava. I thought I was going to have to hire a moving truck to get it all to the airport."

Ava picked up a framed photo of her and Molly taken just the week before they went to Prague. She traced a finger over Molly's face. "I miss you, Mol."

She put the picture on top of her clothes in the suitcase. After a moment, she shook her head and put it back on the nightstand. It would be best to leave behind anything that could distract her from her current case.

Thoughts of both her mother and Molly had been reawakened. As she carried her case file bag and her suitcase to the front hall, she let the memories of them run free. Better to do that at home than in Kentucky.

The afternoon passed with Ava alternating between memories of her missing friend, her mother, and analyzing the case at hand.

By the time she called her father that evening to inform him of her impending trip, she was chomping at the bit to get to Hidden Cove and get her hands on the actual files. She didn't like navigating through the digital files, even though she was good at it. It was simpler for her to use the paper files. She much preferred to get her hands on the evidence instead of digitized pictures of it on her computer or phone screen.

"Hey, Dad. How are you this evening?" She flopped on the sofa and curled into the corner with her feet tucked close.

"As well as I can be, I guess. How about you? Did you take my advice yesterday?"

"I did. That's why I called, actually. I am doing my job."

He chuckled. "Okay, that's good. An FBI agent who is doing her job is always a good thing."

Although he couldn't see it, she grinned and rolled her eyes. "I mean, I found a case to work, Dad. It's in Kentucky, though, so I'll be heading out first thing Monday morning. I don't know how long I'll be there."

"Kentucky? Rural or city?"

"Oh, I think it's about as rural as you can get. Fullerton approved everything, and all the plans are in place. I have a decent hotel room booked indefinitely. And there is an officer already assigned to me from the local police department. Agent Sal Rossi will accompany me, too."

Hank had always worried whenever he thought she would be working a case alone. He said he didn't like the idea of his little girl out there all by herself, and it didn't matter if she had a gun and was adept at martial arts, she was his baby girl and he would always worry.

Ava wasn't sure how much it eased his worry that she would have two other people with her, but she hoped it would do him good to know it. Especially after what had happened to her mother—and herself, too.

"You just be extra careful out there, Aviva. You can ask your Uncle Ray how outsiders are viewed in some of the more rural places."

Again, she gave a slight eye roll. "Yes, Dad, I do know. I know firsthand. Don't worry, though, the officer is local and Sal has worked the area for over a decade. She knows her way around the locals. Besides, if I wanted to deal with city people all the time, I would have been a socialite, not an agent." It was her turn to chuckle.

"Still feisty. That's a good sign. You'll call me when you get there, right?"

That had usually been her mother's line. Just a short phone call or text to let her know Ava made it to her destination safely. A lump formed in Ava's throat, and she nodded. Realizing she was on the phone and he couldn't see her nod, she cleared her throat and said, "I will, Dad."

"All right. I love you, Aviva. Stay safe, warm, and don't you dare hesitate to call if you need anything."

"I love you, too, Dad."

She put the phone face-down on the sofa cushion and rested her head against the back. As she relaxed, flash-shots of the crime scene behind her eyelids caused her to flinch. She pushed those thoughts away with a sigh and tried to relax again, hoping it was a sign that she was falling asleep. Rest would be a most welcome guest.

The next time an image occurred, it wasn't so much of a flash. It lingered and turned into a dream. Dustin Johnson lay face-down in front of a cold fireplace, blood pooling around his shoulders and face. A ghostly forensic team collected evidence and shot pictures as she moved toward the body with a building sense of dread.

In the flash of a camera, the body was no longer Dustin Johnson. It had morphed into the body of Elizabeth James. Ava stopped in her tracks, her thighs turned to rubber, and she crumpled slowly to the floor, a scream trapped in her chest.

In the next camera flash, the body turned into that of her missing best friend, Molly. The tips of her blonde hair were floating in the puddle of blood.

The scream tore loose from Ava's chest and she flung herself forward on the sofa, waking just in time to catch her balance and not hit the floor.

Someone was screaming as she looked frantically around the room. The lingering dream fell over the room like a mirage. She finally realized the scream was coming from her own throat, and she clamped her mouth shut.

The dream evaporated, and she was sitting in her living room, perched on the edge of her couch with tears wetting her cheeks.

A quick glance at her phone screen told her that she had only been asleep for forty-five minutes at best.

CHAPTER FOUR

THE SUN CRESTED OVER THE HORIZON ON MONDAY MORNING, bringing life and warmth over the snow-dusted tree-tops, as if thinking it alone was enough to curb the buildup of December snow. The world was only beginning to wake, but Ava was already speeding down the interstate.

She hadn't slept much. The anticipation always got the better of her when she started working a new case. That it was a cold case mattered very little. In her mind, the active, recent investigation made it all the more nerve-wracking. She was certain the two were related. There were too many similarities evident from the sweeping overview of the new case she had access to.

She would have access to more files and, consequently, a more in-depth view of that case once she reached the Hidden Cove Police Department. The plan had been for her to arrive at the hotel around eleven that morning, and then go to HCPD and pick up the files along with her ride-along officer.

But it was barely eight AM and she didn't feel like waiting around for hours. The little difference in timing wouldn't be so bad, she thought. They could get an early start and pound the pavement instead of wasting half the day. She was sure they wouldn't mind getting going early.

But shortly after entering the station, she found out that idea had been wrong.

The officer at the front desk wasn't entirely displeased to see her, but he wasn't the most accommodating in the world either. It was like the man had a permanent scowl that seemed to darken somehow as she approached. Not wanting to play the time-honored game of chicken between local and federal law enforcement officials, Ava simply presented her badge to him and requested to speak to the chief. The man eyed her with a look somewhere between disdain and surprise and then left her there in the lobby to go talk to the chief.

Several minutes passed before she finally was allowed back and escorted to the chief's office. He was older, and surprisingly pretty tall. His face was red and coarse in the way that told Ava that he'd spent much of his life outdoors. His nondescript graying hair was beginning to thin at the top, but his eyes remained a bright, clear green. Much like the desk officer, his scowl also seemed permanently affixed to his face. He was drumming his fingers impatiently while listening to someone on the phone and looked none too pleased about her interrupting him. When she stepped into the room, he motioned for her to take a seat.

After ending his call, he grabbed his coffee cup, sloshing some of the dark liquid onto the papers on the blotter.

"Damn it," he grunted, picking up the papers and shaking the coffee off them onto the floor. Ava watched in silence, careful to keep the grin off her face.

His scowl deepened. "Do we have business this morning, ma'am?" He dried the papers against the leg of his jeans, still holding the cup of coffee aloft and to the side.

"Yes, sir. My name is Agent Aviva James from the Federal Bureau of Investigation." She offered her credentials.

Giving the badge a cursory glance, he nodded. "Tell me, does your birth certificate have your first name as Agent?" One silver eyebrow shot toward his receding hairline, and the ghost of a smirk played at the corner of his mouth.

Is this his sense of humor? she wondered as she put her badge away. Deciding to err on the side of humor, she chuckled and shook her head. "Not that I'm aware of, no."

Finished with his paper-drying episode, the chief lifted out of his seat just far enough to extend a hand over the desk. She shook it.

"I'm Chief Grady. Refresh my memory. What am I doing for you today?"

She thought about asking if his birth certificate listed his first name as Chief, and quickly decided against it. "Chief Grady, I'm supposed to pick up the evidence from the 509 Pleasant Hill double homicide. The one that happened a few months back."

He nodded. "That's right. I had forgotten about you coming to investigate it. We didn't request the FBI's involvement. Mind me asking why the Bureau's taken an interest in this case?"

"You did ask for the FBI's help with a similar case about five years ago, though," she pointed out. "As I understand it, that murder took place in the same house under eerily similar circumstances. I believe the two might be connected."

Chief Grady laughed. It was a big sound in the small office. "Well, I highly doubt that. Five years and two completely different families? Lotta years for a killer to wait for his next victims just so he could kill 'em in the same house. Don't you think?"

Curling her lips inward and pressing them together, she only arched her eyebrows. She didn't want to come off as combative on her first meeting with the local chief of police.

He shook his head. "I'll call evidence and see if they have your boxes pulled. The files will be in Detective Hopson's office. He's been working on it. Can't say he's too happy about the feds waltzing in and taking it from him, either."

He picked up the phone. Ava bristled. The feds didn't just waltz in anywhere and take over as if it were a dance and they were cutting in. She disliked that analogy, she hated the snide way PD anywhere used the phrase, and she loathed it when local law enforcement showed contempt for the Bureau. She was there to help. Why couldn't they understand that?

Local detectives were always swamped with cases, and that made it nearly impossible to devote a hundred percent to any single one.

If the tables had been turned, she thought she would have been thrilled to have the FBI helping her with cases. Of course, she wasn't in this line of work to make a name for herself as many local-level detectives were, either. She was in it to serve justice. She couldn't care less whose name got a gold star placed by it as long as they made the world safer.

Chief Grady huffed and shook his head as he hung up the phone. Taking another long draught of coffee, he smacked his lips and forced a smile. "Chev's on his way. He'll take you to evidence to get the boxes. Seems somebody decided to show up a few hours early and they hadn't pulled the stuff yet."

"Yes. I got an early start. Is that a problem?"

"Not for me, no. Not at all," he replied, though the way he said it made Ava somehow doubt that. He nodded toward the door where Chev stood. "Glad to meet you, Agent James. If you need anything else from us—"

Ava interrupted, "My ride-along. I'm supposed to pick up my ride-along so we can get started. And Agent Sal Rossi was supposed to meet me here. Has she been here yet?"

Chev spoke up. "I'm your ride-along." He extended his hand but not a smile. "Officer Chev Redding."

"Aviva James." She shook his hand and smiled. It was unreturned. He simply nodded once, gripped her hand, and let go.

"Come on, we'll go get those boxes. Hope you've got a big trunk."

"What about Agent Rossi?" she asked as she followed Redding down a long, narrow hallway.

He shrugged. "Can't say. Haven't seen hide nor hair of another fed today. May not show up until the scheduled meeting time." He turned sideways and pointedly looked to his watch. "Which is what? About three hours from now, would be my guess."

Fighting the urge to remind him who she was, Ava rolled her eyes after he turned around again. She remained silent until they had descended two flights of stairs and entered a dank corridor that felt more like a dungeon passage than a hall.

"You keep evidence down here in the dank and musty dark?"

Seeming to take offense, Redding stiffened. "Our coffers ain't as padded as those of the FBI. We're lucky that we have this basement to use as storage. And this only holds the evidence from the cases we are actively working on. Cold cases and old closed cases are shipped across town and stored in the basement of Town Hall."

"Doesn't the damp degrade the papers and boxes?" She thought it must if the items remained there for long.

"Nah. We don't keep anything down here long enough for that to happen. Not usually, anyway. I guess working for the Feds, you're used to bigger and better, but here in Hidden Cove, Nowhere, Kentucky, we're small. The town's small, the cases are usually small. Nothing we can do about that. Not that I'd want to change it at all. I like small just fine, and if you're gonna be here in our fine little town, I'd suggest you get used to it. We don't do things the way y'all do up in the big city."

For the second time in a half-hour, Ava bristled. She wanted to tell him it seemed as if there was some small-minded thinking going on in his fine little town, but she knew it would only escalate the situation. The last thing she needed was to be on bad terms with her ride-along. She wished Sal would hurry and put in her appearance. It would be nice to have another agent around who might understand the workings of the Bureau a bit better than Officer Chev Redding.

The officer in charge of the evidence didn't speak, didn't bother even making much eye contact with Ava as he unlocked the door and turned back to the paperwork he had been looking over.

The room was larger than Ava had imagined but smaller than most she had been in. Being a new agent, she hadn't been in many local PD evidence rooms, and the ones she had been in were central to larger counties and municipalities.

Officer Redding walked straight to the boxes labeled with the Johnsons' names and case number and pulled them from the shelf. He handed one to her and grabbed the other two. He carried them to the door and turned to her with an eyebrow raised. Taking his meaning, she moved past him and pulled the door open to let him step out first.

"Thank you," he said.

"You're welcome." She followed him back out of the basement area in silence.

They stopped outside Detective Hopson's office. "This is where you'll find the case file and any notes that go with it," Chev grinned and nodded toward the closed door. "I'll let you have the honor of disturbing Hopson."

Suppressing a huff of irritation, Ava knocked sharply on the door.

Without warning, the door was jerked inward hard enough that the inrush of air pulled her hair forward. Gasping, she took a step back to avoid what she thought was going to be a collision, and she nearly dropped her box.

A gruff, older man stood there looking highly displeased. "Well, don't just stand there and blink at me. I'm busy. What the hell you want?"

Chev snickered and stood against the wall, facing the opposite side of the hall.

"I'm Agent Aviva James with the FBI. I'm supposed to—"

The detective scoffed, rolled his eyes, and interrupted, "Yeah, yeah, yeah. I don't need the laundry list. Name was sufficient." He disappeared into the room.

Ava stepped to the threshold and watched as he yanked open a drawer on a tall filing cabinet, pulled out a thick file folder, slammed the drawer, and turned back to her. He tossed the folder onto his desk.

"There's all I got. I'm sure you'll tear into it like a starving dog on a raw steak, but that's totally up to you. My notes are in the back. Glad you could relieve me of some work." He shoved glasses onto his face and plopped back into his seat, pulling another file toward him.

"I think there's a connection between this case and—"

Without looking at her, he nodded and said, "A cold case. Which I had nothing to do with. Rogers was on the cold case. I got nothing for you there." He looked over the rim of his glasses at her. "You mind?" He pointed to the papers in front of him. "I need to work. I don't have the luxury of having my time wasted on something pointless."

Ava snatched the file and slammed it onto her box, a little angrier than she'd intended. "Pointless? You think it's pointless to solve cold cases, detective?"

He glared at her and stood slowly. "No, I do not, *Agent* Aviva James. Not when it makes sense, anyway. What is pointless is having me waste months of my time putting a case together and doing all the legwork just to hand it off to you so you look like you swooped in and saved the little backwoods detective with your investigative superpowers. That's what's pointless." He sat again. "By the way, you're welcome for doing all the heavy lifting there." He pointed the business end of his ink pen at the file on Ava's box.

"I am honestly not trying to seem like a hero, Detective Hopson. I'm only here to help. The FBI was called in on the cold case, that's what triggered this investigation. And, yes, I have found enough similarities between the cases to say there is a high probability that they might be connected."

The absolute last thing she wanted to do was make enemies, but everyone in Hidden Cove already seemed intent on making her out to be a bad person with ulterior motives who wanted to undermine their work. She also did not have the time nor the inclination to deal with the ornery detective at that particular moment.

"Right, right. Heard it all before, agent. It's nothing personal. I just don't like that you're here taking over. Have a good day, and if you need anything…" He smirked and pointed to the phone on his desk.

Seeing that it was only a waste of time to try smoothing things with him, Ava pursed her lips and nodded. "Thank you."

"Shut the door on your way out, please and thank you."

Ava wanted to at least slam the door, but she played the role of the bigger person and shut it normally. Officer Redding stood grinning over his boxes at her. His cheeks were flushed and he seemed overly jolly.

"Something funny, officer?" Ava shot heatedly as she spun on her heel and headed for the exit.

"Welcome to Hidden Cove PD, Agent James. You have now been initiated. Hopson is the resident curmudgeon."

"Oh. Nice to know. A bit of warning would have been nicer."

"What, and miss that fun encounter? No way."

It might have been funny on a day when she had enough sleep and wasn't worried sick about her mother. But as it was, she was running on caffeine and pure willpower and completely fed up with the situation. "Where is Detective Rogers now? Why isn't he working this case?"

"He works two counties over. Better pay over there. He left two years ago and all the load fell into Hopson's lap. There's a junior detective bumping around here somewhere. Hopson probably has him cleaning out the car or whatever to keep him out of his way."

Shaking her head, Ava opened the exit and let Chev go ahead of her.

"Two counties over. Would he be any more willing to speak to me if I have questions about the cold case?"

"No idea. He ain't nearly so mean and gnarly as Hopson, though."

"Good to know."

She opened the trunk of her car with the fob. "Just put them in there, please." She dropped hers in next to them and closed the trunk. "Are you ready to go, or should I come back after I've settled in at the hotel?"

"Do you know how to get to the hotel?"

She waggled her phone between her thumb and forefinger. "GPS."

"Ah, well, then you can just come on back. You have to anyway to meet up with Agent Rossi, right?"

"I do. Thanks for helping me with the boxes. I'll see you in a few hours." She wasted no time getting in her car and heading toward the hotel. She could only hope the people in charge there were less pessimistic about her arrival than Redding and Grady had been.

Uncle Ray had warned her years ago, when she'd first said she wanted to become an agent, that she would be singled out, no longer part of the masses, and lots of times she would feel ostracized because of her title and who she worked for.

Even back then, she had assured him she could handle it. And she could handle it. Sometimes it was difficult to take without saying what she wanted to people, but so far, she had done a stellar job of maintaining her professional demeanor, even as those around her seemed intent on poking her with a sharp stick. She was proud of that. As proud as she was to be working for the Bureau and making a difference in the world, albeit in small steps.

"Eye on the big picture, Ava," she reminded herself aloud.

The hotel was small but neat. Likewise, the room was small but neat and everything looked clean. Not the Hilton or the Ritz for sure, but the atmosphere was one of familiarity and comfort among the staff and the very few guests. Certainly more welcoming than the police station had been.

A young man helped Ava get all her boxes into her room, which was on the third floor. She tipped him a twenty, thanked him, and shut the door.

With the boxes and files separated into two sections of the bed, Ava sighed. There was a lot of work to be done.

Flipping the lids off the cold case boxes, she bent to the task of sorting and laying out the evidence down one side of the bed. As she flipped the lids off the boxes from the newer case, her phone dinged. She stood straight, agitated at the interruption, and took out her phone.

The text message was so plain, so ordinary, that it took her a couple seconds to process what it was. And when the realization sunk in, the world started swimming.

It was from her mother. At least she believed it was from her mother.

I'm okay. Don't follow me. Just wanted you to know I'm fine. Tell Dad I love him. Love you, my little dolphin trainer.

CHAPTER FIVE

AS SOON AS HER BRAIN PROCESSED WHAT SHE WAS READING, AVA shot a message reply and waited.

Nothing.

Only her mother called her *my little dolphin trainer*.

Ava's mind raced as she tried to recall anyone who ever might have heard her say those words. It had become a thing between Ava and her mother only after she'd joined the Bureau. Ava had indeed wanted to become a dolphin trainer. Way back when she and Molly were young. Other than her father, Ava could think of no one who had ever been present when Elizabeth called her that. It was like their private little joke.

If she had been at home, Ava would have rushed to her father and shown him the message. Being so far away, she called him and told him about the message. They both cried a little. They both hoped a lot.

"You know how your mother is, Ava. She's onto something and doesn't want you involved. Please honor her wishes. I'm sure it's in your best interest, for your safety."

"Dad, how can I just sit on this? I have to do something."

"Then turn it in. Show it to the proper people and let them do their jobs. She said nothing about that. She isn't asking you to hide anything from the Bureau, she simply doesn't want you personally trying to find her."

"What could she be doing that's so secretive?"

A long silence passed before he finally said, "My best guess is that she is checking out some lead that nobody else is checking out. With her connections all over the world, there's no telling what it is or where it will take her. We just have to believe she knows what she's doing and that she's being careful."

"Do you think it could have anything to do with the gala murders?" Ava's stomach knotted as she thought about her mother investigating something that might lead her right into the midst of such monstrous and ruthless people.

"Honey, I've been wondering that since the day she went missing. I hope not, is all I can say, but it's not impossible. I don't want to jump to any conclusions, though. It could be something to do with the corruption of the local government in South Africa, or the suspicions of money laundering in Argentina, or even claims of drug-running through the Ukraine border. You just can't know. I'm just hoping it's something on the less-dangerous end of the spectrum."

"Me, too, Dad." But that's not the feeling she got from the whole thing. She feared it was something even more dangerous than she and Hank had thought of.

Her phone beeped and she looked at the screen. "Dad, I have to get back to work. Call you later."

She answered the number she didn't recognize. "Agent James."

"Agent James, this is Agent Rossi. I'm at the station. Do you want me to bring Officer Redding and meet you at the hotel? He said you had only left a short time ago. You're probably not even settled in yet."

Ava allowed a glimmer of hope to grow that she finally had someone to speak civilly with about the cases. "Agent Rossi, that would be excellent, and I would owe you one. I'm elbow-deep in evidence right now."

"See you in twenty."

Ava thought about calling the Bureau and telling them about the message. After hemming and hawing for several minutes, she did so. Her father was right—nothing in the message said that the investigation couldn't continue. Only that Ava personally couldn't follow up on it. She already figured that the phone her mother had texted from wouldn't be traceable, but it was worth a shot. Maybe the analysts down in Headquarters could find something.

After the call, she would have to fill out paperwork online and her phone would have to be analyzed. Nothing new there.

As promised, Agent Rossi and Officer Redding arrived within twenty minutes. She let them into her room and introduced herself to Rossi properly. The woman was tall, with jet black hair and hazel eyes. Her handshake was firm and confident and her smile pleasant but very professional. Ava liked her instantly.

"Cold case on this side, newer on this one," Ava said, motioning to the bed. "Separated out into case files, suspect interviews, evidence, and supplementary documents."

"I see you've got a system," Rossi noted wryly.

"You want a table or two to put that on instead of the bed?" Redding offered. "I can have them bring one or two up and we could set it up over there in front of the window. They can take that round sitting table out."

Shocked at his much more helpful attitude, Ava nodded, smiling. "That, Officer Redding, would be a great idea. Thank you."

"Just Chev is fine. I mean, we're going to be working together while you're here, might as well be on a first-name basis, right?"

"All right by me."

It took another twenty minutes to swap tables, but the setup was much better than the bed. Three people going over evidence and files on a bed would have been awkward, she thought.

After two hours of going over and comparing the two cases, Chev spoke up. "Doesn't the Bureau let y'all eat? I'm starving."

Ava and Sal exchanged a look and laughed.

"All right, then. You're in charge of grabbing the food since you're local," Ava told him. "We'll get together what we need while you're gone. After, I want to get the lay of the land around here. I don't like not being orientated."

Chev left happily with their food orders.

Sal picked up Ava's notepad. "So, what are you thinking here? Same perpetrator? Or coincidence?"

"I'm thinking I don't put much belief in coincidences," she replied, echoing the lesson drilled into her head from her missions with Emma.

"Me neither. What would this be, though? A serial doesn't seem to fit. Not with five years between kills, anyway."

Ava shook her head. "I don't know. The murders in this one house are all we're seeing. What if there were more and we just haven't seen them because they're not directly linked to either of these cases?"

Sal frowned and nodded. "That's possible, I guess. Did you ask if there had been similar cases here?"

"Ha! No. I think I was lucky to get the files and boxes. They weren't exactly thrilled that I was coming in and *taking over*, as they put it."

Laying the notepad on the table, Sal shook her head. "They never are. Especially since you're a woman. The men seem to have a real problem with that sometimes. Took me a while to get used to it. Just don't let it get to you."

"I don't. Or, rather, I try not to." Ava used the notepad to jot down a list of tasks for the next day. Asking about other similar cases was at the top of that list.

"The leads in the current investigation amount to exactly zilch," Sal sighed.

"Same as the leads in the cold case." Ava finally put the notepad down again and reached for the interviewee list from the new case. "Can you hand me the interviewee list from the cold case? I want to compare the two and see if anyone is the same."

Sal handed her the list. The list for the newer case was longer and more detailed. She would have expected no less from Detective Hopson. He seemed to be a stickler for such things.

"Robert Mitchell. He's the neighbor. Same now as then," she mused. "He alibied out both times." She quickly searched her notes and found what she was looking for. "Here it is. Five years ago, he said he was on a nighttime fishing trip hours from here." She flipped through the newer file and located his new statement. "Says this time, he was visiting a friend out of town."

"Has a knack for being out of town when someone gets murdered, eh? Married?"

"Nope. Divorced, no kids. Lived at his current address for nearly two decades."

Sal nodded, seeming to pick up what Ava was putting down. "Maybe he should be questioned again."

"Just what I was thinking."

Sal turned pages and lifted evidence from the newer case. "It looks like this case was headed for the icebox, too."

"I hope we can prevent that."

Chev returned with the food. Ava hadn't been sure what to expect from Hidden Cove's rather limited selection, but the several large, steaming boxes of pad thai, shrimp fried rice, and tofu curry quickly placed any worries she'd had to rest.

"That smells incredible," she groaned, suddenly realizing just how ravenous she was. She'd only had a protein bar for breakfast at some point in the wee hours of dawn.

"Hidden Cove's finest," Chev smiled, setting up each box on the counter and passing out plates and forks to each of them.

"And here I was thinking about all I could expect was hamburgers and french fries," Ava told him.

He shrugged. "You'd be surprised at what this little town can offer."

The trio spent most of the afternoon slurping down noodles and discussing possibilities of the cases being related. Redding was against the idea. Other than Robert Mitchell still being the neighbor, nothing else lined up.

"Five years ago, the husband was shot dead, the wife went missing, and they had no kids. In the new case, the husband was shot, the wife was shot numerous times, and they had a three-year-old girl who was left alone."

Ava nodded. "Exactly. In both cases, a gun was used and never recovered. The husbands were killed in the living room. Did you notice the victims' names were similar? Five years ago, there was Dustin and Katherine Johnson; the new case was Derrick and Krystal Jakobson. Dustin and Derrick, Katherine and Krystal, spelled with Ks. Robert Mitchell was the neighbor, and both times, he was conveniently out of town. In both cases, the women were the last to suffer their fates. And the perpetrator was a man."

"How do you know that?"

Ava pulled papers from both cases and handed them to Redding. "It's right there. The women are the ones who called nine-one-one in both instances. That means they had time to see what was happening, grab a phone, run, hide, call emergency services. In the transcripts, the victims both said that *he* had a gun, *he* was in the house."

Chev's face reddened. "You're right." He rubbed his hands together and smiled a big-howdy-friendly smile. "I say it's time to show you around and let this rest for a while." He walked to the door, obviously done with the casework for a while.

"All right. Give me the dime tour. I just need to know the basics. Town Hall, Library, good cheap place to eat, you know, the essentials."

"Got it."

Ava could have found all the places with her phone map but felt more confident having a local show her around. She didn't want to be staring at a screen to find things. She wanted to see it through the eyes of the people who lived there.

When they got halfway through the town, she laughed to herself and at herself. She could have found every place in Hidden Cove that she would have needed simply by walking down Main Street.

"Big ol' business district, eh?" Redding asked, grinning at her.

"Oh, yeah. Huge." She shook her head and grinned back. "You could have just told me everything was on Main Street."

"And miss this fun tour? No way. I feel obliged to tell you that we only have five traffic lights in Hidden Cove, and we are sticklers about people trying to run them. A yellow light does not mean you're supposed to put the pedal to the metal and try to beat the red light."

"I'll try to remember that," Ava laughed.

On their way back to the hotel, Chev pointed out a tiny laundromat two blocks from where Ava was staying. "You'll want to keep quarters for doing your laundry. Hotel don't offer the service, and this is the only place in town. The machines don't take cards like the ones in bigger cities."

Lolli's Laundry sat squashed between a coffee shop and an antique shop, both of which were larger by far than the laundromat. The paint on the bricks above Lolli's was faded and chipped pink, written in a scrolling script that made it hard to read. The windows sported a permanent milky haze across their faces and grime along the bottoms. The sidewalk in front was chipped and cracked and looked to be a walking hazard.

"How long has Lolli's Laundry been there?"

Chev snorted a short bark of laughter. "Longer'n me, and I'm thirty-seven. My mom used that place when she and Pop were first married and the only appliances they owned were a cookstove with a short and a fridge."

"That long. Wow." It was such a contrast from the gleaming metropolis she called home. Nothing seemed to have any history in the city. All the businesses at least gave the impression of being new and shiny, always being gutted and renovated every few years to chase the new trends.

Back in DC, that laundromat would have become a tax filing office, then a burrito joint, then a cell-phone repair shop, then a vape shop, back to a burrito joint, and then a kombucha bar, all in the span of a decade or so. But there was something to the permanence of a place like this in Hidden Cove. Even though the paint was chipped and fading, it felt real. It felt like history. In small towns, Ava could actually touch the history of a place, if she wanted.

That evening, after Sal and Chev left, Ava paced her room and wondered about her mother. She checked her messages for the millionth time to see if by some miracle there was a reply from Elizabeth. She knew there wouldn't be, but that didn't keep her from hoping and checking.

A little after one in the morning, she laid aside the casefiles and her notepad. There was no ballistics report for the newer case. She needed that. If the same gun was used in both crimes, that would be a monumental revelation, as the gun from five years ago was never recovered.

She jotted another line of text on her task list and closed the notepad.

Taking the flash drive, she plugged it into her laptop and pushed the earbuds into her ears.

"Nine-one-one, what's your emergency?"

"Someone's broke into my house. Oh, my gosh! I just heard a shot!"

"What's your address?"

"Five-zero-nine Pleasant Hill Drive, Hidden Cove, Kentucky."

"Okay, ma'am, the police are on their way. Stay calm and lock the door to the room you're in, and please stay on the line with me until they arrive."

Ava listened to the recording again, listening for background sounds. The panic and fear in Katherine Johnson's voice were obvious before the gunshot. After the shot, her tone was one of sheer terror.

She heard thudding footfalls and the sound of Katherine's heavy breaths as if she were covering her mouth and the phone with her hands as she hid. A scream tore through the silence just before the call disconnected.

Once more, Ava listened.

Where are you hiding, Katherine? she wondered. *Which room did you go into?*

Concentrating only on background noises, she listened yet again. Something was there. Obvious. Right in front of her, but she couldn't put a finger on what she should be understanding from the recording.

The last time she listened, Ava realized the woman's scream had an echoing quality to it, as if she were in a cavernous room. Or, perhaps, a room bare of any decorations and furniture. There was nothing to dampen the sound of her scream.

Removing the earbuds, she propped her chin on her folded hands and stared at the computer screen.

"What rooms in a house would echo?" She mulled it over. The Johnsons had lived in the house long enough to make it a home, meaning it had been fully furnished. The evidence photos showed that much. Most of the rooms were carpeted, which would dampen sounds even more.

She pulled the evidence photos and went through them again, looking for a room that would have made the woman's voice echo. The kitchen had vinyl flooring, but that was the only room that seemed to fit a sound profile for echoing.

Why would Katherine be in the kitchen after calling the emergency dispatch? There was nowhere to use as a hiding spot. The pantry wasn't large enough to stand inside, and none of the cabinets looked big enough for an adult woman to fit into.

The master bath was carpeted and the walls were lined with decorations. Ava doubted that would be conducive to the sort of echo she had heard in the call, but made a note to check it when she went to the house.

She went back to the photo of the kitchen and scoured it for a clue, anything that might have been missed, anything that said Katherine had been there during her 911 call.

There was nothing.

Frustrated, she tossed the pictures to the table and made her way to the bed. She had no illusion that sleep would come easily, but she was mentally and physically exhausted. She had to try to sleep.

"Fake it, 'til you make it, Ava," she mumbled as she pulled up the covers and closed her eyes.

CHAPTER SIX

AVA WOKE IN A COLD SWEAT. THE DREAM FADED AND THE HOTEL room came into clear focus. She forced her breathing into a semblance of normalcy as she threw back the covers. Her phone said it was six in the morning and she groaned that it was already so early. She had slept, albeit fitfully, and suffering through a terrible nightmare.

In the nightmare, her mother had been the woman making the emergency call. It had been her mother in sheer terror and screaming. She heard every sickening detail: every shaking breath, every panicked footstep, every crack of gunfire. It ended in a scream, and Ava couldn't tell if it was hers or her mother's.

The horrible dream had started over immediately. The next time, though, it came with visuals. Elizabeth James stood in the kitchen of 509 Pleasant Hill Drive with a phone pressed to her ear, eyes wide, face pallid. Ava heard the thudding footfalls coming closer and began screaming for her mom to run out the side door, to just get away. Elizabeth couldn't hear her daughter, though, and backed toward an open doorway beside the pantry as the footsteps advanced. Ava pitched forward, trying to pull her back to safety, but she tumbled backward, down into the darkness beyond that open doorway, her scream echoing in the night.

Ava wanted the dream to fade away into the land of forgotten things, but she felt it might have contained a message about her mother. She was a federal agent, but she was also a woman who believed there were things out there that no one could see and that science couldn't adequately test.

As she prepared for the day ahead, Ava let the dream live on in her mind's eye. It was difficult to see her mother so scared and to hear her scream, and just because Ava was awake didn't mean she could see and hear the remnants of the nightmare any less clearly. She pushed it aside as well as she could, but it remained there.

She called Agent Rossi as soon as she had gathered everything for the day. "Feel like going to the scene?"

"I was hoping you'd ask," Sal replied. "I like to go to the scene and get a feel for the real-world logistics of what we might be dealing with. Things just make more sense if I actually do a walkthrough."

"Same here. We'll take my car. I'll be out front in five."

"Meet you there."

Sal had taken a room on the first floor of the same hotel. It was almost an hour drive for her to get back home, and she had told Ava that she would rather stay in Hidden Cove than do all that unnecessary driving. She was single with no kids and had said it would just make more sense to stay.

Ava hadn't disagreed, but she did wonder why Sal was single. It wasn't her business, so she didn't pry, but a woman as obviously smart and pretty as Sal should have snatched up some lucky man a long time ago, Ava thought. Then she chastised herself for thinking like her grandmother. Her grandmother would not have approved of Ava's chosen career, either. In her opinion, women were to be gentle, kind, loving, raise the children, and cook at least two meals a day for their family. Needless to say, Ava had never agreed with that mindset. She'd witnessed firsthand the friction between her mother and grandmother because Elizabeth had chosen to work in the UN instead of the PTA.

Sal had two large coffees in hand when she got in the car. She offered Ava one.

"Thanks. Where'd you get these so fast?"

Sal pointed to the side of the lobby as Ava backed the car out of the parking spot. "Back left corner, there's a little table with an ancient coffee pot. There were packets of creamer and sugar, but I didn't know what you liked."

"Black is fine." She maneuvered onto the road and into absolutely no traffic. They stopped at the first traffic light, and Ava looked around. "I can't tell you how long it's been since I've seen this little traffic. There's one truck there," she pointed to her right, "and I see three cars way down there," she chuckled, pointing to her left. "Very different from the city."

"If traffic was like this in cities, they wouldn't be cities, now, would they?"

They laughed.

Ava used the GPS to guide her. The turnoff for Pleasant Hill Drive was where the pavement also stopped. The rest of the road seemed to be gravel, and the road was long. They passed a big farmhouse on the right. In the fields behind the house, so distant they seemed small, tractors crawled through fields spewing great whorls of dust into the dry air.

On the left, they passed two small clapboard houses built close to each other.

The porch of one sagged. The boards had turned almost black from years of use and exposure to the elements. Tattered curtains hung in the downstairs windows, and the one upstairs window was broken out, giving the place an abandoned air.

The other house was in considerably better condition with a bright, fresh coat of white paint. The porch was under a roof, and the whole of the small structure looked sturdy.

Ava drove slowly along a winding portion of narrowing roadway for five minutes without seeing another house. Then, on the right, a quaint, small, one-story brick came into view. The yard had been meticulously trimmed and landscaped. Small evergreen bushes lined the property in lieu of a fence, except the portion near the next house. There was a long section of privacy fence there.

On the other side of the privacy fence sat the house Ava was looking for.

"This is it," Ava said.

"Nice place. Handsome house, though not my color of choice. Big front and back yards. Looks freshly painted, too."

Ava parked as close to the front porch as she could get. Yellow police tape flapped in the breeze anchored to shrubs and trees. More yellow tape formed an X over the front and side doors, which also bore the security seals.

Sal produced a pocketknife and cut the security seal on the front door. "After you," she said, putting the knife away.

Ava and Sal walked through the house. With evidence photos in hand, Ava stood at the edge of the bloodstain in the living room. "Almost the same place as the first victim five years ago," she pointed.

"Weird as heck, I'll give you that," Sal commented, eyeing the photos and then the carpet. "Both men were found face down and as if they had been heading in that direction." She pointed behind Ava.

Ava looked over to the room and nodded. "The den. Both men had rifles in that room."

"Didn't do much good in either case."

Ava walked to the stairs and headed up. The master bedroom door had been broken off the hinges. Someone had propped it against the wall. Probably necessary to evaluate for further evidence in the room, she thought.

Sal made a disgruntled sound. "You know a little guy couldn't have done that. That's a heavy door. Can you imagine how scared she must have been?"

As a matter of fact, Ava could imagine. She could imagine very well how terrified the poor woman must have been as she huddled on the other side of the door with a phone pressed to her ear, hoping against hope that someone would save her before he broke it down.

"And, she had a baby hidden in the bathroom to boot." Sal sighed raggedly as she stepped past the large bloody spot on the carpet in the shape of a torso.

"He shot her three times. Why so many times? He only shot the husband once."

"Personal maybe?" Sal moved toward the bathroom.

"He left the baby alone, though. Usually, if it's a love-grudge, the baby is either killed or kidnapped."

"Maybe it wasn't a love-grudge, maybe it was a drug deal gone wrong. Maybe she owed him money."

Ava shook her head. "I don't think it had anything to do with drugs. There was nothing stronger than ibuprofen found in the house, and the only alcohol was an anniversary edition bottle of wine that was at least two years old. It hadn't even been opened. They seemed to be level people all the way around."

"Level people don't usually have or make many enemies, and this just doesn't feel random. What the hell happened here?"

Ava shook her head, at a complete loss. "Let's check out the kitchen again."

In the kitchen, Ava opened base cabinets, checked the pantry. There was nowhere that would have made a decent hiding place for Mrs. Johnson five years ago. The pictures from both cases showed that the kitchen had not changed in appearance save the fact that some of the cabinets had been refinished.

The image of her mother falling through a doorway flashed in her mind. "The basement!" Ava announced, opening that door.

"What about it?" Sal followed.

"I listened to the emergency call from Katherine Johnson in the cold case. She dropped the phone, screamed, and then it disconnected. But when she screamed, it echoed. I've been looking for the room that would cause her voice to echo that way. It had to be the basement."

"Were there photos of the basement?"

"Not in the files I received. I'll remedy that, though. I want shots of each room from different angles." Ava pulled out her phone and took several shots of the unfinished main room of the basement. A smaller room in the back corner housed the water heater and a heating and cooling unit.

In one of the flashes from her camera, a dank odor wafted to her nose, causing images to crop up that she would have preferred to ignore. They were too strong to be ignored, though, and soon overwhelmed her.

The musty odor of damp earth that has dried many times mixed with the smell of human sweat. Not just sweat, but adrenaline-riddled, fear-induced sweat of many people crammed close together for a long time.

Molly lay on the floor beside her in near darkness. The tips of her beautiful blonde hair dripped with blood.

Footsteps approached, voices spoke in a language she should have understood, but could not. Men entered the room. Large, rough hands jerked her around as if she were no more than a ragdoll.

All the while, Molly lay motionless and barely breathing on the cold floor.

"Agent James!"

Ava was thrust from the terrible memory into the stark reality of the basement. She whipped her head toward Sal. "Yes? What is it?"

"Didn't you hear me?"

Heat rose from the collar of her shirt. "I'm sorry. I was zoned for a minute there."

"Lost in your own little world, eh? I asked if there was a reason they didn't give you pictures of the basement."

"Oh, I don't know. I'll have to ask Detective Rogers, I suppose. He was the one on the case, and he no longer works at Hidden Cove PD. He's over in Randall County."

"You okay? You look really pale. Like you're about to pass out."

"No, I'm fine. Just tired. I didn't sleep so well last night." It wasn't exactly a lie. She had slept, but not well.

"I feel you. I get that way every time I start a new investigation."

"Let's go back up and look over the list of people from the cold case again. I'm still missing something and it's driving me nuts."

An hour later, with no new connections between cases found, Ava and Sal made rounds of each room, shooting pictures from every angle possible.

"I'll have these printed out later today if I can get Redding to show me where that's possible around here."

"Well, I didn't see a Kinko's anywhere, that's for sure," Sal chuckled humorlessly as she headed out the same door they had entered.

"Hey, I think I want a few shots of the outside, too. This is a long drive. I don't want to have to come up here every day or two to check things out when I can have the photos hanging on the evidence board."

"Is PD going to give you an office space to work in?"

"I won't have it for a few days yet. They're clearing out a small storage room, from what I gather." Ava had not been surprised when no one mentioned the promised office space upon her arrival. She had been too

AVA JAMES AND THE FORGOTTEN BONES

upset with their attitudes toward her to even remember she was supposed to have an office.

"Good thing we're versatile."

"Tell me about it. I was ready to work this case sitting in the middle of the bed with all the files and evidence scattered around me."

Sal laughed, this time with humor. "I can't say a word about that. I've done it more than once, and more than I care to admit. That's why I sleep alone. Hard to have room for another person when your bed's constantly covered in case files and miscellaneous paperwork."

Stopping just short of the car, Ava turned. A light had just gone on in her head. "Oh, my God. Do you think that's what people mean when they say someone is married to their job?"

"Mm-hm. Sure is, Agent James," Sal nodded. She opened the passenger door and got in.

As she started the car, Ava looked at the house and property again, trying to memorize as much detail as she could. "This place isn't a vacuum and doesn't exist in one. It's here. I just have to find it."

"Still thinking the two are connected?"

"Indeed, I am."

CHAPTER SEVEN

WITH TWO WHITE EVIDENCE BOARDS FINALLY SET UP IN HER makeshift office, Ava unpacked her notepad and all the photos she had. Setting up a timeline of events took her over an hour as she meticulously attached pictures to each point of the line. Below the timeline, she put up pictures of interviewees and under each face, a copy of their official statements.

The walls were only large enough to place one whiteboard per wall, so the two met in a corner. She had worked in chronological order so that the cold case's board was on the left, the recent case on the right. Between the boards, she had used a piece of white posterboard to plot the similarities of the two.

After finishing, she sat at her desk and gathered phone numbers for the people she would interview for the cold case. Keeping everything chronological would help her pick up on whatever details the original investigators might have missed. Skipping back and forth in time would only cause confusion.

Lunchtime rolled by without Ava noticing. At three, she moved from the whiteboards to her desk once more, becoming frustrated. She pored over the pictures labeled Then and followed the line to the Now photos of the crime scenes and the house.

Nothing had changed, nothing stuck out, but she still had that feeling that she was missing something fundamental. Beginning to doubt her prowess as an investigator due to her inability to see what had to be right in front of her, Ava went to the window and stared out.

That's when she noticed a group of officers walking toward the parking lot and another walking toward the station.

"Shift change," she muttered as she put her fingers to her forehead and groaned.

Grabbing her phone, Ava walked out of the office, stopped in the hallway, and returned to grab her notepad. She could make a few preliminary calls while taking lunch. Maybe even stay out of the office for the rest of the day to see if it cleared her head some.

She drove to Calhoun's Country Kitchen, a place Redding had shown her on the grand tour of Hidden Cove proper. It seemed like a fine enough place if a little humble, certain to have enough grease to get her through the next week. The restaurant sat alone at the edge of a gravel lot. The back of the building was right up to the edge of a steep embankment.

There were only three vehicles in the lot, and from their placement, Ava thought they were most likely the employees' cars.

She pulled up close to a large side window and peered in before deciding it would be a nice, quiet place to grab a bite and make a few calls.

The pay counter was on her left as she walked in the front door. A bent, frail, elderly woman sat on a wooden stool behind the register. She smiled at Ava, and her many wrinkles bunched at the corners of her mouth and eyes.

"Well, howdy, Miss. Just sit wherever you want and Jilli will be with you shortly."

"Thanks," Ava smiled as she looked for a corner seat where she could make calls and not have all the noise from the kitchen.

She found a seat and pulled out her phone. She dialed Dean's number but hesitated before pushing the call button. If he asked what she was up to, would she tell him about the current case? Would she divulge that she was stuck, had hit a wall, and couldn't figure it out?

Would it be worth involving him in this case? It had been some time since they'd spoken, but things had always been good between them.

Instead, she pushed the button that darkened the screen, laid the phone on the table, and stared out the window at her dusty, bug-riddled car hood. It was too soon into the case to hit such a standstill, but there she sat with that very problem.

Movement across the room caught her attention, and she watched as the aged hostess made her way painfully slowly toward the kitchen at the back. The server cleared her throat and Ava started.

The pretty waitress looked to be around twenty, with golden-blonde hair that shone and hung to her waist in gentle wavy curls. An image of Molly flashed through Ava's mind, and her heart clutched.

"She's slow as molasses in January, but she refuses retirement," the waitress started in a thick Southern accent, her eyes moving toward the hostess.

"She certainly has determination," Ava smiled, embarrassed that the girl had seen her staring at the older woman.

"She's seventy-seven this year. She owns the place. Her name's Callie Calhoun, my granny." She shook her head and continued, "My name's Jilli, I'll be your server today. Do you know what you want?"

"That's awesome. I hope I can get around as well as she can when I'm her age." Ava grinned and glanced toward the old woman with renewed respect. "I know I want sweet tea to drink, but I need a menu. First time here, and all."

Jilli took a menu from another table and handed it to Ava. "I'll be right back with your tea."

She took a cursory look over the menu items only long enough to confirm they had the meal she had most often when she was working.

Jilli returned, took Ava's order, and chuckled.

"What?" Ava asked, smiling.

"I totally expected you to be one of those women that orders some frilly little salad with the dressing on the side. If I had the cheeseburger and large fries, I'd gain ten pounds just like that," she laughed and snapped her fingers.

"Careful now. I like my frilly little salads sometimes, too," Ava joked.

It still amazed her how friendly people could be, how familiar they could act with total strangers in small towns. Maybe small towns weren't as bad as she had once thought.

The waitress bounded back to the kitchen to get started and an idea struck. She lifted the phone again. If the conversation with Dean went in a direction she didn't like, she'd use the meal's arrival as an excuse to get off the phone.

She hit the call button and put the phone to her ear, staring once more out at her dirty car.

"Hi, Dean, it's Ava."

"Long time, no see. How are you, Ava?"

"I'm okay. How are things? How's everyone?"

"Good, good. Xavier's... well, he's Xavier. And Emma's Emma, and Sam's Sam."

"How descriptive."

She could almost hear his shrug through the phone. "Things have been relatively quiet for once, which is nice. We miss you, though."

"I miss being there, but I think transferring was the right move for me." At least she believed that ninety-eight percent of the time. The other two percent, she spent wondering what in the world she was doing trying to make it as an agent and doubting that she could. When she had doubts, memories of her and Molly in Prague, and thoughts about what might be happening to Molly now, spurred her on and made her strive to be a better agent.

"Did you need something? Is everything really okay?"

"Yeah, I just called to find out how things are going."

"Mhm." The statement seemed to linger on an unasked question, but when he opened his mouth next, what he actually asked took her completely off guard. "What's happening with that gala murders case? Anything new?"

"There have been a few leads," she told him. "Everybody now thinks this ring is much larger than first suspected. It might even span several countries, from what we're learning. As of this moment, we may have a good lead of this same crime ring being active in Barcelona, and possibly in the Ukraine, as well. But that's all way above my pay grade now. There are seasoned international agents chasing down those leads."

"Barcelona and Ukraine? The ring must be huge. Gah, how many people work for these degenerates?" It was a rhetorical question, naturally.

"Maybe thousands, if it's as large as we think."

The thought was a sobering one. The idea of thousands of people out there trafficking humans as if they were nothing more than crops of vegetables angered her to her core.

In her silence, Dean cleared his throat. The background noises on his end faded as he asked what she'd been expecting him to. "Ava, how's it going with your mother? Any word at all?"

"She sent me a message from what I'm sure was an untraceable phone. I know she's alive, but have no idea where she is. I don't even know what country she's in, let alone what specific area."

"You're sure it was your mother who messaged?"

Ava could tell from the tone change that Dean's interest had been piqued. "Yes. She said something that only she, my father, and I would understand. That's the only reason I believed it was her. The Bureau team investigating her disappearance have it all, and they're trying to trace where it was sent from, but if I know my mother as well as I think I do, they won't find it."

Jilli returned with Ava's food. Seeing that she was on the phone, the girl placed it quietly on the end of the table and disappeared to the back again. The smell of the food set Ava's stomach rumbling and made her mouth water.

"I'm sure they'll locate her when she's ready to be found. Maybe beforehand, if I know the Bureau as well as I think I do." He chuckled at his own wit. "What do they have you doing up in Harlan? Anything interesting?"

Moment of truth, Ava, she thought. "I'm working a case in Hidden Cove, Kentucky right now."

"Talk about traveling the world," he cracked. "They took you off Barcelona and put you in the Appalachians?"

"You know, it's not so bad. I'm currently sitting in front of what the sign outside says is the best burger in all of Birch County."

"Sounds like a treat. You'll have to take me along sometime."

"Maybe I will. Tell everyone I say hello. I've got to go, but I'll be in touch again soon, I'm sure."

"All right. Talk later, Ava."

They ended the call, and Ava moved her plate closer, ready to eat and get a move on the case. Talking with Dean was akin to grounding herself in reality. She thought no meditation session in the world could have done more for her focus and determination. And reminding herself about the leads from the gala murders gave her plenty to think about when she needed to get her mind off her investigation for a while.

Barcelona and Ukraine, she thought.

Both places had been reported as hotspots for human trafficking. Of course, she mused that any tourist destination was a possible site for kidnappings and other nefarious events. Tourists were easy targets for crime rings of all sorts.

But what about small towns like this one? She wasn't so naïve as to think crime could never descend upon a place like this. Her first impressions of Hidden Cove only seemed to paint the town as a complicated place.

Sure, the police officers were surly, but they always were. Jilli and Callie Calhoun seemed nice. There were cute shops on Main Street, though not many, and a surprising amount of diversity in the local cuisines. It didn't have some of the amenities of city life that Ava was used to, but she wouldn't blame it for that.

Which only made her more curious about the murders at 509 Pleasant Hill. What secrets did that house still hold?

CHAPTER EIGHT

Sal Rossi walked into the diner and looked around. Ava had spotted her as soon as she had pulled into the parking lot. Sal raised a hand to Ava as she walked to her table.

"Chief Shady Grady said he saw you leave and head toward town. Mind if I join you?"

"No, of course not. I had to get out of that office for a while."

Sal nodded. "It's a bit on the claustrophobic side." She waved for Jilli and ordered coffee. "Any plans for this afternoon?"

Pushing aside her half-eaten food, Ava nodded, then immediately shook her head. "This case. Or, rather, *these* cases. I have to figure out what I'm missing."

Jilli brought the coffee. Sal thanked her. She took three packets of sugar and dumped them into her cup, took three more and dumped them in, then three more.

Ava gawked as she opened and poured five of the little creamers in the mix and stirred.

"Would you like a side order of insulin and a shot of overnight in the hospital to go with that, Agent Rossi?" she asked, only half-joking.

"I know. I should just order a cup of hot chocolate. I'm addicted to the caffeine, though."

"And obviously the sugar. If I did that, I would be swinging from the rafters all afternoon." Ava laughed as Sal turned up the cup. "What did you have in mind for the afternoon?"

Setting her cup down, Sal nodded in the direction of the lot. "I thought, if you wanted, we could go to the house and roleplay."

Ava mulled over the thought, wondering if that could be the catalyst she needed to find the clues she needed. Weighing the possibility of wasting the afternoon in the small office space, or possibly wasting it at the crime scene, she decided on the latter.

"That, Agent Rossi, sounds like a good way to end my day."

"Should we pick up Redding? You've been leaving him at the station the last couple of days, I hear."

Ava rolled her eyes and groaned. "He's a big boy, he can handle it. I know my way to the house. No need to bring him along."

Sal finished her coffee with a nod and waved for Jilli to bring a refill. "You can't take things he says personally. I really don't think he means to come off as insulting, or even borderline insulting."

Ava scoffed. "He does, though. Not enough to get under my skin too bad, but he's just bad enough to be annoying. Annoying equals distraction. Distractions, I do not need right now."

"It's your call."

They left the restaurant and headed to the house on Pleasant Hill. As they passed the big farmhouse with all the fields, Ava asked, "Is this really inside the city limits?"

"Far as I know, it is. Otherwise, you'd be dealing with the Sheriff's department."

"Yeah, that's why I was asking. This doesn't seem like city limits to me, though. I'll double-check, although I don't know why the police department would have all the files if it was county jurisdiction."

Robert Mitchell, the closest neighbor, still seemed to be absent. The doors were closed, and though the blinds had been opened, Ava saw no movement within.

"Which first? The cold or the new?" Sal asked as they stepped inside. She looked around the living room carefully as they stopped in its center.

"I've been working from cold to new, and it's not working for me. Let's roleplay through the recent case and work back to the cold case."

Ava flipped through her notepad and nodded. "Okay, I'll be the perpetrator, you're Derrick Jakobson." She pointed toward the fireplace. "I've just come through the front door, that makes the most sense. I have a gun."

Sal stands with her back to Ava. "Did we argue? Did you say anything to me? Or did I just spot the gun and take off?"

"Krystal saw or heard enough to know she needed to call 911, so, let's just assume words were exchanged. You probably yelled at some point, alerting her to the intruder, hence the call."

Sal held up a hand. "What if the wife and kid were in here with him? Maybe that's why he was headed in that direction. He was behind his wife, who was probably carrying the kid, trying to rush her upstairs and protect them as best as he could."

Ava lit up. "That's good! The perpetrator broke in. They saw the gun, panicked, and the dad was shielding them as they ran for the stairs. Okay, I shoot you and you fall at the fireplace."

"One shot," Sal said. "I'm down, and you're not interested in shooting again. You just head for the stairs where you saw Mom and kiddo go."

Ava moved around Sal, trying to get into the perpetrator's mindset. "I follow you upstairs," she announced. "Derrick might have been my main target, but there is a witness. I have to take care of that. Tie up the loose end." She made her way upstairs with Sal right behind.

"Or maybe I'm the main target," Sal told her as they ascended the stairs. "Maybe you only killed Derrick to get him out of the way."

"Either way, I still follow you."

They turned into the master bedroom doorway. Sal went in, closed the door behind her, and crouched low, holding her phone to her ear. She started whispering in the same tone of voice as the panicked 911 call and then raised her voice. "Can you hear me in here?"

"Well enough to tell that you've called the cops," Ava called through the door. "The door is locked. I panic and break it down. I have to end that call before Krystal can give them a description of me."

"So you shoot her three times," added Sal, gesturing to the blood-stained carpet and spattered wall.

Ava pointed her fingers like a gun and pantomimed firing three shots. "One, two, three."

"A small space like this, those shots would have been incredibly loud. Especially to a small child," Sal pointed out.

Ava nodded, turning to the bathroom. "The kid's in there. I hear her crying. She might not be old enough to give my description to the cops, but I can't know that for sure. But I leave her anyway. I don't even try to get in there. I just..." she let her voice trail off as she turned to Sal. "I just what? Leave? Did the cops show up and scare me off?"

"If that happened, how did you get out unnoticed? There's no door that isn't in view as cops pull into the yard high and low sides. Surely someone would have spotted you darting off into the woods."

"K-9 unit didn't get a hit anywhere near the woods, either," Ava said, shaking her head again.

"Nothing was stolen, nothing was rifled through. Dogs only hit in the house and driveway," Sal said, looking over the notes. "That means you drove here and left in that same vehicle."

"Check the notes. I think it took the cops about twenty minutes to get here after the call."

Sal thumbed pages, finally stopping on one and then nodding. "Twenty minutes."

"So, I would have had plenty of time to kill the parents, collect valuables, and make my way back to the vehicle. If, that is, robbery had been my motivation. But why shoot Krystal *three* times? She was a small woman. One shot would have been sufficient, and less likely the neighbor would have paid much attention to a couple of random popping noises versus one, a pause, then three in quick succession."

"Maybe you already knew the neighbor was away. If you had watched the house for a few days, you likely would have seen that he was packing gear into his Jeep for the trip."

Ava bobbed her shoulders and huffed. "Let's go through it again. This time, the perpetrator and Derrick argue. Krystal and baby are upstairs. It's possible that she was getting little Jayda ready for bed."

Sal nodded. "We're facing each other. I see you have a gun, so whatever the argument is about, the killer is serious about it."

Ava advanced. "I'm angry enough to kill over it."

"Money? Love triangle? Jilted lover? We've already ruled out drugs."

"If it had been money, I would have taken your valuables after shooting you. I would have searched for money stashed in drawers and made a mess of the place," Ava pointed out,

"That only leaves a matter of the heart."

Ava nodded, but it didn't feel right, and she said so. "By all accounts, the Jakobsons were happy. He went to work and came home. She worked two days a week at the local elementary school as a teacher's aide and took Jayda with her. She went there and home. Otherwise, they attended church once or twice a month, frequented a few restaurants as a family, and did their shopping and errands at a few places. They were known. Familiar. Both grew up around here. Everyone knew them and seemed to think they were stable in their relationship."

"All right. How about financially? Were they solid there, as well?"

"From all the paperwork, they were. They weren't rich by any means, but they did have enough money set back to buy this house and get renovations done by contractors." Ava felt her eyebrows inching toward each other, bunching up the skin between them. Her grandmother would tap that spot with her finger and scold Ava, telling her it would cause ugly wrinkles when she was older.

Sal put a hand on her hip. "So, why the hell did you break in here with a gun while I was watching TV one evening, just living like an everyday Joe? What had you so upset that you killed me and my wife?"

Ava delved deeper into the mindset of the killer. "Not you."

She darted back upstairs and Sal followed to find her standing in front of where Krystal Jakobson was found. Ava looked down at the blood-stained carpet. "It was her. It was all about her. She's the one I'm so angry at."

"Okay, why?"

"Something she did made it personal. That explains the overkill."

"Or panic. If she was screaming as frantically as I imagine she would have been, maybe he panicked and shot more times than he intended."

Ava shook her head. "No. Look at the door."

"Broken off the hinges. Panic action."

"Nope. If he had panicked, there likely would have been blood, skin, hair, something from the killer left on the door where he threw himself into it, pounded with his fists. There was no DNA material at all. That means he was calm, just determined. He kicked until the lock and the frame gave way. She was holding it from the other side, trying to keep him out, but she was so small, she would have been no match. He launched into it, and in its weakened state, ripped it right off the hinges. The victim would have been thrown back, the door on top of her."

Sal nodded. "She struggled to get out from under it. The killer threw the door aside and put three bullets in her before she could get up."

"That matches the blood spatter patterns. The bruising to her right cheek wasn't because he struck her. It was from the door. She was leaning against it with all her weight when he rammed it the last time."

"That still doesn't answer what the very well-liked woman did to anger him so badly that he killed her and her husband."

"And orphaned a three-year-old girl," Ava added.

Ava put additional notes in her book, walked through the bedroom again, and then went downstairs.

"Let's go over a scenario for the cold case."

Sal was again the victim in front of the fireplace. Ava was the perpetrator.

"Is there a confrontation that turns deadly? There was no forced entry this time. Did we know each other, or did you wheedle your way in somehow and then kill me?"

"Going out on a limb here. We knew each other. You didn't feel threatened by me, and let me in willingly. It's dusk dark, so you had to be comfortable enough to invite me inside knowing your wife was here, too."

Sal looked down at the notes again. "Friends and family all have alibis. None of them were here. Who were you to me?"

"You were suing your old friend for a preventable injury. That's the only enemy we know about, and he wasn't really an enemy, they were just no longer friends."

"But if I was costing you money and hurting your rep, you might get angry enough to end the lawsuit in a less civilized way," Sal prodded.

"Alibi. The guy was on vacation in Florida with his family," Ava countered.

"Correction. He was seen early in the morning, at seven, on the day before the murder. That was caught on security footage at the hotel in Florida. There's no other footage until about two the next morning when he's seen going to the car and carrying in a small bag. It's unlikely but there is a pretty big gap there."

"We can check flights to and from here. He wouldn't have had time to drive here, kill the Johnsons, and get back to the hotel. It would be around ten or twelve hours one-way. That's my best guess."

Sal jotted the note to check the flights. She pulled out her phone and put information in. She turned the phone so the map showed. "You're good. Ten and a half hours, it says."

Ava grinned. "Now, I've shot you, you're lying dead in the living room. Where is Katherine? She heard the shot, but she knew to call the cops before that. She said a man had broken into their house."

"But there was no forced entry. Did she hear the two men struggle?"

"Maybe, but there wasn't anything broken, and Dustin was facedown, shot from the back."

"He was leaving the room. Running for the rifle."

Ava nodded. "Maybe. Or, his wife heard a commotion and was coming down the stairs and he was trying to warn her."

They went back upstairs. Ava closed her eyes, trying to mentally push the first case out of her mind and focus solely on this one. It was hard, given they'd just gone through such a detailed re-enactment in this very house, but she wanted to make sure she wasn't getting any wires crossed. She stepped into the bedroom and remembered the echoing scream she heard over the recorded call. "Sal, scream. Just a short burst of a sound."

"What?" Sal raised an eyebrow in confusion.

Ava nodded and made a hurry-up motion with her hand.

"Seriously? You want me to scream?"

"Yes. The echo I told you about. I want to hear if your scream echoes in here."

Sal shook her head and yelped loudly.

Ava shook her head. "This isn't where she was when she called the cops."

They moved from room to room, Sal giving that same loud, sharp yelp in each one.

"She wasn't upstairs." Ava thumped down the steps.

"Well, if she'd been in the living room or the little den where the rifles were kept, the gunshot would have been louder."

"I know. Let's try the kitchen. It was my first thought."

Again, no match. There was a slight echo, but no match for the one Ava had heard.

Sal looked through the notes. "Okay, it took the cops almost a half-hour to get here."

"No. I have to find that room." Her gaze lit on the basement door. "The basement," she said, heading for the door.

Sal sighed but followed. "Walking up and down all these steps, I won't have to worry about my calorie intake for a week."

"Hey, now, this was your idea," Ava chuckled as she stepped into the bare, unfinished room. "Okay, do it."

Sal yelled.

Ava brightened. "That's more like it. Do it again, but stand over there in the corner."

Sal moved and did as asked, her eyes giving away the fact that she was more interested.

Ava grinned. Working on this case had almost made her forget that rush of excitement when she figured something out, put together some missing piece of the puzzle that others had overlooked.

"Katherine Johnson was hiding in the basement when she called the cops. I'm certain of it. The sound isn't exact, but it's close enough that this had to be the room."

"Now that we know where she was, where did she *go*?"

Ava bit her lip and walked the length of the main room. "If he took her, where would he have taken her? And why were there no signs of a struggle?"

"Maybe he knocked her out and carried her." Sal walked up the stairs as if carrying something over her shoulder. "Even if he was a big man, I think he could've carried her over his shoulder up and out of here without much trouble."

"If he hit her hard enough to knock her out, where was the blood?

What did he hit her with? Where did she land?" Ava turned, looking closely at the floor and rock walls, doubting she'd find much of anything. Between time and the family who later moved into this house, all the evidence would have crumbled to dust long ago. But that was the hard part of cold cases. It was like trying to cross a tightrope with a blindfold and hands tied behind your back.

"You think there's any possibility she's still alive out there somewhere?"

Ava shrugged. "I don't know, but I think maybe she was the killer's target. He entered the house that evening with the intent to kidnap her."

"Dustin was shot just to get to her," Sal stated, frowning up at the door.

"That would be my guess. If he had meant to kill them both, he would have. She would have been lying here, or at the very least, there would have been evidence of a struggle." She tossed her hands up in irritation. "Now I have more questions than before."

"Sometimes, it's like running in quicksand. That just means you're doing your job, Ava."

"I want to interview the people in the cold case tomorrow."

She already knew she would start with Robert Mitchell. Had he been home during either of the incidents, he would have surely heard the gunshots and the women screaming. Since his was the only house close enough for that, she would start there and work her way to the others.

CHAPTER NINE

AVA DROVE OUT BY HERSELF TO ROBERT MITCHELL'S HOUSE AND knocked.

The man made his way slowly to the door and looked out at her for a moment. He opened the door, eyed her up and down, and stepped to the porch.

Dressed in a red flannel shirt, worn, faded jeans, and work boots that had seen better days, he seemed an ill-fit for the manicured little house. His cheeks were grizzled with days' old stubble that he scrubbed at with one hand. Adjusting his hat by the stained bill, he cocked an eyebrow at her. "If you're selling something, you can just light on outta here. I ain't interested, Missy."

"Mr. Mitchell?" Ava smiled.

"Lady, listen, if you're here to sell Avon, go away. I ain't married, and I ain't interested." He turned, hand on the doorknob, ready to walk away from her.

"Agent James with the FBI, sir. If you're Mr. Robert Mitchell, I would like to talk to you."

He turned. An expression of complete shock sat comically on his rough, weathered features. "You're with the FBI? What in the hell d'you wanna talk to me about?" He adjusted his cap again.

Ava nodded toward the house above his. "I'm working on the cold case. The Johnsons."

His eyes hardened as he glanced in that direction and back to Ava. "I talked to the cops about a million times back then. That detective hounded me for months." He let go of the doorknob and pointed to her black portfolio. "I'm sure you have all my information in there. Including the statement I gave at the time. Now, I'd like nothing better than to help you, too, but I wasn't even here when that happened. So, good day. You can see yourself to the car." He stepped inside the house.

Ava put her foot against the door before he could pull it closed. "I'm not here to harass you, Mr. Mitchell. I'm re-interviewing everyone from that case."

"Who'd you interview before me?" He raised both eyebrows, and Ava got a clear look at his grey-green, angry eyes.

Why was he so defensive? Had the police and Detective Rogers harassed him so badly during their investigation that he was automatically up-in-arms with her? Or did he have something to hide?

In her brief hesitation, she gave herself away. Before she could say anything, Robert scoffed. "That's what I thought. I'm the first one. But o' course I am. Was back then, too. Even after I told them where I was. I ain't got anything to tell you, lady."

"It's Agent James, Mr. Mitchell, and I'm not going away. I *need* to talk to you. The only reason you're the first interview of the day is simply because yours is the only house close to theirs. I have other interviews slated for later in the day. I just thought I could learn the most from you." She smiled pleasantly. "Now, may I please come in and just go over a few things with you?"

He scowled at her foot for a moment before finally shaking his head and relenting. "Come on in, but make it short. I have a life, too, you know."

"Yes, sir. I'll be as brief as possible."

"Good." He walked to the kitchen table and pulled out a chair. "We can sit here. I wasn't expecting company, the rest of the house is a mess."

"Thank you. No worries. I completely understand. I should have called, but most people won't even pick up if it's a number they don't recognize." She opened her notepad and flipped through the legal pad of notes.

"I'd be one of 'em," he laughed, sitting back and crossing his heavily muscled arms over his barrel chest.

It was not lost on Ava that he was of a size and demeanor that could have broken a door off its hinges. It also was not lost on her that he could have whacked a woman over the head and carried her easily out of that basement. She decided it was in her best interest to keep buttering him up.

"You and me, both, Mr. Mitchell. Too many telemarketers and robocalls nowadays."

He nodded. "Ain't that the truth."

"Okay, Mr. Mitchell, just to confirm, you're divorced and have lived here a little over two decades alone. Correct?"

"Why that's important is beyond me. Me and my wife bought this place, and we were divorced before we got the boxes unpacked, so she never really lived here."

Ava nodded. "I'm sorry to hear that."

"Don't be. We didn't get along all that much by then. I thought the house would be a fresh start for us, but I was wrong."

"You are forty-eight?"

He nodded. "Be forty-nine next month. Feels like I'm a lot older, though." He chuckled dryly.

"How well did you actually know the Johnsons?"

Blowing air through his lips, he adjusted that hat again, leaving it cocked with the bill pointing toward the ceiling. The reddish-brown of his hair was heavily streaked with silver over his temples.

"I knew Katherine, that was the wife. Her family owned the house. Her parents did, anyway. That's what they told me not long after I got acquainted with them. They bought it cheap and were 'bout as happy as pigs in mud."

"Did you visit with them often, or vice versa?"

"Nah. Not really. In case you didn't notice, we're the only two houses for quite some distance in either direction, though. Bein' young, I think they just needed someone besides each other to socialize with every now and then. We would sit on either my porch or theirs and have a beer together sometimes. We had a couple of barbecue dinners up there. She wasn't much of a cook, but Dustin was good on that grill."

"So, it's fair to say you were pretty close with them?"

"No. A couple of dinners together and a few beers over the summer don't make me close with anybody. I didn't dislike them, if that's what you're asking. I didn't wish any bad on them, either. I liked them as good as any forty-five-year-old divorced man can like a newlywed couple half his age and all full of giggles and dreams for their future. They never know that it's all just pipe dreams. Fairytales. There ain't no happily ever after."

He pulled the bill of his hat back down and leaned his elbows on the table. A sadness entered his eyes as he stared at his massive, folded hands.

"Okay. You were just well-acquainted. Got it." She scribbled furiously in the notepad. "Did the Johnsons have any enemies that you were aware of?"

"Just that guy Dustin worked with. It was his business partner or some darn thing."

"Why were they enemies, do you think?"

"Dustin was suing the guy. Don't recall all the details now. Like I said, they were business partners and at one time had been friends from what I understood. Dustin got hurt on a job. Said it was the other guy's fault. He was in the middle of suing when..." he motioned toward the house, "well, when they were killed."

"Was the friend-slash-business partner's name Jack Kearns?"

Robert nodded. "It was a weird name I can't ever remember until I hear it, but that's it, I'm sure."

"MJ Welding was the company name?"

He nodded again.

"How were the Johnsons' finances?"

"How the heck am I supposed to know that, lady? I don't stick my nose where it don't belong. I have enough troubles of my own without adding those of my neighbors to the list."

"I just thought you might have noticed if they were struggling due to Dustin's injury. He couldn't work, she had to take care of him. Did they sell off anything like cars, boats, appliances?"

There were no notes in the case files about such deals, but that doesn't mean they didn't happen. People often don't record cash transactions.

He shrugged. "If they did, I didn't notice."

"All right. Tell me about that day."

"The day they were murdered?" He adjusted his hat again and turned sideways in his chair.

"Why do you keep saying that *they* were murdered, Mr. Mitchell? It was only Dustin who was killed. Katherine is still *missing*."

Rolling his eyes, he answered, "Well, if she's not dead, I bet she's wishing she was."

"Why do you think that?"

"If a man murders a husband and kidnaps the wife, do you really think he intends on taking her to his castle and treating her like a frigging queen?" His tone had gone combative, and the color in his already ruddy cheeks heightened.

"You have a point, Mr. Mitchell. But I work in facts."

"Cold and hard, right?" He smirked but didn't relax.

"The colder and harder, the better. Facts always lead to the truth. So, tell me about that day. The day Dustin Johnson was killed and his wife disappeared."

"What do you want to know exactly?" His breathing had kicked up a notch, and his pupils dilated slightly.

"Let's start with where you were."

"Just like I told them back then, I was camping and hunting miles and miles from here."

Ava remained quiet and just nodded, trying her hardest not to let the alarm bells ringing in her head show on her face. His statement didn't match up with the official statement she had on file, but she didn't want to give that fact away.

He lifted the hat, ran his hand over his hair, and jammed the hat on again. "Listen, I like to hunt. My buddy was with me. He can tell you."

"What's his name?" Ava didn't have his name in her records.

"Alan Watkins." He shifted, his gaze flitting to something behind Ava several times. "Are we about done here? I got things I need to be doing right now."

"Almost, Mr. Mitchell. I'm trying to hurry." She flipped pages, and read notes. "What were you hunting miles and miles from here?"

"Deer. What's it matter? I wasn't here." His eyes narrowed and focused on her.

"Just wondering. You hunt deer with a rifle?"

"Unless you think I could run one down and cut its throat."

She shrugged and grinned. "Just asking. Just doing my job, sir. Some people use bows." She knew she was getting under his skin. That was her intention. Agitated people are more likely to let things slip. Helpful things.

"I hunt deer with a rifle." The skin between his eyebrows bunched and his gaze started flitting to that spot behind her again.

Uneasy, and recalling how she had been intent on doing the interviews alone knowing it could be less than safe, Ava tried to strain her ears for any out-of-place sound. Between the crows cawing outside the window and the drone of the ceiling fan, she could imagine someone sneaking stealthily up behind her.

But that would be stupid on his part. The feeling of being watched, and stalked, wouldn't go away. The fine hairs on her neck stood up. Turning her head to the side as if reading a note at the bottom of one of her many pages, Ava turned her eyes as far in that direction as she could without turning her head completely away from him.

She saw nothing. But the room wasn't washed with light. It was dim and there were shadows that could easily veil a person, making it nearly impossible to see them with peripheral vision alone.

Her gut told her the interview was over. She had all the information she needed for the moment. It was time to exit gracefully and not tempt fate.

Closing the notepad, she stood and smiled as agreeably as she could manage and extended her hand to him.

A brief look of confusion mixed with an equally brief expression of relief as he shook her hand.

"Mr. Mitchell, I would like to thank you for letting me take up your time. I think I have everything I need for now, though. Is it all right if I come back if I find more questions?"

Standing slowly, he pursed his lips and sighed. "Sure, I guess so. Just call next time. These kitchen chairs are hard."

"You have a deal." She headed for the door and Mitchell followed. As she opened the door, it occurred to her that he might have one more answer for her. "Mr. Mitchell, is Pleasant Hill Drive part of the city or the county? Do you know?"

Immediately he pointed to the property line of trees just past the crime scene house. "You see those woods right there?"

She nodded.

"About fifty feet on up the road is where the county line begins." He turned and pointed down the road. "You saw that big farmhouse and land down the road?"

She nodded again.

"Everything from the top of that property line to the other side of town is city limits. The boundary lines are all hinky and it gets confusing, but we're in city limits here." He leaned forward. "Truth be told, maybe if they'd been in the Sheriff's jurisdiction, this thing woulda been solved. City police department ain't much pumpkin in my opinion."

"Thank you, Mr. Mitchell. That helps me a great deal. You have a good day."

"You, too." He stepped back inside and closed the door.

As she was backing out of the driveway and thinking about Robert's odd turns of phrases, she glanced back at his door. She could just make out his ghostly face as if he were standing a few feet from the door watching her.

A shiver ran up her spine.

His alibi didn't match what he'd previously stated. In her records, he had said he was on a night fishing trip on a lake. This time, he said he'd been camping. As far as she was concerned, his actions made him seem guilty of something.

Whether it was murder and kidnapping, she still had to figure out.

But one thing was for sure: Robert Mitchell had moved to the number one spot on her suspect list.

CHAPTER TEN

O N HER WAY TO INTERVIEW JACK KEARNS OF MJ WELDING COMPANY, Ava's phone rang. As a rule, she did not answer while she was driving, so she pulled off the shoulder of the road even though there was no other traffic and the road was mostly straight. In the hill country of Kentucky, a straight road was unusual. Nevertheless, she took her driving safety seriously and pulled over before answering the call.

"Agent James here," she said without looking at the caller ID.

"The lead for the Ukraine looks solid," said a voice that immediately registered as Xavier Renton's.

"Would it kill you to greet me when you call?" she asked, smiling at her fond memories of the odd-acting Xavier. The two of them had been paired up on a mission to Windsor Island to bring down a drug kingpin along with Dean and Emma. Ava wasn't nearly as close to the group as the others, but she was glad to have him as a friend she could rely on.

"You have caller ID. My name should have been on your screen in large font," he replied without inflection, and matter-of-factly.

"I was driving and didn't take time to look at the screen." She sighed. She had missed Xavier and the others more than she realized.

"That explains why it rang so many times. The Ukraine lead looks solid," he repeated.

Straight to business. That was Xavier, though.

"What have you found out about it? Is Molly there? Any sign that she might have been?" She bit her lip. Question overloads were likely to cause him to disconnect the call. "Sorry. What have you found out about the Ukraine lead?"

"It's a hotspot for human trafficking. One common route that we followed went from Ukraine and crossed the border at Petrovce and on into Slovakia. Then they went through Southern Czechia. From there, Munich."

"Where did they go after Munich?" Her pulse raced at the mere mention of Czechia. Prague, though many years ago, was still very vivid, very fresh in her mind.

"That's where we had a problem. They seem to be splitting large groups of trafficked people there and they go in all directions. There's no discernable pattern of routes. It will take a long time to track down even one route."

The silence grew as Ava waited to make sure Xavier had finished his train of thought. When she was certain he had, and she had mentally drawn lines along the plotted course he had spoken of, she asked, "Was there any sign at all?"

"There were lots of signs, of course. How else would we have been able to track them? Any activity leaves signs."

Closing her eyes, Ava leaned her head against the seat and breathed deeply. Dealing with his Mr. Spock-like ways was tough at times. Sometimes he was extremely literal, sometimes he was extremely metaphorical. She didn't know how Dean and Emma managed to understand everything he said. "I meant, were there signs that Molly had ever been on this route at all?"

"We thought we spotted her on a section of grainy security camera footage outside a hotel in Germany. The footage is being rendered and enhanced so we can study it further before making a definitive decision about it."

"Did she look all right?" Ava's heart skipped as she thought about Molly still being alive. For years, she had feared the worst.

"She was black and white and grainy on the footage. No real details except that the woman turned her head once to look over her shoulder. That's when I saw her face. I think it's Molly. If it is, she has lost a lot of weight and they cut her hair, but at least she is alive."

"Thank you, Xavier." Her chest was tight with emotion and her thoughts were racing.

"You are welcome," he said.

"Will you let me know as soon as you figure out if it was Molly on that footage?"

"Of course I will. I called you this time as soon as I had information that was useful."

Chuckling, she replied, "Yes, you did. Is there anything I can do? Anything my prior experience can shed some light on? Anything at all?" She hoped he would have anything else for her, any tiny nugget of information to share. Although she knew that wouldn't happen, she still hoped. As it was, she'd hired Dean in a private investigative capacity, who'd roped Xavier along for the ride. Neither had the resources of the Bureau to work with, but at the same time, being free from those constraints was what made them so good at what they did.

"No. Nothing at all. We have it covered thoroughly."

"All right. If there's anything I can do, don't hesitate to call me day or night."

"I won't. Bye, Ava."

Xavier hung up the phone before Ava could say more. He didn't even give her a chance to say goodbye. Again, that was just his way.

Placing her phone in the console, Ava pulled back onto the road and tried to concentrate on MJ Welding Company and Jack Kearns.

Her thoughts kept going back to her and Molly in elementary school. Fall break. The wonderful aroma of apple cinnamon pies and spiced cider and pumpkin rolls filled the house all that week. Molly spent most every day at Ava's house. It had been a delightful week of stress-free, worry-free homebound goodness.

Back then, Molly's mother had been a pretty woman with a loving nature and a bright smile. She had helped Elizabeth with the food preparations before Thanksgiving Day when the feast was devoured by family and friends. Molly and Ava had sneaked in before the big dinner and taken an entire apple cinnamon pie. They had snuck it into Ava's room and sat on the floor watching a televised parade while they ate the stolen treat.

Ava laughed aloud at the memory. Just when the two of them thought they were getting away with it, her mother opened the door that day without warning and Molly dropped the pie in surprise. Both girls tried to shove it under the dust ruffle of the bed before it was seen, but to no avail.

Elizabeth had been a little disappointed, but not angry as the girls worried she would be. Their punishment? They couldn't have apple pie after dinner. They would just have to settle for pumpkin roll. Ava's mom had delivered the punishment as if it were a serious one, and the girls had fallen out laughing when she left the room again.

She would give anything to laugh again like that.

CHAPTER ELEVEN

THE TURN FOR JACK KEARNS' RESIDENCE APPEARED SUDDENLY ON the right side of the road. Ava was so lost in memories that she nearly missed the turn. She slammed on her brakes and made a hard right turn, grimacing as the tires slid in the gravel and kicked up a cloud of snowy slush.

The one-story brick ranch house seemed almost out of place compared to the other houses in Hidden Cove. It reminded Ava of a 1950s-era California ranch-style house, with its long front and wide, stubby chimneys. The kind of place that seemed better suited to a mid-twentieth century actor than an owner of a local welding company. She drove up the circular front drive wondering why this unusual house was here. The other homes in the neighborhood were mostly of a farm-style from the late Victorian through mid-century, and most of them showed their years.

A large stone fountain adorned the center of the gravel entry, and the whole of the property was meticulously manicured. Someone had cleared the snow from the drive, but not the yard, and it was blanketed, even, and pretty. It was a perfect, unbroken plain of white, not marred by footsteps or animal tracks. It told her that someone with wealth lived there and that person, or persons, took great pride in their residence. It also told her that this house had no children, who certainly would have run around constructing snowmen and fighting epic snowball battles in the wide yard.

Ava rang the doorbell. It echoed into the house with no response. Ava waited for a full minute, then another, and decided to ring the doorbell again. This time, a man immediately replied by yelling, "Yeah! Hold your horses!"

The man appeared on the other side of the central oval window. The etched ivy vines on the pane framed a man of average height, average weight, with black hair and bushy black brows which were drawn down close to the bridge of his nose as he scowled at her without opening the door.

"What do you want? I'm not expecting any visitors, and if you're selling something, I don't want any. There are signs at the drive entry. No soliciting. No trespassing. Goodbye, lady." He turned to go.

"Mr. Kearns!" Ava held her identification to the glass, her fingers burning from the icy, relentless wind.

Mr. Kearns stepped closer, eyeing her suspiciously over the top of the badge wallet. He leaned close and squinted at it, then looked back to her with wide eyes.

"FBI? What's this about?" He still made no move to open the door.

Was he scared? Did he have something to hide? He couldn't guess she was there about a five-year-old cold case, so what would he be worried about so instantly?

"I'd like to ask you some questions about a case. A cold case. I'm re-interviewing everyone from that case to see if I can close it."

"I don't know anything about any case. Cold or otherwise. I don't have time to play pitty-pat with a rookie, female FBI agent. Go get your training hours in somewhere else." He turned again with a huff and eye roll.

"Mr. Kearns, I am not training, and this is a case you know about. I think you're pretty familiar with the case in which your ex-business partner and ex-friend was killed five years ago," she snapped, her blood boiling. The man was rude to the nth degree.

It made her think once again at the wide contrast in receptions she'd received since arriving in Hidden Cove. Some of the residents of the tiny town seemed friendly, the type of people you could just knock and borrow a cup of sugar from. But some of them were frosty at best, even outright hostile to outsiders. Once she'd warmed up Robert Mitchell, he'd basically turned out alright. She could only hope Jack Kearns would do the same.

He stopped and turned to outright glare at her for a moment. She nodded toward the door. "May I come in? We could speak out here if that suits you better."

He opened the door and looked up at the sky. He shook his head. "I'm not standing outside freezing in the snow for this crap. I guess that means you're coming in. Wipe your shoes." He turned, leaving Ava to follow or not.

She stepped inside. "Would you like for me to close the door?"

Without looking back, he shrugged. "Unless you were raised in a barn and don't know better than to leave it open." He took a hard left, again, not waiting for Ava.

Raised in a barn? she thought. Taking one look back at the door, she left it wide open and walked down the short hallway, made the left-hand turn, and ended up in what she could only describe as an overly male-centric office.

Three boars' heads and five deer heads were mounted around the top of the room. All those glassy, dead eyes accusing anyone who dared enter their afterlife domain. The walls were paneled in dark walnut, and a T-Rex of a mahogany desk took up almost the entire left side of the room. The right side of the room sported six slender floor-to-ceiling windows covered by blackout curtains. The bearskin run on the floor took up the center directly in front of a massive fireplace, where a low fire crackled. She was grateful for the heat.

He poured himself a drink from the old-style cellarette designed to be a globe when closed. Ava turned to look for a seat and saw there was none close to his desk. He obviously didn't entertain guests in his home office. She saw the musket hanging over the mantel. It seemed authentic, at least from a distance.

"Well?" he asked, turning to her. He closed the globe pointedly and smirked.

"No, thanks," she replied, thinking he wanted to know if she'd like a drink.

He waggled a finger at her with a laugh as he stepped to his oversized leather desk chair and sat. "I wasn't offering you a drink. You're on duty, as they say. If you have questions, best ask them before I lose interest in being courteous. A pretty face will only lend you a little leniency in my home, sweetheart."

Bristling, she gripped her notepad and gritted her teeth. If this was being courteous, she didn't want to see his discourteousness. "My name is Agent James, if you please, Mr. Kearns." She walked to his desk and plopped her notepad on its edge, shoving a horse and rider statue out of her way.

"Hey! Watch the finish, please, *Agent James.*" He grabbed the figurine, lifted it, and ran his fingers over the desktop to check for scratches.

"Oh, sorry. Here we are." She smiled at him, giving him her best sarcastic pretty face imitation. "Dustin Johnson. Ring any bells?"

Scoffing, he flopped back into his seat. "Lots of 'em."

"Tell me about your relationship with Mr. Johnson."

"We were friends. We went into business together. Then we weren't friends. The business went under. He got himself killed. Now, you're sitting here wasting my time with questions I've already answered and that you should have in your fancy little notebook."

"MJ Welding Company went out of business when, Mr. Kearns?" Ava poised her pen over the paper. That was a bit of information she had not come across in the files.

"Two years ago. Don't you do your research?"

"I do. That wasn't in the files I had access to. Thank you." She took the note. "Why did you two stop being friends?"

"Because it's a really bad idea to go into business with friends or family. That's why."

Ava bit her lip and nodded. "So, why was he suing you?"

He put his glass down and furrowed his brow at her again. "For an accident he said I caused."

"An accident in which he was permanently injured?" She kept her head down as she wrote.

"Yeah, the lucky jerk."

"Why lucky?"

"Because he should've been dead. That fall alone would have disabled most men, but the wall frame falling across his back should've killed him, or at least paralyzed him. It wasn't my fault, either. That was never proven."

"Were you trying to buy out his half of the business before the accident?"

The glass whammed the desktop that he had been so protective of only moments earlier with a resounding crack. The sudden loud noise caused Ava to look up sharply at him. "I'm not accusing you of anything, Mr. Kearns. Simply trying to get the facts straight."

"Right. Yes, I was. I could've taken the company and made it phenomenal. I was going to expand to other areas of construction. He was a local boy who wanted to keep his business small and *local*. Stupid, in my opinion. There was more money, millions, to be made by expanding. Expansion is key in any successful business."

"Mm," she acknowledged as she wrote. "So, I'm supposing you have an alibi for the day of the murder?"

"Then you would be supposing correctly, Agent James."

"And, that alibi was what?"

"I was on vacation in Florida with my wife and kids. Let me guess, you didn't have access to that, either."

"I did. I just had to make sure you told me the same thing as you told the other investigators then." She smiled at him. "So, where are your wife and kids? I haven't heard or seen anyone else."

"Well, that might be because we're divorced and the kids live with their mother. That happens sometimes. Darnedest thing, ain't it?"

Another tidbit not in Ava's current repertoire. "It is. Sometimes for the best, though, don't you agree?" She smiled again. In this case, she bet that it was for the best. At least for his wife and kids. She couldn't imagine this man being a loving father and husband. "Trivial question, more for curiosity's sake than anything else, but why did you two call your company *MJ* Welding instead of DJ, or JD, or some variable of your initials?"

He actually laughed and leaned back in his chair, putting both hands behind his head. "That's a funny story. When we were really young, Dustin and I, we were both welders, as I suspect you already guessed. Being the FBI, you might've *known*. Anyway, we worked at the same company.

When anyone asked us what we did for a living, we'd answer, 'just welding'. Meaning we were just grunts, entry-level workers. When we went into business together, we were drinking coffee together one morning and trying to figure out the name for our company. Dustin got laughing, and said we should name it More Just Welding, because that's really what we were still doing; just welding, only more of it. From there, we whittled it down to the letters so we could keep it as sort of an inside joke just between the two of us."

He sighed and his smile failed by slow degrees until it had disappeared. Suddenly, he was the sullen, hateful man he'd been since Ava had met him. All traces of his good humor and good memories vanished as if they'd never existed.

"You got any other questions? I have things to do." His gaze trained on his whiskey glass.

"Is that how you afforded this place, Mr. Kearns? MJ Welding Company?"

"Partly. Why? Are my finances under scrutiny for some reason?"

"No, just wondering again. I mean, your business went belly-up, and I just thought maybe it had been doing exceptionally well before Mr. Johnson's accident and all."

"Well, if you'd care to have a look, you'd know I have my fingers in a lot of pies, Agent James. A smart man never puts all his eggs in one basket. I've worked my entire life for what I have. Nobody ever handed me a thing. I'm a little smarter now, and I have a *financial advisor* who helps me play the stock market and such. Does that put an end to all your many and varied little wonderings?"

"I think I have what I need for now, Mr. Kearns. Do you mind if I call around again if I have more questions?"

"As a matter of fact, I do, but feel free to try the front door just like you did today." He smirked and waved a hand toward the hallway. "I'm sure you can find your own way out."

Closing her notepad, Ava nodded. She walked out of the office, down the hall, and out the open front door, smiling at the snow blowing gently into the entry and onto the rug where she wiped her feet. She left the door that way as she stomped through the gravel and got into her car.

She imagined that Jack Kearns didn't have many friends in Hidden

Cove. Not with his nasty attitude and lack of manners. She could only imagine how he'd have treated her had he *not* been, in so many words, courteous.

Armed with the information about MJ Welding Company's closure, Ava headed to the company's old office building. The drive took her the better part of an hour. Not due to its distance, but due to the curvy, snow-covered mountainous roads she had to traverse. She had to slow to a snail's pace through several steep curves to keep from sliding off the edge and over a drop-off. It seemed the state of Kentucky had something against such commonplace safety features as guardrails.

Pulling up to the site, she saw that it was indeed closed. The tall chain-link fence surrounding the property was littered with trash that had blown against it and gotten stuck, branches that had fallen and bent it nearly to the ground in some places, and sported a human-sized hole to the left of the gates. Someone had used snips to cut through the fence. That meant there were no active security cameras, she surmised as she looked to the buildings and utility poles nearby.

There was no need for her to enter posted property illegally, as she figured there was nothing of importance to the case there. Mr. Kearns wouldn't keep anything hidden there that might be found by a bunch of teenagers looking for a place to drink some booze and not get caught. The man was a greedy jerk, but he was far from dumb or careless.

He had been trying to buy out Dustin's part of the company. When Dustin wouldn't sell, it was possible that Jack caused the accident, and from what she gathered from talking with the man, he thought Dustin should've died. His part of the company would've gone to his wife in that case, and Jack could've likely strong armed Katherine into selling out. Then when Dustin not only survived but sued Jack, it would have been motive for Mr. Kearns to kill him. Or rather, have him killed, since he had been seen at a hotel bar in Florida the day before the murder.

The more she thought about it, the more Ava thought it might have been plausible for Jack Kearns to have hired someone to kill Dustin Johnson. That would have kept his hands relatively clean, at least as far as his absence from Hidden Cove on the day of the killing. He could swagger around his Florida hotel bar, being seen by all the patrons and the security cameras, setting his airtight alibi. Unless Ava could prove he had hired someone to do the dirty work.

But was their dispute really worth killing a man over? The faint glimmer of nostalgia that had passed through Jack's eyes, even if just for a moment, seemed to prove that at one point, he was capable of being friendly. Maybe even of having friends. Had things deteriorated between them so badly that he would construct an elaborate murder plot and hire a hitman to commit the deed?

It was an angle she would pursue. Jack Kearns moved onto her suspect list.

CHAPTER TWELVE

Back in her makeshift office at Hidden Cove PD, Ava stared at the case boards. She walked along the one filled with pictures and evidence from the cold case. She was missing something vital but couldn't put her finger on it.

She worked on organizing her new interview notes and placed them under the relevant pictures on the first board. The new pictures she and Sal had taken at the house were on her desk. She took the pile and arranged the newer shots over the top of the older ones on the cold case board.

As she hung the living room picture, she compared the angles and the bloodstains between the Johnson case and the Jakobson case. The stains were eerily similar even in their pattern. What sort of mind went to the trouble of planning out two nearly identical murders in such detail? Even as she chased down a motive for the Johnson case, how would there be enough motive between both of those cases? Or were the two truly unrelated, and the male victims' placements were coincidental?

She could already hear Emma Griffin's famous words about coincidences running through her head.

Next, she moved to the pictures of the basement and hung that one over top of the cold case photo. Something niggled at the back of her mind about the pictures, but her phone rang before the thought fully formed.

"Hello?" She pressed the phone between her ear and shoulder as she proceeded to hang the pictures on the first board.

"Hey, Ava, it's Sal here. Where are you? I went by PD to meet up, but they said you were in the field and weren't sure about your exact location."

"Sorry. I'm at the PD now. Working on the cold case and getting ready to hang the pictures we took on the new case board to see what I can come up with. Did you happen to see Detective Hopson while you were here?"

"No, I didn't. Have Redding call Hopson, if you need something from him. That man can be a character to work with."

"Yeah, so I've noticed. I was going to check if he had found anything new in the Jakobson case."

"Did you find anything new in the Johnson case?"

"Maybe. I talked with Robert Mitchell and the lovely Jack Kearns," she said, adding an uptilt to her voice on the last name so it was clear that she was being sarcastic.

"I take it Kearns was less than thrilled to see you?"

"That man is less than thrilled about everything. How long until you get here?" Ava flipped the photo of the basement on the Johnson case board. Old photo. New photo.

"I'll be there in ten."

Ava told Sal that would be great, and they disconnected. She lifted the new basement photo one more time, and it hit her what the problem was. The old photo didn't show any sheet vinyl flooring, but there had been vinyl down at one time. She and Sal had seen the small pieces stuck to the adhesive in one of the corners while they were there doing re-enactments.

She pulled the old photo down and examined it in the light of her desk lamp. She saw no sign of vinyl. Only the light grey, smoothed concrete.

She moved to her desk and pulled out a magnifying lens to get a closer look at the corner. No adhesive, no vinyl pieces.

Mulling over the difference, she waited for Sal to show up. As soon as the other agent walked through the door, Ava held out the two pictures. Sal gave her a cocked grin and took them.

"Okay, what am I looking for here?"

"There were pieces of vinyl stuck to adhesive in the corner when we were there. Did you see it?"

Sal nodded. "Yeah. The tape was just around the edge of the room. I wondered why they hadn't used regular vinyl adhesive to secure the flooring in place all over the room instead of just the edges. I figured they weren't sure they would leave it and didn't want the mess of scraping it up later. Why?"

"It wasn't there five years ago. No sign of it, and no vinyl rolled up anywhere in sight as if they were getting ready to lay it down, nothing. Nada."

Sal studied the pictures for a moment and then walked to the stack of new ones. Flipping through them, she nodded. "You're right."

"So, who put the vinyl down and then removed it again?"

Sal looked up at Ava. "And why?"

Snapping her fingers, Ava stood. "Exactly. If the Johnsons didn't have it down, that means the Jakobsons must have done it. But they had only lived in the house for three months when they were killed. It seems like a long shot that they went through the trouble of putting it down and turned right around and tore it back out. It doesn't make sense. They were trying to fix up the house and make it their own."

Sal laid the stack of pictures down on the edge of Ava's desk. "And they weren't loaded with money they could just waste that way, either. Everything points to them being pretty frugal."

Ava tapped a finger against the desktop as she thought. "We need to check the Jakobsons' financials and see if they had purchased the vinyl and when. And we need to find out if either of them was handy enough to install it, or if they hired someone to do it."

Sal took out her phone and added the directives to a list, nodding. "I can check on that. You can work on whatever you were doing before. I'll get back to you by the end of the day with this, hopefully."

"You think you can really get their financial information that quickly?"

Sal shrugged and smiled. "Hey, it's a small town. Everybody knows everybody else's business. If I find out they purchased it, all I have to do is go to the store they visited and get the receipt info. They might even have security footage. Who knows? It's only been a few months since this happened. People want the case solved; they'll be willing to help."

Ava smiled. "It's nice to work with someone who knows their way around here. I feel a little lost and really awkward trying to even talk to people here."

"Lighten up. You're still the new kid in town, the *outsider*. They'll warm up to you soon enough."

Ava rolled her eyes with a scoff and crossed her arms as she leaned against the desk. "Well, I'm not going to hold my breath. No one has done much warming up to me yet."

"Redding did," Sal reminded her with a small smile. "Trust me, you'll be fine. These rural towns are naturally mistrustful of *others*, people who weren't born and raised in the town. Most of them are harmless enough."

Ava pointed to the two whiteboards. "Well, at least one person isn't harmless. Maybe more."

Sal nodded solemnly. "We'll figure out who did this, and then this little community can go back to being safe. Or, at least safer than it seems to be right now." She opened the door and exited quickly, heading to do some legwork, which Ava had noticed seemed to always make her happy.

Ava took up the stack of pictures again and set back to work matching the new to the old and examining each in great detail.

The living room hadn't changed at all since the Johnsons lived there. The dark paneling, dark floor, the same cream-yellow ceiling, all of it was the same. Only the furniture and décor had changed.

The kitchen still sported the same loud and abrasive yellow and orange flower print wallpaper, the same tile flooring, blond oak cabinetry, and beadboard ceiling. The fridge, stove, wall oven, and dishwasher were leftovers from the Johnsons' stay at the house, which, to Ava, was another sure sign that the Jakobsons were either just very frugal people, or they kept the items to save money. Large appliances were expensive, but Ava thought anyone would likely swap the old ones, the ones that a murdered man and his missing wife had used for new ones.

She shuddered. If the Jakobsons had been from out of town, they might not have known about the Johnson case. But the Jakobsons were locals. They had been renting an apartment in town during the time of the Johnson case. There was no way they didn't know about it.

They did everything they could to save money. So, what was going on with that vinyl? Ava wondered as she finished looking through the other photos.

Standing, Ava stretched and stifled a yawn. It was time to find Detective Greg Hopson, resident curmudgeon.

Walking down one hallway and turning onto the next, Ava saw Redding walking in her direction with his head down. He didn't look up as he neared her, only moved to the side as if to pass her.

"Officer Redding?" she asked, mainly to force eye contact.

His head snapped up. "Agent James." He stepped closer to the wall and went around her.

Ava turned to watch him, wondering what the heck was going on. "Chev," she yelled after him.

He turned, his cheeks flaming, his eyebrows arched high. "Yes, Agent James. Is there something I can do for you?" His hands went to his hips.

"Is Detective Hopson in?" She chucked her thumb over her shoulder, indicating his office farther down the hall.

"I didn't stop to look. Would you like me to backtrack and go stick my head in his office for you?" The smirk on his face was out of place.

Ava didn't know what had happened, but Redding was intent on taking it out on somebody. "I was just asking." She turned to go before his anger rubbed off on her and she started biting back at him. Agents were supposed to hold themselves to higher standards than other people. It wasn't easy in some circumstances.

"Listen, if you need me, call. I have to go. Sorry for…"

Ava turned and eyed him warily. He was motioning with his hand. "For being a jerk?" She smiled.

His eyes opened wide, his mouth opened and closed, he blinked twice slowly. Then he chuckled and the chuckle turned to a laugh.

Ava didn't laugh but did hold her smile. And her composure.

"Yeah. For being a jerk. I'll explain later, though. Gotta go." He turned and disappeared around a corner toward the back exit near the cruiser parking lot.

Turning back to her task, Ava straightened her jacket, bobbed her shoulders to loosen the tension in them, and took a couple of deep breaths as she neared Hopson's door. Her nerves were on edge, and she didn't want it to show as she entered the detective's analytical and grumpy line of sight.

She knocked on the door. Three short raps. And waited. She counted to five and then knocked again. After five more seconds of hearing nothing, she pressed her face close to the door. "Detective Hopson? Are you in there?"

"Not unless I figured out the secret to bilocation," he grunted from directly behind her.

She jumped and hit her knee against the door. She grimaced and sucked air through her teeth, then righted herself and regained composure. "Well, now. That would be something, wouldn't it?" The heat flamed up her neck and into her cheeks.

He nodded toward the doorknob. "Mind if I go into my own office?"

Stepping aside, Ava sighed and thought about walking away without asking him anything. He had managed to embarrass her and make her look like a bumbling rookie within twenty seconds. And the self-satisfied grin on his face was proof that he had intended to do it.

He opened the door and stepped inside. "Did you need something?"

"No, I just thought I'd stand at your door and knock and then call out to you for the fun of it. You know, my job got rather boring and I thought I'd have some fun." She glared at him.

Laughing heartily, he swung the door wide and stepped to his desk, still laughing. "Well, get your shorts out of a tangle and come sit down." He sat in his chair and then went serious. "Better hurry before the humor of the situation wears off, though. If that happens, I'll just be a jerk until you leave."

She believed him, and she didn't sit. "I just wanted to ask if you'd learned anything new in the Jakobson case."

Lacing his fingers together, he rested his arms on the desk and sighed. "I thought you were concentrating on the *cold* case. The Johnson case."

"I am. I'm also trying to connect the two cases, as you well know."

His lips pulled into a deep frown and he studied his hands for a moment as if in deep thought. Ava nearly turned and left the room, thinking he wasn't going to speak further to her.

"Agent James, do you seriously think the two are connected? I know I gave you some guff, but I don't think you're dumb."

"That's a load off my mind, detective. Thank you." She didn't bother to even smirk.

"See, that's what I'm talking about. You know how to handle yourself, yet I can see that you have to be new. You're too young to be old hat at any of this. But the Bureau must've seen something in you to turn you loose on these cases. So?"

After a moment of scrutinizing his expression for signs that he was only leading her into some confession he could ridicule, she nodded. "Yes, sir. I think there's a distinct possibility they're connected. I don't know why or who just yet, but I'm getting there."

He shook his head and looked back at his hands. "Five years apart."

"The similarities are too profound to be ignored."

"Coincidences. Especially if you're talking about Mr. Johnson and Mr. Jakobson both being shot in the living room by the fireplace. Both men kept their guns in that little room they were heading toward when they were shot. Home invasions. That's it."

"What was stolen, then?"

"What do you mean?"

"If they were home invasions, what was taken? Where's the list of missing items?" The tension returned to her shoulders. Why did she feel the need to prove her theory to Hopson?

He shrugged and gave a humorless chuckle. "No one knows what was missing other than Mrs. Johnson. Maybe she went off her rocker and murdered her husband five years ago, and then killed the Jakobsons, too."

"Why would she do that?" Ava had also thought of that scenario, but it didn't work out.

"Because that was her house and she didn't want anyone else living in it. If she couldn't have her family in it and be happy there, she'd be damned if anyone else would do it," he mused. "Hell if I know."

"Statistically speaking, women don't kill with guns. Nor do most women kill both parents of a crying child and leave that child abandoned, alone, scared with the bloody corpses of her parents."

"Why not? Women these days are liberated. They can do any old thing a man can do. Right?"

Holding her temper, she clasped her hands in front of her. "It's not how most women are hardwired, detective. They tend to poison their victims. Whatever is least gory. Did you find anything new? Or is it don't-share-with-the-new-kid day at the Hidden Cove PD?"

He laughed again. That time it was full of humor. "No, I'll share if it will get you out of my hair; what little I have left of it, anyway."

"Thank you."

"Ever heard of the cornbread mafia?"

"Yes, I have. It's a colloquial term for the grassroots, homegrown types of organized crime rings that run through the South. Mainly, from Tennessee to Georgia. Why?"

"God Almighty." He shook his head. "Sometimes, you're scary, Agent James."

She held a level gaze, but she was secretly thrilled to know she had gotten under his skin even if it was just a little.

Taking out his pocket notepad, he flipped a few pages and put on his readers. "Rumor around town is that Jack Kearns has ties to the cornbread mafia. One of the members," he squinted to read slowly, "Asher Patterson, is in jail over in Bellamy County, if you want to have a go at talking to him. Of course, I don't know how much he'd be likely to tell a woman." He hooked the glasses with his forefinger and shut the notebook. "No offense. Just saying."

"Why wasn't that in the case file? That name isn't in there anywhere."

"And you'd remember if you saw that one name out of the hundred or so?"

"I would. Asher, in Hebrew, means fortunate or lucky. Seems to me that Mr. Patterson has been neither since he's locked up in prison." She smiled.

Hopson's eyebrows raised until he looked comical, and then he made an effort to recompose his expression and shook his head again. "Like I said, you're scary sometimes. No wonder you're with the Bureau. Patterson's name wasn't in the original case files because I just got this information today. This morning, as a matter of fact."

"Why would someone give you information on Jack Kearns if you were investigating the Jakobson case? Kearns is linked with the Johnson case." She squinted at him, accusing him of running both cases at once with her eyes.

"Because there was a shipment of bad drugs that hit the streets a few weeks ago. Killed one man, put a woman in ICU, where she's still barely clinging to life, and turned a nineteen-year-old into a vegetable. I am also working on that case. The informant said Kearns had a hand in getting the drugs here. When I questioned him about the legitimacy of the claim, he said Kearns had been part of a trafficking ring for years. Everyone on the bad side of the law pretty much knows it, too."

Ava thanked Hopson for the information and opened the door to leave. "One last question. You might have no idea, but it never hurts to ask, right?"

"The only dumb question is the one not asked," he replied, striking a pose reminiscent of a long-ago scholar.

"Do you know who put the vinyl flooring in the Pleasant Hill Drive house? Who put it down, or who took it back up?"

"I didn't know there had ever been vinyl down there. Just concrete from what I saw."

"Thanks again." She closed the door and went back to her office as she dialed Sal's number.

Sal picked up. "Ava, Derrick Jakobson bought the vinyl two weeks before the murders. He had laid it with the tape, knowing he would probably take it up again soon. A friend says he was going to reno the entire basement. The friend says Derrick never got the chance to remove it, though."

"He was killed first."

"Yep."

"If we're sure the friend is correct, and Mr. Jakobson didn't tear the flooring up, that means it's likely that whoever killed the Jakobsons also ripped up the vinyl."

"I'm ninety percent sure he was telling the truth. There's nothing for him to gain by lying. Not that I can see, anyway."

"So, we're going to work the theory that the killer, or killers, ripped up the flooring. Now we need to know why they would do that."

CHAPTER THIRTEEN

BEFORE AVA COULD GET OUT OF THE OFFICE FOR THE DAY, HER PHONE rang again. It was her Uncle Raymond. Her father's brother had been somewhat of a mentor over the years. His long and distinguished career in the Bureau was what first put her on to this line of work so long ago.

"Hi, Uncle Ray," she said as she sat in her chair, knowing the conversation would last longer than it would take for her to get to her car.

"Hello, Ava. I talked to your dad."

The tone of his voice was fatherly. It held the note of an impending lecture, and she could guess what it would be about. "You did? That's," she hesitated, then continued, "nice," she finished lamely.

"Mm. Yes. I wanted to ask you about your mother."

And, there it was, just as she had suspected. "All right. Ask away, Uncle Ray." She grinned, hoping the little rhyme would at least take the edge out of his voice. It did not.

"Do you know anything about her case that you didn't tell Hank?"

"No. I told him all I know. Why?"

"He thought maybe you did know more and just were afraid to tell him for some reason. That didn't happen, did it?" His tone was worried and warning at the same time.

"No, it most certainly didn't. I told him everything. Why the interrogation, Uncle Ray? Has something come up? You're starting to worry me." She gripped her phone and sat rigid in her seat. Had he found out something more than she had known? Was he getting ready to reveal that something terrible had happened to her mother after all? He wouldn't do that over the phone, she thought, trying to remember to breathe.

"Nothing has happened. I didn't mean to scare you, Ava. Your father is just worried that you know something more than you told him and that you'll act on whatever that is. Frankly, I'm just as worried. I know how stubborn you can be."

"Me? Stubborn? That's the pot calling the kettle black, isn't it?"

"Yeah, well, it's not me we're discussing here, is it?" His tone was mostly warning that time.

"I promise, I do not know any more about Mom's case than what I told Dad."

"All right. I'm taking you at your word on that. I believe you. Now, are you planning on trying to do something half-cocked and crazy?"

"You mean like try to go find her on my own?" Incredulity leaked into her voice, and she didn't bother trying to disguise it. Ray should know that she wouldn't do that. Not to her father, not to herself. Sure, she had taken to spontaneous actions when she'd been younger, but the Prague incident had all but taken the spontaneity right out of her. Nothing like being kidnapped and trafficked to make a person go through life being hyper-aware afterward.

After Prague, she had painfully thought out, searched every angle, and tried to process every possible scenario of any major action in her life. Especially her professional life. She didn't want to endanger herself, but more importantly, she didn't want to endanger her family, team members, or her chance at being able to finally bust the trafficking ring that had taken her and Molly in Prague all those years ago.

"Yeah, that's exactly what I mean," he said bluntly.

"Well, you don't have to worry about that, Ray," she sniped, biting off his name a little harsher than needed. "I know nothing, and I'm not going to go out on my own looking for her. As much as it pains me to say it, I'm sitting here working every day, waiting, watching, expecting news from the Bureau about my *mother*. Do you have any idea how useless I feel? And, shame on you for thinking I would still be as careless and reckless as I was at eighteen. I've grown up a lot since then, and I deserve a bit more faith than that. I'm a federal agent, same as you are!"

Surprisingly, she sniffled. Tears did more than sting at her eyes. A tear zig-zagged from the corner of each eye, and she swiped angrily at them.

"Ava…" He sighed. "You're right. I'm sorry. I wasn't thinking as a professional, but just as your uncle."

"I accept your apology."

"I promise, I did not call to upset you. I never said you were careless or reckless. Not even in Prague. You were both young, not reckless and careless. I worry about you. So does Hank. You're all he's got right now. He has a right to worry."

"He's got you and Kay, too," she replied sullenly. She turned her gaze to the cold December landscape outside and tried to focus on the harshness of the world around her. If that didn't work, all she had to do was look back at the evidence board. The world was a hard place. She didn't have time to indulge in emotional breakdowns and teary-eyed sessions of self-loathing.

"You know what I mean. I love you, kiddo," he said softly.

"I love you, too, Uncle Ray." Her tears dried quickly as she regained mental control and focus. "How's Aunt Kay? I haven't talked to her in a while."

"She's a hard woman to keep up with, that's for sure. But she's doing great. Or at least she seems to be. She worries about you too; especially since what went down with your mom."

"Well, tell her not to worry. I'm fine. I was worried that she wouldn't be doing so well after the gala."

"She's a lot tougher than we give her credit for, I believe. She's planning on traveling to a fundraising function soon, also. I tried to talk her out of it, but you know how she gets over her charity."

"Isn't she worried in the least?"

"She says that no matter what happened, she's determined to keep up her good work. She says now more than ever, it's time to do what's needed to rehabilitate the Avilion Foundation's good name. And she says the world needs more good things, and as long as she can provide a sliver of good, she's going to keep doing it."

That sounded like Aunt Kay. Ava smiled. "I'm glad she's holding up so well. Remind me to never underestimate her fortitude again. Where's she heading this time?"

"It's in Maine. They haven't set a venue yet. I guess they're still working out the logistics and technicalities of the event and making sure everything is on the level. Too tedious for my blood."

"It's perfect for her, though. She loves working out all the details, I think."

There was a pause, and Ava could imagine Ray smiling as he thought about his wife. Theirs was a love story for the ages, and sometimes Ava was a bit envious. Would she ever have a relationship as strong and enduring as theirs?

"So, Hank tells me that you're in Kentucky for a while."

"Yeah, I'm in Hidden Cove. Ever heard of it?"

"Can't say that I have. Is it a small rural place?"

He was back to being just good old Uncle Ray again, and Ava was glad. She knew how to talk to regular Uncle Ray without getting emotional.

"Thought you'd never heard of it," she said laughing.

"I take that as a yes. Why did they send you there?"

"I'm working on clearing cold cases, and one of them led me here. There was a recent double homicide, and it happened in the same house as the murder-disappearance did five years ago."

"Oh, so you're thinking the two might be linked? Small-town serial killer?"

"I don't know about the serial part. Heck, I'm not even sure there's a connection. I just *feel* there's a connection. All the similarities keep playing out as mere coincidences, but you know what I think about those."

"Me, too. I don't think they exist. If there are similarities, then, there's probably a connection. It might be tenuous, maybe barely visible, and you might have to dig deeper than anyone ever expected to find it, but it's probably there. Trust your gut but follow the facts. Remember that."

"That's what you taught me. You and the Bureau, that is. I feel like the answer, the connection, is right in front of me, but I'm not seeing it.

Of course, the PD here still has Detective Hopson working on the recent case, and he doesn't like to share information."

"What about quid pro quo? He gives you info, you return the favor."

"He's not interested in the cold case. Not in the slightest. A lot of them seem to resent that I'm even here, and even more have double resentment because I'm a woman. It's like I've stepped back into the 1940s."

Ray barked out a laugh and then tried to stifle it by moving the phone away from his face. Ava waited for him to get it out of his system.

"I'm sorry, Ava. You know law enforcement is still largely considered a man's world. It sounds like you're dealing with some men who are intimidated by your title, your smarts, and possibly by your doggedness. You don't take no for an answer, and you go over everything with a fine-toothed comb so many times, it's scary."

"Really? That's three times today that I've been told I'm scary. Definitely not the perception I have when I look in the mirror. Guess I better start working on that, huh?"

"Not at all. Those are some of your most admirable traits as an agent. That's what got you where you are in the Bureau. You don't give up. You don't quit just because something seems daunting or difficult. You dig in and do the dirty work until the job is complete. Take pride in being who you are and don't ever try to change yourself just to fit in better. No matter where you are, be yourself and do it your way. It's worked so far."

"Thanks, Uncle Ray. It's good to have some support."

"We all need a little moral support sometimes. If you need anything, on those cases, or otherwise, just give me a call."

"I will." But would she? Would she be able to ever admit to Ray or anyone else if she thought she wouldn't be able to close out the cold case? Would she ever be able to admit that she had failed miserably at an assignment? She would not. That's why she fully intended to stick with it until she figured out every possible angle so she could get at the truth. If the cases were connected, and her first instinct had been right, that would be awesome. If they weren't connected, and she still closed the cold case, that would still be good.

They talked for another fifteen minutes, mostly about the weather, and the upcoming traditional New Year's celebration, which they thought would be best to postpone in the absence of Elizabeth and the uncertainty of her situation.

After she put her phone back in her pocket, Ava gathered her things from the desk again, zipped her jacket, and pulled on her thin driving gloves. As she walked through the corridors to the exit, and the dreary evening scene unfolded before her, she sighed.

It would be good to get to the hotel where it would at least be warm.

CHAPTER FOURTEEN

I N THE HOTEL ROOM, AVA KICKED OFF HER SHOES, DROPPED HER COAT on a chair, took off her jacket and tossed it to the edge of the bed, and collapsed heavily into one of the chairs at the table. Redding was right. It was a lot better than the small round table that had been in the room before.

She thought back to her conversation with Xavier about the Ukraine lead. Had he really seen Molly? If Ava had been there, looking at the footage, she would have known if she was looking at her friend, or if it was a stranger. Either way, whoever was in that footage needed to be saved. Justice needed to be served.

Then she wondered if she really could've recognized her friend after so long a time. Molly had been captive for years. There was no telling what kind of torture she had endured, what trials and tribulations she had suffered since Prague. Most likely, every day had been a battle for survival. At least until Molly figured out how to survive.

If she had figured out how to survive.

Shaking her head, Ava groaned and rubbed her eyes as if to blot away images that cropped up in her mind. If her friend were to survive such an ordeal, she would surely never be completely normal again. Her life would have been ruined in such a way that normal would no longer play a part in her world. Perceptions would become irreparably damaged and skewed, and she would likely have a host of physical problems to go along with the diminished mental state.

Forced drug use is a common way for traffickers to make their victims more docile. Pair that with the ruthless beatings for even slight infractions in the beginning, and you get a recipe for an obedient victim who desires only to do what they have to in order to keep from being hit again. The forced drug use nearly always ends with the victim having to suffer through detox once—if—they are rescued. Most relapse within the first year. This starts the cycle in which the victim finds themselves using again within a few months of getting clean. Sometimes, it goes on for the rest of their lives.

Many victims, while still in captivity, simply give up and find a way to commit suicide. Ava couldn't blame a single person for choosing the only way out of a horrific situation, but she didn't think Molly would do that. Molly was always so determined, facing challenges head-on. But so many years had passed that she couldn't be sure. She couldn't even be sure how she would have reacted to such circumstances had she not gotten away when she did. But she *hoped* Molly had not done such a thing.

Even if it meant that she would have to be Molly's caregiver, sidekick, nursemaid, or whatever for the rest of their lives, she wanted and needed her friend to be alive. She needed to see her again to apologize for not getting her out of there, for leaving her behind and then not being able to get her free.

Ava's chest tightened and the air was suddenly too thick. Her stomach clenched and her vision swam. She had left her best friend behind. Everything that had happened to Molly over the years was ultimately Ava's fault for not dragging her out too.

It didn't matter that there had been no feasible way for that to be done. It didn't matter that they both might have been killed if they had tried and failed to escape. It didn't matter. None of the possibilities mattered. Not now. Not six years later, while Ava sat in her warm hotel room paid for by the federal government while she investigated a cold case in relative comfort and safety.

God only knew where Molly was or when the last time was that she had been warm and comfortable and unafraid. Did she have any friends? Was there even one person she could talk to without worry and fear? Or was she completely alone in a group of other victims so demoralized and abused that they acted much as their captors did?

But now there was a lead.

Ava took her fists from her eyes and stared at the snow outside the window for several moments, letting her thoughts follow whatever paths they could, like rabbits hopping in the snow.

"There isn't *one* lead," she stated into the emptiness. "There are *two* leads. One in Ukraine, the other at a hotel in Germany. Molly's passage could be traced through both places. If that was her on the footage."

She dug for her phone and rang Dean. He didn't answer. She left him a message to call her back as soon as he could.

In her car, there was a small box far back in the trunk. She had brought it with her despite knowing it could become a distraction. She simply could not part with it for an indeterminate amount of time. She always had to have its contents close. Just knowing it was there brought a modicum of comfort.

Sliding on her shoes, Ava pulled her coat around her shoulders. She headed to the car to get that little box, shivering and huddling low as if there were watchful eyes somewhere in the distance. Once she was safely back within the hotel, she brought it back into the room and set it on the end of the table.

The Prague files were all there. It was a small box because sadly, there was little evidence. Her personal journal was there, too. Things she had remembered after the event and after the initial investigation, along with personal insights and feelings that had only been of interest to her. Most of it had been seen as useless in the investigative process by law enforcement. Nevertheless, she had kept it, and she added to it every once in a while, when a sliver of some unpleasant memory would surface that she wasn't sure she had previously entered.

Running her hand over its worn cover, she said, "Maybe one day, you'll reveal a key that's been there all along to solving this case."

Maybe.

For about the ten-thousandth time, she searched diligently through all the files, searching for anything that would scream Ukraine or Germany at her, but there was nothing. She put away the official files and opened her journal with a bit of trepidation. There were things in that journal that dredged up old feelings. Feelings she didn't like and memories she liked even less.

But it was time to face it once again.

If there was a sliver of hope that what she had written could help even one of those trafficked women, it was definitely worth it in her mind.

As she read about the dungeon-like holding cell she had been kept in, her body reacted with chills. It had been six years, but the events had seared themselves permanently in the back of her brain. She could recall everything. Every minute detail.

The sound of water dripping in the darkness. The dank odor of old, wet earth filling her sinuses. The shadows in the corners of the room, so vivid as if she were still in that place. Space and time meant nothing. Instantly, she could hear the terrified whimpers, feel Molly's weak breathing as her side rose and fell in almost imperceptible movements, and see the men who had taken them.

An idea popped into her head at that. The men. If she could recall their faces, maybe she could see if she recognized one or more of them on the footage.

Steeling her nerves, Ava clenched her fists and forced her eyes to close. A cave-like dungeon splashed across her mind's eye. Dim red lights that seemed to be on strings were the only illumination.

The tips of Molly's beautiful blonde hair darkened by her own blood caused Ava to open her eyes. "I can't do this."

She stood and paced the room, trying to talk herself down. The terrible thing had happened years ago, and she was safe in a hotel in Kentucky. Those men couldn't hurt her. Her brain knew that, but her body still refused to believe it.

Several minutes passed as she walked back and forth, breathing deeply, convincing herself that she was okay and that the exercise in memory recall was absolutely necessary.

In the chair again, she leaned back and closed her eyes, focusing on recalling only the men who had taken her and Molly from the street. Only their faces. They were big men. Of course, she and Molly had been teenagers at the time, and she supposed most men would have seemed big to either of them.

One man stepped close to her face. She could see him only in her peripheral vision. He had a large head and dark brown or black oily hair that flopped down to his jawline in semi-curled clumps. She was sure she had seen a few streaks of grey in that hair under the dim yellow glow of the streetlight before everything went dark.

The other man, possibly the one who had manhandled Molly, had been taller and broader than her own assailant. His hair had been cut so short he almost looked bald. The streetlight had shone sideways through it for a millisecond and it showed like peach fuzz.

Gasping, she opened her eyes, and she was back in the hotel room, her heart racing furiously at reliving the moment she had realized her life and Molly's life had changed forever in a bad way.

"He wasn't bald. His head was shaved close, but he wasn't bald." She took up a pen and scribbled furiously in her journal, wanting to make sure she recorded the details while they were fresh. She laid the pen aside afterward and sighed. "If I can still recall any details fresh after six years. Wouldn't stand up in court, maybe, but now I know he wasn't bald anyway."

Both men had characteristic Czech pointed noses and face shapes and hair color. Nothing set them apart as being anything other than Czech citizens that she could tell.

Closing her eyes again, she tried to focus on her time in holding and transport when her eyes hadn't been covered. The men didn't care a whit that the victims could see them. Why would they care? It was too late for any of the women to do anything about it. They had been successfully snatched, hidden, and were being moved. The men had guns, and there was no doubt they would use those guns if someone tried to scream for help or escape.

To Ava, it also meant that whoever they worked for was very powerful and influential. Why else would the bad guys not worry about being caught as they moved the girls around cities and took them in and out of holding rooms while they marched ahead, beside, and behind with guns in their hands?

"Because they are either above the law, or their boss has the law bought off," she murmured, keeping her eyes shut.

She followed the memory, lived it, felt it, all the way into the next holding room. Some of the girls had been shuffled farther down a concrete corridor lit with a few long fluorescent lights. The walls were cinder block and unpainted. It was cold. Their footsteps and sniffles echoed. When the men yelled orders at them, the words reverberated menacingly.

Had she understood those orders? No. But she had obeyed them as if she had understood. At the time, she remembered thinking that she could almost understand them, and she thought it had been her fault for not studying the language more. If she'd only studied more seriously, for longer hours, or if she had only reached out to a tutor so she could practice the use of the language, maybe she could've understood what was being said, and then she could have led authorities back to the men.

Was that really why she couldn't understand them, though? Was it because she had slacked, or were they perhaps speaking a language other than Czech?

She let the memories continue, paying special attention to the short commands she heard. Finally, she had what she needed. A short phrase that perhaps she could research and figure out if it was Czech, or if it was some other language.

Clim ouf vee es still. That's what the order had sounded like. She had known the man meant for them to get on the floor and be quiet. He had motioned for them to sit and then had put his finger to his lips, and then waggled the gun over their heads and laughed before walking out and locking the door. The sound of that lock engaging was perhaps the worst sound Ava had ever heard in her life.

Prisoners often say the sound of the cell door locking behind them for the first time was the worst thing they'd ever heard, but they had committed crimes. With illegal activity, it's always a possibility of capture and incarceration. It's an inherent risk to getting involved in crime in the first place. But Ava and Molly had not been involved in anything illegal, so they had no thoughts of ever being locked up anywhere.

In her mind, that made the sound of the locking door even worse than it had ever been described by any prisoner.

"*Clim ouf vee es still,*" she grunted out, trying to make the words sound the way the man had. *"Clim ouf vee es still."* She couldn't, but she had the gist of the sounds, she thought.

Pulling up a translator on her computer, she typed in the words phonetically and came up with nothing. She knew she was probably spelling the words incorrectly, but she wrote them in her journal anyway. Pulling up the online translator app that made it possible to speak in English and have the person you are speaking to hear your words in another language, she spoke the words as best she could. The translator couldn't even make sense of what she was saying. The auto-detect gave suggestions for Danish, German, Russian, Afrikaans, among others, but nothing definitive.

She closed the app and sat back, grinding the heels of her hands into her eyes again. "All this effort, and nothing? Really, Ava?"

Frustrated, she repeated the phrase with the inflections moved around and still couldn't quite make it sound as the man had spoken it. If she could see the words written down, it might be different, but she couldn't. Not until she knew what language had been used, anyway. She didn't think it had been Russian or German, though. She had heard enough of those two languages to be familiar with how they sounded when spoken. Very distinct, in her opinion.

Brushing her teeth before bed, she looked up at her reflection and, around the toothbrush, said the phrase and imitated the man's motions. It was a bit better. Maybe she would eventually figure it out, but she thought it was time to quit for the night.

She hadn't eaten her dinner until almost eleven, and that had been an order of stale nachos topped with gloopy cheese and a watered-down fountain drink from the all-night gas station at the edge of town. The meal had been followed by a big dose of *the chalky stuff.* That's the name she and her father gave to the generic brand of Mylanta when she was a teenager and had caught a stomach bug. It was the only thing that had eased off her malaise, and so, she had held her breath and swallowed the chalky, white liquid with a grimace. Years later, nothing had changed. She still held her breath and grimaced.

The next day was going to be a busy one. She needed all the sleep she could get. And sleeping would be out of the question if she had to taste those stale chips and that pitiful excuse for cheese all night.

CHAPTER FIFTEEN

FOR THE THIRD TIME IN AS MANY DAYS, AVA DARKENED THE DOOR OF Frank Lauter's house at the crack of eight in the morning. She'd found he had moved since the Johnson case five years earlier.

As with so many of the residences in Hidden Cove, it was out in an isolated rural area with woods close to the house, a creek on the property, and a house that looked as if it had been built around 1940 or so. It was a single-level home, clapboard siding, which needed some significant repairs and a fresh coat of paint, and featureless. Not exactly what Ava had expected as the home of a contract handyman.

But just like the last two days, she knocked on the door to find it empty.

She gave it one last look around, not particularly loving what she saw. Old tires stood propped against the side of the one-car garage to the left of the house. A Chevy Cavalier sat inside, but it had no tag and no back tires. Ladders, none of which looked usable any longer, lay toppled between the house and garage, cluttering the narrow concrete pathway there.

Five-gallon paint buckets had been stacked seemingly everywhere. There were three metal thirty-gallon trash cans beside the front porch, and they all were too full for the lids to fit on them. Instead, the lids were merely balanced on top of the trash bags.

And yet besides all this, she couldn't seem to find hide nor hair of Mr. Lauter.

She headed back to her car in frustration and got behind the wheel, ready to head for her second stop of the day, which she already had the sinking feeling was going to be another bust.

Frank had a solid alibi, or at least as solid as he could have, for that evening. His pregnant girlfriend, Stephanie Halliday, had sworn he had been with her all night. And now it was Stephanie's house she was headed for.

The drive wasn't long, given that Hidden Cove was such a small place. Making this trip for the third day in a row made it pass by in a blur, and when she knocked on Stephanie's door, her suspicions were confirmed.

Just the same as her ex-boyfriend, Stephanie was nowhere to be found in her house for the third day in a row.

If Ava's records were correct, she would have a child of four or five years by now. She had to wonder if it was even worth trying to track the broken couple and question them. They had never been on anyone's suspect list, and she thought it likely that they never would be. She would eventually question them, but there were others she wanted to talk to and she couldn't very well do that if she spent all her time hunting for the elusive Stephanie Halliday and Frank Lauter.

Enrique Ponce had been relatively simple to locate. He had been at his office on a back street in town. He was a small man with a constant smile. English was his second language, and although it was broken and jilted, she had no trouble understanding him at all. He apologized several times for stopping to think of the right word, but his friendly smile never faltered. He was charismatic and didn't seem in the least bit sketchy. Every question she asked, he answered willingly.

"That day, I was working at Dr. Williams' office. Had to trim shrubs, cut grass, and use a blower on his parking lot. There was a lot of work there, and he pays a lot, so I always go to make sure it is finished the way he wants it. You can check the records if you want to."

He pointed to his office filing cabinets. "I keep them all here for the last twelve years. Some are in boxes, but active clients' schedules and invoices are still in here." He was leading her toward the office as he spoke.

Ava nodded and followed. Stepping into the office, she was stunned at the number of filing cabinets. They were the four-drawer type, and in the far corner, they were stacked two high. Enrique saw her looking at them with trepidation and laughed.

Walking to them, he slapped the top one then the bottom one. "Bolted to each other and the wall behind. Won't fall. All safe." As if to prove his point, he pulled on the top one. It didn't budge.

"Ah. That's good to know," Ava noted, still preferring to keep her distance. She wondered how many times he had to go up and down a ladder to access the top cabinets, or if they were part of his storage system for older files.

She laughed to herself. *Even landscapers have a cold case department, it seems*, she thought.

Enrique flipped through several files in three different cabinets before locating Dr. Williams' file from five years ago. He turned, handed it to her, and put his hands on his hips, smiling proudly. "You never know when you will need a file. That's why I always keep them."

Ava was again amazed when she opened the folder. The records were more detailed than she had ever imagined. Dates, times, prices, places, payments, supervisor name, and employees on shift for each day were all listed in meticulously neat handwriting.

She took a photo of the open file for completion's sake and handed it back to Enrique. "Thank you, Mr. Ponce." She handed him her card. "If you happen to think of anything, don't hesitate to call me. You're sure you didn't notice anything out of the ordinary in the week before the murder? Not even a car or truck that struck you as suspicious? A person perhaps walking by that you'd never seen around there, or that stuck out in some way? Maybe paying a bit too much attention to the house or what you were doing? Even the tiniest detail like that would be a huge help in solving this."

He shook his head, and for the first time, his smile vanished. "I wish I paid more attention, but we were very busy and had other jobs we needed to hurry to that day, as all days. I hope you find who killed Mr. Johnson. He was a good man, and his wife was a good wife. Beautiful, always kind, offered us sweet tea or lemonade every time we went that she was there. Nice, good people. So tragic."

Ava nodded. "Yes, it was a tragedy, indeed. Thank you again, Mr. Ponce."

"Welcome. Happy to help." His smile returned.

As she stepped back into the blowing cold, she reminded him to call for even the smallest thing he recalled. He promised he would, and put her card in his wallet, patted it, and put it in his back pocket.

A huge scraper truck sped by the lot. It had rooster-tailed snow into a ridge the entire length of the lot. She knew there had to be a curb there somewhere, but couldn't tell exactly where it ended. Clamping her teeth, she eased her car forward, hoping the undercarriage would survive if she hit the curb. Which she did. There was an ugly scraping sound as she had to pump the gas to move it over the snow and the concrete to keep from becoming stuck.

Her palms sweated as she gripped the wheel for the next two miles, waiting for another ugly sound from under her car as something fell off, or from the engine compartment as something keeled over in there. She had no idea how much damage she'd done, if any. After the two-mile-mark, she deemed the car in good shape and relaxed a bit.

Most of the roads had been freshly scraped and salted. Travel was easier than it had been in the past few days. Earlier in the week, the roadways had been closed to regular traffic. Even parts of the interstate had been closed down due to the heavy snowfall and low temperatures that plummeted enough to freeze several inches of ice onto the pavement. Sal had headed home in anticipation of the storm during that time, and their only communication had been via phone and email. And as luck would have it, it seemed another snowstorm was just beginning to brew up.

Even their lead with the vinyl flooring had gone stale. They couldn't verify that the friend really knew whether Dustin had put down the vinyl or not. Therefore, they also couldn't be sure he really knew that Dustin had wanted to take it up. After all, he hadn't been there. They had only discussed it over the phone.

With all that leading to dead ends, she and Sal had little to go on. It was mostly just staying in contact. Fortunately, Ava didn't mind talking to Sal. It was nice to be able to just talk to someone about whatever's going on, not necessarily always about work. A couple of times, Ava had come close to speaking about her mother but had stopped short both times. She supposed some things were just best left unsaid, and the case of her missing mother was one of them.

Taking a chance that she might get lucky, Ava drove by Stephanie Halliday's house again. She pulled into the short, wide gravel and dirt driveway facing the front porch. It was screened and looked to be in good condition. To the left of the porch was a set of large windows with the curtains pulled back. She could see a television playing a cartoon on the far wall and the top of a long sofa just under the windows. A floor lamp gave a warm glow from the corner. On the other side of the porch was a single window looking in on a kitchen. The overhead light shone, and Ava could see a woman moving around inside, but thought she seemed too old to be Frank's ex-girlfriend.

"Or maybe not. You never know," she muttered as she put the car in park and got out.

The wind had eased up some but still felt as though it blew in from an iceberg. She hugged her coat to her front as she walked to the porch. Thankfully, the screen door wasn't locked and she had a bit of refuge from the weather as she stepped inside.

She knocked on the door, and a little boy with big round eyes and a headful of light brown curls ran to the door and smiled up at her through the glass. He fumbled at the knob with his chubby fingers, his tongue caught firmly between his lips at the corner of his mouth.

An older woman with greying hair in a bun at the back of her neck came from the kitchen on the other side of the hallway. She was wringing her hands through a kitchen towel as she scolded the boy.

"Remmie! You don't open the door for strangers. You know this," she admonished him as she pushed his hands away from the knob.

"But Granny! The lady's cold out there." He pointed at Ava.

"Shush up, now, and you go on back in there with your cartoons. Go on!" She shooed him away, suffering a barrage of childish protests as he went.

The woman looked at Ava with a studying scowl but didn't immediately reach for the door. "May I help you?"

"I'm Agent James with the FBI, ma'am. I'm looking for a Stephanie Halliday. Is she here?"

The woman shook her head. "Why you looking for her?"

Ava understood at once the woman thought Stephanie might be in some kind of trouble. "She's not in any trouble, ma'am. I was hoping to ask her some questions and see if she might be able to help me with a cold case I'm working on."

After another moment of hesitation, the woman unlocked the bolt, gave Ava another doubtful look, then unlocked the chain and opened the door. "Follow me to the kitchen. We can talk there." She cut her eyes toward the boy in the living room, who was clacking two toy cars together as he watched the cartoon on television, never looking in their direction.

Ava nodded. "Thank you."

In the kitchen, Ava was struck at how old everything looked. The appliances were all in seemingly good condition, but they were straight from the sixties, maybe a few years later. The linoleum was the color of faded limes and parts had been worn completely away, revealing a solid whitish-grey underlayment. These bald places were in front of the sink, under the head of the table, and in front of the stove. It was a little shabby and showing its age, but the place was immaculately clean and smelled of fresh lemons. Ava supposed that was from whatever cleaner the woman used.

"I'm Elsie, Stephanie's mother. What's she gotten herself into now?"

There was no offer of a seat. "She hasn't, Ms. Halliday. Not that I'm aware of, anyway. I'm investigating a homicide that happened a little over five years ago on Pleasant Hill Drive."

She nodded and looked relieved. "The Johnsons. That was such a shame. I reckon they were good people. At least from what little I knew of them, and from what everybody else said of them. Why's the FBI on that case now? Did something new come up?"

"Not really, no. I've been assigned to a cold case unit, and we're just trying to close as many of them as possible."

Scoffing toward the window, she nodded again. "Seems like all your cases would be real cold right about now. So, why are you traipsing around out in this mess looking for my Stephanie? You never have said."

"I am interviewing everyone again from that case. Just making the rounds, taking notes, and hopefully, I can piece together something useful."

"Well, she ain't here right now, and she won't be until later tonight. Maybe even tomorrow if the snow keeps coming down. She don't have a good car, and sometimes she sleeps in a room at the back of the restaurant bar where she works. She didn't have a thing to do with what happened to that family, though. I never understood them questioning her the first time, and I don't understand you wanting to do it now."

"It is just routine, Ms. Halliday. Where is the bar?"

"Next county over."

That's helpful, she thought sarcastically. "Between Birch and Randall County?"

"Nope. Other direction." Ms. Halliday stepped into the hall and leaned to look in on the little boy.

"And what county is that?"

"Good Lord," she groaned, shaking her head. "Outsiders. Couldn't find your way down a one-way street, could you? It's called Pine Oaks."

"What's the name of the bar?"

"It's a restaurant with a bar. Morty's." She sighed with irritation, rubbed her forehead, and nodded toward the door. "If you're done? I have supper to cook. I have the boy to look after, you know."

"Yes, of course. Is he Stephanie's son, Remington?"

"Guess you got his name from your files?"

"Yes, I did. It's an unusual name. I like it."

"We call him Remmie." She hurried to the front door and put her hand on the knob. "I wouldn't suggest driving to Pine Oaks. Roads ain't a bit safe over that way once the snow hits. They don't scrape and salt the way they do over here, and if you don't mind me saying so, your little car don't look like it knows what to do in the snow."

Ava chuckled. "It doesn't, but I assure you, the driver does. Thanks for your time and your concern, Ms. Halliday. Have a good evening."

The door shut behind Ava the instant her foot cleared the threshold. She huddled inside her coat and walked back to the car.

"Well, come on, car. Since you don't know what to do in the snow, I'll take the lead. To Pine Oaks it is."

Laughing and shivering, she cranked up the heater and pulled out her phone. She pulled up the map and got directions for Morty's. It would be a forty-five-minute drive. She eyed the sky. Low, white snow clouds with an under-tint of grey. The weather wasn't going to let up anytime soon. Three-quarters of an hour there and then back. The layer of snow already laying on top of the scraped road gave her pause.

She thumped the steering wheel with the heel of her hand. There wouldn't be enough time to get there, talk to Stephanie, and get back before the sun set and the temperatures fell into single digits again. She would have to wait until the next day.

Maybe Stephanie would be home by then. Maybe.

The only people on the original cold case list she had left to interview were Stephanie Halliday and Frank Lauter. She had added Asher Patterson to that list because of the information about Jack Kearns' involvement with drug trafficking in the area. If there was trafficking of any kind going on, it was a distinct possibility that there was human trafficking as well. That meant she might be able to track down Katherine Johnson. If she had been taken, and all indications were that she had, she might have been trafficked through Patterson's gang.

As Ava drove back toward the hotel, she wondered again if it was even worth her time to go back out and talk to Stephanie, or to Frank. They seemed legit, they both alibied out years ago, and she didn't believe they could give her anything new.

Except she had to double-check everything. She didn't take her job lightly. She didn't like to leave out anything. All the boxes had to be checked off her list, or she wouldn't be able to rest.

Not that she was exactly getting a ton of that these days.

CHAPTER SIXTEEN

THE NEXT DAY WAS DEVOTED TO GETTING THE LIST OF SUSPECTS FOR the Jakobson case. Ava was not looking forward to talking to Hopson. There was no excuse for one man causing her so much stress, and he seemed to enjoy every moment of it.

So she went for the nuclear option. It was her last resort. At eight-o-clock sharp that morning, Ava brightly welcomed herself into Hopson's office, taking him two huge jelly-filled donuts and a large coffee.

"Are they poison?" he asked with a curl of his upper lip.

"Of course not. Just thought it might be nice on such a nasty morning."

He leaned back in his seat grinning like the Cheshire cat. "All right, what do you want? Or, what do you *need*?"

She feigned shock. "I'm shocked, detective. Can't a girl just be bringing you donuts and coffee to be nice?"

"Not on your life. Even a rookie like you knows better than that."

"Fine. I need to interview the suspects in the Jakobson case."

"I'm working that case."

"Yes, sir, that you are. But I need to interview them, too."

He laughed and shook his head. "You're working the cold case. Why on Earth would you need to do something I've already done with the new case?"

"Because I know there's an overlap. I think that could reveal the thread that's holding these cases together."

"That thread, Agent James, is only that these two couples lived in the same house. Plain and simple. I might be inclined to let you look over my interview notes, but keep your nose out of my case. I don't need your help." He pushed the coffee and donuts toward her. "And take these out of here. I'm diabetic, and I don't drink coffee."

She didn't know he was diabetic, but who didn't drink coffee? "The coffee's black. No sugar. No creamer."

He shook his head and pointed to the items then at his door. "Good day, Agent James."

She could pull rank on him, but really didn't want to do that. Working with a department where nobody liked or respected her was hard enough. If she pulled rank and forced him to let her in on the case, it would compound the problem. She had been allowed to pursue the two cases only because there was a tenuous connection. It was only the house, just as Detective Hopson had said, but it was enough to give her the authority to step in whether he agreed or not. She would just have to change tack and figure out how to get him to agree. Obviously, being nice only deterred him even more.

She picked up the coffee and donuts and headed out the door without a word. When she reached the end of the hall and started to turn a corner, Hopson barked her name from his doorway.

"James!"

She turned on her heel, making sure to wipe away the flash of irritation on her face before facing him. Hopson had a way of getting under her skin, and frankly, she was tired of trying to be nice to him, although she didn't want things to be any more difficult at the police department than they already were for her.

She'd seen the looks that some of them gave her, she'd heard their half-whispered remarks as she passed by them, but she wouldn't give up and allow them to bring her down or cast doubt on her own abilities as an agent. She would hold her head high, uphold her duties, and continue to do the best job possible in the name of justice. Even if it meant having to deal with the likes of Hopson.

And it seemed that's exactly what she would have to do.

She stood there holding the coffee and donuts in her hand, not speaking or walking back down the hall. She bobbed her shoulders as if to ask what he wanted.

He motioned for her to return to his office. It took her a few seconds to assess the situation. He could have been doing that to see if she would follow his unspoken command like a trained monkey, or he could have been seriously wanting to rectify his attitude. Even when she started back toward him, walking slowly, she was unsure which he would do once she got there.

"What's the big idea? If you give a man coffee and donuts, you don't just take it back and walk away."

"You're diabetic and you don't drink coffee," she replied flatly, feeling her frustration rise to her face.

He patted his round belly and laughed. "I just wanted to see how gullible you were. Does it look like I worry a whole lot about what I eat, James?" He took the box and the cup from her and walked to his desk. "Now, did you get both of these for me, or is one of 'em for you?"

"Both for you. Just like I said before." She flopped into a chair and let her hands land heavily on her thighs. The man was almost more than she could deal with. She still didn't know if he was diabetic and making a joke of it, or if he wasn't diabetic and had outright lied to her. Calling her gullible was not a good idea, either. It only angered her more. Striving to remain professional, she cleared her throat. "So, the interviews?"

He slid a folder toward her. "I've already done them all. The official notes are in there. Knock yourself out." He devoured the first donut in a matter of seconds and washed it down with a huge swig of coffee.

Ava took the folder. It was pitifully thin, in her opinion, but she had what she needed. The names and addresses. "Thank you. I'll get these back to you by the end of the day."

"They don't leave my office. That wasn't part of the deal. You can read them in here and leave the file when you're done."

"I don't have my notepad with me."

"Then I suggest you hurry on back to your little office and get it," he countered, wiping jelly off his chin with a paper napkin.

Unbelievable, she thought.

Still not wanting to pull rank and simply demand the files, she tried to play the game his way. Redding wasn't around much, and she thought that maybe she could at the very least earn herself one friendly face in the midst of all those who seemed eager to dislike her and the Bureau for which she worked.

She wasn't out to take anyone's job, she wasn't there to gain praise, and she certainly wasn't there to steal anyone's thunder, as they say. She merely wanted to do her job, and none of them seemed to realize that. And, she certainly was not gullible. Her job was second nature to her; she knew what rights she had and what rights she did not have, and having Hopson constantly playing games with her about it was getting old.

She headed to her office, but she didn't 'hurry along' as Hopson had suggested. That was a directive given to a kid in school, and his snide remark had not been lost on her even though he had delivered it in a good ol' boy tone and fashion with a smile and nod. Before long, she would be able to consider herself a veteran initiate of being on the receiving end of the good ol' boy jibes.

Before even entering the Academy, she'd been warned by several people how tough it would be to be a female agent. Ava had stubbornly set her chin against it all and continued. Endurance became her saving grace back then, and that would never change. Whatever they could dish out, she could handle. Mostly with a smile on her face because she knew she was in the FBI for the long haul, no matter how many good ol' boys she had to deal with.

And, when she had returned, his office was empty and locked. No one seemed to know where he'd gone and he didn't answer his phone. She hadn't expected him to. "Just another gullibility test, I suppose," she grumbled on her way back to her office.

Ten minutes before she would leave for the day, Hopson knocked at her door. "Here's what you were really after this morning, Agent James." He handed her two sheets of paper.

On the papers, he had the names and addresses of all the suspects in the Jakobson case. She eyed him warily.

He grinned and nodded. "I know you had no interest in my notes. You're going to do the interviews for yourself. Again, knock yourself out. And, by the way, you can stop blowing up my phone now." He turned and walked out, leaving the door open.

Ava thought about thanking him but decided against it. He would probably see that as a weakness. Something else to look down on her for. Instead, she read over the list and put numbers beside the names. One through nineteen. Several she didn't know, but some were the same as in the cold case.

It would take days to talk to everyone on the list. She spent the first four days concentrating on the new names. They all checked out. Nothing suspicious about them or their activity at all.

The last three days, she spent going over her notes in the interviews she had already conducted. She had stuck to questions about the cold case in those instances, but had recorded the way the people had acted, her impressions, and if she thought they had something to hide.

Robert Mitchell rose immediately to the top of the list. He'd acted suspiciously, his alibi was different, and for a few moments in his house, she was sure that someone had been behind her. But maybe that hadn't been why he had been looking over her shoulder into that other room. Perhaps there was something there he didn't want her to see. Something that might make him look guilty in the cold case—or maybe in the new case.

"Maybe in both cases," she mused aloud.

He hadn't been open to her visiting him again about that case, either. Though he hadn't said so in those exact words, she knew he wouldn't be happy to see her again whether or not she called him first. He had no desire to talk to her again, and those hard kitchen chairs had very little to do with the reason why.

The photos of the basement drew her to the evidence boards again. That tiny scrap of vinyl in the corner still nagged at her. What was it about a simple piece of vinyl that bothered her so much? She still couldn't put her finger on the problem. So what if the Jakobsons had put it down and then taken it back up almost immediately? What did it matter? It was a dead-end lead, and she felt that it was overly distracting and useless, but was unable to put it to bed.

Reaching out, she took hold of the newest picture, meaning to take it down, get rid of it, put it away so it wouldn't be there calling to her to find out about that minuscule piece of vinyl stuck in the corner. The living room is where the murder had happened, after all. That's where her attention should have been focused.

But something stilled her hand. She didn't know why yet, but that picture needed to stay right where it was.

She let go of the corner with a sigh and the photo drifted back against the board into place. She decided she would have to make a conscious effort to avoid focusing too much of her time and attention on it.

She dialed Robert Mitchell's number and waited for him to pick up, already knowing he wouldn't. On the fourth ring, his voicemail did the job for him. Rolling her eyes, she left him a short message asking that he return her call as soon as possible and that she needed to speak with him again. Shaking her head, she put the phone back in her pocket and left the office for the day.

Feeling as though the day had been an almost complete waste of time as far as the cases went, Ava drove to the hotel and collected her laundry. The hotel offered laundry service for a fee that the Bureau would've paid for, but she did not altogether trust that her clothes would come back in the same shape they left. She hadn't seen a very warm welcome, and she didn't exactly relish the idea of someone doing something to her clothes as yet another way of getting at her. She would do her own laundry down at Lolli's Laundry.

Staying away from the case for an hour or so might do her some good, she decided. Sometimes she had to walk away and do something totally and completely unrelated to a case for a while. When she returned, oftentimes, the puzzle was easily solved. She just needed to clear her head of the clutter-evidence and leads that seemed to gather there, forming a veil through which it was difficult to see clearly.

CHAPTER SEVENTEEN

AVA ENTERED THE LAUNDROMAT AND LOOKED AROUND, SEEING WHAT it must have looked like back in the sixties, and then what it had become. A former shadow of itself.

Lolli's had been a cute place once upon a time. It was painted and decorated in cotton candy pink, powder blue, and white that must have faded sometime before Ava was born.

Now it was a fading, worn memory of a time when women would gather to talk over the latest female-oriented magazines, smoke cigarettes, and decide whether to spend the money on a new Hoover vacuum or buy new drapes for their living rooms—which would have been offered for sale in the magazine with full-color pictures and ads depicting smiling housewives whom they wished to emulate.

At least the ancient machines were clean. A sterile, bleach-like smell permeated the whole of the interior, and the windows could've used a good cleaning. Cobwebs fluttered in corners hanging thick with lint and dust. The white paint on the cinder block walls had turned a light, nicotine brown over the decades and the powder blue had faded to gray with hints of blue. The cotton candy pink still held to its integrity, but there were smears, smudges, and places where chips of paint and block had been broken away, probably by repairmen.

At the back of the small room, there was a window that looked into a tiny office. A chair and desk on one side of the room left no space for anything other than a person in there. Nobody was present in the office, though, and Ava suspected that it was typical of this establishment. She didn't mind. The time alone would be nice.

A dispenser hung crookedly on the wall next to the bank of dryers. Ava took out a roll of quarters and walked to it. One tiny pouch of Tide was two dollars. She openly gawked at the price and then looked at her basket. She had two loads. It would cost four bucks just to buy the washing detergent. The softener was one pouch for a dollar-fifty. Even in the city, she could have gotten a better deal than that, she thought.

"Jesse James used a gun," she scoffed and tore open the roll of change, "Guess highway robbery has gotten more sophisticated over the years." She sank almost half the roll into purchasing the items she needed and moved to the washers. Washing would cost her another five dollars, and she was suddenly thankful that she had her own washer and dryer at home.

The thought of her home, of being back home, brought on a bout of wishing she were there. Usually, she was unbothered by such thoughts. She'd never been homesick, but this feeling was pretty close to it, she imagined.

By the time she had her clothes loaded into washers, thoughts of her mother had taken over her mind completely.

She took out her phone again and dialed her mother's cell number. Not that it would do anything different than it had the hundreds of times she had called it before, but she was compelled to do it. There was always that one in a million chance that her mother, or someone, would answer.

The phone beeped several times and an automated message came on saying the number she had dialed was out of service. Ava hung up before the message played through. She'd heard it before. The investigators had heard it. Her father had heard it. It always said the same thing.

Knowing didn't stop the ache in her heart when she heard it, though.

She called her father. When she was feeling especially down and useless, calling him had become a go-to measure to thwart the depression. That had also been her mother's forte. Once upon a time so long ago. It seemed she had been missing forever, and that their lives would never go back to being normal.

Hank answered.

"Hi, Dad. Just thought I'd call and check on you."

"Is something wrong, Ava? You sound different."

Sitting straighter, Ava cleared her throat. "It's cold and I'm at a place called Lolli's Laundry, so there's probably a bit of an echo."

He chuckled. "Lolli's Laundry. What are you doing? Moonlighting at a laundromat?"

Even though she had felt like crying only moments before, and although she knew her father couldn't feel much brighter under the circumstances, he had successfully made her laugh within seconds of answering the phone.

"No, but sometimes I think that would be easier than what I am doing." She sighed before she could stop herself.

"Ah. I know that sound, and I recognize that sentiment, too. What's got you down, kiddo?"

She wanted to tell him all of it. The sexist, belittling treatment doled out by the older men in the police department, especially Hopson's part in it. The inhospitable attitudes of the residents. Feeling like a greenhorn rookie when she wasn't. Most of all, she wanted to tell him again how awful and useless she felt in her mother's case. But she wouldn't do that. He had enough to worry about without adding her personal emotional woes to the pile.

Since he had obviously figured out that something was wrong, she thought it best to glaze over the situation and move on to what really mattered. How was he doing? That was the big question on her mind. She had only called to check on him and soak up some much-needed comfort from hearing his voice and knowing he was okay.

"I guess it's just the nice Hawaiian weather and this cold case. Between the two, I'm feeling a little less than convinced about how I'm handling it all."

"Well, at least the weather's nice, eh? It's snowing and nasty out this way."

Again, she laughed. Hank always found a way to pull a smile out of her even at the worst of times. It was one of the reasons she loved her father so much. She sighed again, but this was of the unconscious variety that usually signaled the end of a particularly stressful situation.

"Now, see? I know that sound, too. That sounds like you're already getting a handle on whatever's bothering you about the case. Wanna talk about it?"

She did. But he didn't need to have the gruesome details on his mind so late at night. He didn't sleep well in normal circumstances, let alone these, and she was certain hearing about her case would do him no favors in that department.

"Nah. It's okay, Dad. Really. I'm fine."

"All right, Aviva. I won't pressure you. I have to know one thing, though."

"Sure. What?" She stood and moved to the first washer and waited for the door to unlock so she could transfer the clothes to a dryer.

"Why are you doing your laundry at a laundromat? I thought you were staying at a hotel. You do know most of them offer laundry services, right?"

"Yes, I know that." She paused for a second, thinking of a viable excuse. One that he might buy anyway. "I just thought it would do me some good to get out of that room and away from the case files. I was starting to feel a little claustrophobic between being in my car, my broom-closet of an office, or the hotel room all the time."

"So, there's part of the problem. Wasn't so hard to tell your old dad, was it? And you're right. It probably will do you some good to take a step back for a while. It always helped Ray when he was having a hard time sorting something out in a case, too."

She wanted badly to let it all out, to whine and complain about the way people were acting, the uncooperativeness of the interviewees, and the unhelpfulness of law enforcement and practically everybody else involved, but she bit her lip. Was she losing interest in the job? Was she losing her edge?

She tossed the basket of clothes into the dryer and closed the door. No, she thought, she was just worn down right now. She was worrying about Mom and Molly and Dad while trying to prove to the men at the

HCPD that she wasn't a rookie. She told herself she'd be okay in a day or two, and she had to believe it. After all, she had to be. It wasn't a choice.

"He says Aunt Kay is getting ready to go to another function for the charity soon," she told him, trying to deflect the direction the conversation wanted to take.

"Yeah. She seems undeterred by what happened at the last big hoo-rah. Me? I'd be hard-pressed to attend another function for a while. Maybe she feels safer knowing she married an FBI agent. Who knows?"

"You never said how you're doing, Dad," she insisted. She'd hoped that nudging him in another direction would work, and it seemed her effort paid off. He finally relented with words that sounded less cheerful than they were.

"I'm right as rain. I wish you'd stop worrying so much about me, Aviva. You've got a lot on your plate as it is."

"I'll always worry about you, Dad. That's kind of part and parcel of being someone's kid. You worry about them when you're not there."

He laughed again. "Now you're starting to sound like a parent instead of a kid. It should be me asking what you ate today, *if* you ate today, and how you've been sleeping, not the other way around."

"Okay, I'll play it your way. But know this is quid pro quo."

"Deal! You answer first, though."

Ava told him in great detail about what she had eaten, where she had gotten the food, how much it had cost, and that it was good, not like fast food. She described how she had been sleeping at least five hours a night, and that she had a good outlook on the case. She wasn't sure if the half-truths were for his benefit, or if she was trying to convince herself of those things. Maybe she was only hoping to speak the positive into being. Manifest something good to combat the bad, kind of thing.

"All right. Your turn, pops. Give it up."

And he did. In just as much vivid detail as she had.

They talked so long that she was loading her baskets back into her car before he even got to the afternoon portion of his daily play-by-play. It was unusual for the two of them to have such lengthy phone conversations. Chatting face to face was different. They could talk endlessly that way, but their calls were normally short and pretty much to the point. This conversation branched into several directions and random tangents. She thoroughly enjoyed it. It was nice to feel some semblance of normality for once.

Ava pulled back into the hotel room just as Hank was asking her what he should make for dinner—sweet potato chicken curry, roasted salmon and squash, or whether he should just give up and order pizza. Ava told him she was likely ordering Chinese herself, so he laughed and they finally hung up to order their respective dinners. A genuine smile lingered on her face as she hung up. She hoped her father had found some sort of solace in their talk as well.

Back at the hotel room, Ava put away her clothes and showered while waiting for the delivery guy to show up. It was good to finally wash away the cold. It was perfect timing as well, because the piping hot box of food was delivered the moment she'd dressed herself again.

Relaxed and warm and with a fresh egg roll in hand, she walked to the tables of evidence and files. There were copies of the photos from both scenes there, and she successfully fought the urge to pick up the basement photos for all of thirty seconds.

She let it fall back to the table and touched the list of people she still needed to interview. Her main priority was Robert Mitchell. Her gut just knew he either had guilty knowledge, or he was outright hiding something in his house that would connect him to something illegal, hence his sketchiness.

She checked her phone, seeing that he still had not returned her call, and she debated ringing him again. It was half-past eleven. She was sure to catch him there but knew better than to call anyone so late. It could be a complaint filed, and a tiny little X by her name as an agent who doesn't adhere to the rules when they don't suit her.

Instead of calling, she placed her phone on the charger and paced the length of the table again. Her journal still sat on the very end. She put it back in its box and slid the box under the table.

It was past time for the day to be over and for her to be in bed. Well, at least it would have been if she had anything resembling a normal sleep cycle going on. She did not.

Just before midnight, she forced her eyes away from the table and all its many and varied interesting tidbits and walked to the light switch. One by one, she flipped off the overheads, then moved to the lamp by the table and shut it off, then to the lamp by the bed, and shut it off.

The bed was warm, the covers were comforting, and the pillow, being one she had purchased at a local retail store, was soft enough. She snuggled down and pulled the blankets to her neck and listened to the icy snow ticking at the window and against the metal door. She should have been asleep within minutes. Lord knew she was tired enough.

But she didn't fall asleep. She may have been able to force her eyes and body away from the table of evidence, but not her mind. It trip-trapped through the landscape of broken and missing puzzle pieces, collecting together an assortment of mismatched junk that made it impossible to lie there and even pretend she was resting.

She did finally doze off, but it was after one. She knew it was past one because she had last grabbed her phone to check the time at one. "If I'm not asleep within another thirty minutes, I'm getting up and working. This is ridiculous," she had announced to the phone, as if it cared.

At three, she woke from yet another nightmare in which her mother was in the basement of the house on Pleasant Hill Drive. Elizabeth had been bloody and pale-faced, her eyes terrified, and she had held out her hands to Ava, pleading silently for help. Ava had run to her, heart pounding. *"I'm here, Mom. Everything is going to be fine now. I'm here,"* she had said as they embraced.

Ava didn't care that there was now blood all over her, too. Her mother was back. That's all that mattered. Then Elizabeth went still, and Ava pulled back to look at her, asking what was wrong. Elizabeth's eyes had gone so wide it looked painful. Her face was a rictus of terror and her mouth drew open far too wide. Ava shook her mother and asked what was wrong again. Elizabeth screamed, but it was the sound of screaming brakes and a car horn that emanated from her mouth.

Ava jerked awake and was on the edge of the bed with her hands out in front of her, the sound of the car horn and brakes echoing around the room. It took a second for it to register that she should not have been hearing those things in the way she was hearing them.

She leaped from the side of the bed, raced to the window, and jerked back the curtain. She had a perfect view of the street and the parking lot. A small pickup truck sat oddly angled with only one headlight burning.

In the center of the hood, it seemed the truck had sprouted a telephone pole. Across the street, with its passenger wheels marred up in the snow on the bank, a Jeep Cherokee sat with its front against a large tree trunk. Its horn was blaring in the chilly night like the cry of a wounded animal.

Normal people stayed in the warmth and safety of their rooms during such events, but not Ava. She was law enforcement through and through. She tossed on clothes without much attention to detail and flew outside to assist if she could.

The man who had been driving the truck looked to be in his mid-thirties. He had shoulder-length hair, a full beard and mustache, and a large, muscular build. Dressed in jeans, work boots, and layered in flannel shirts, he also seemed like he could be a rough customer. He stood outside his truck, glaring at the Jeep Cherokee across the way.

From somewhere in the distance, impossible to tell how far away, came the distinct warble of an ambulance siren. An officer was trying to get the driver to sit down until it arrived, but he insisted on staying on his feet. Probably the result of the adrenaline rushing his system, Ava noted, and moved toward the road to check out the Jeep.

The officer yelled, "Hey! You can't go over there, miss!"

She flashed her badge and answered, "FBI," and kept moving.

The Jeep was in much worse shape than the now-defunct little Chevy truck. The front was crumpled in the center and the driver's side had collapsed inward, making the metal wrinkle like an accordion's side. The driver was still inside. The steering wheel was closer to him than it had any right to be, and he looked unconscious.

A lone officer stood with his back to her, assessing the situation. Other sirens joined the ambulance's warble, and the place was soon filled with flashing lights as they approached.

"Is he alive?" she asked the officer.

He turned to her, startled. "Agent James, what are you doing out here?" Officer Redding looked up at the hotel. "Never mind. He's alive, but just barely."

"Should we get him out?"

"No. They'll do it when they get here. We have to have a neck brace and a backboard in case anything vital is broken, you know."

"Right," she said, feeling her own muscles thrumming under the on-slaught of adrenaline. "Do you know him?"

Redding nodded, a worried look in his eyes. "Small town. We all mostly know each other, even if it's just passing acquaintances. This is Charlie Halbert, local contractor. Does renos and such. Used to work pretty regular, and then people stopped building houses and such, and I guess business slowed down. He's comin' from the direction of the bar." He looked back to the direction the truck had come from, his face clouded by disappointment. "My guess is he was hittin' the bottle pretty hard tonight."

"I'm sorry, Chev. I hope your friend is okay and recovers quickly." Ava didn't know why she did it, but she put her hand on his upper arm. Usually, she resisted the urge to touch anyone when she was in the role of Agent James, but Redding had seemed upset, and she thought he needed a reassuring hand.

He looked at her hand, and then at her. "Thank you, Agent James. I knew you weren't the hard-nosed bitch everyone said you were." He nodded toward Halbert. "He's not exactly my friend, though. I know him pretty well. He's done some work for my family over the years. He's more my dad's friend, though. I hope he's okay, too."

The ambulance and other officers had parked and there was a bevy of commotion as everyone rushed to the Jeep. Every person there knew Halbert. They worked for a half-hour to get him out of the wreckage and secured onto a backboard. He was then rushed to the back of the ambu-lance and placed on the stretcher, which they loaded inside.

Halbert's face and chest were soaked with blood and his face had an assortment of cuts and gashes. She figured they had come from the break-ing windshield. His broken nose was likely from the impact of the steering wheel. He hadn't been wearing a seatbelt. His right leg had an extra bend below the knee, and that pants leg was dripping blood.

Two emergency technicians began working on him, and the two from the other bus were assessing the man at the truck. Ava wondered if the workers and officers also knew him. As she walked back toward the hotel, she glanced at the tag on his truck and saw Pine Oaks written across the bottom. Not Hidden Cove as everyone else's seemed to have. Her mind immediately latched onto Ms. Halliday's information about her daughter

Stephanie working at a bar, or rather a restaurant that included a bar, over in Pine Oaks.

Ava looked at the skid marks from the truck's tires and saw that he had been coming from the right direction. She wondered if he had perhaps given Stephanie a ride home.

She turned to look him over again, setting his face and build into her mind. He wasn't another restaurant or bar employee, and though some would perhaps look badly on her for the quick assessment, she didn't think anything about him fit the profile of a successful business owner, either. So, him being the owner of the restaurant didn't fit.

He could've been a patron who gave her a ride, or he could have been an acquaintance of Stephanie's.

Or he could have been no one. Just someone who happened to be driving from that direction.

In any case, if the snow didn't slow down, she wouldn't be able to get back out to Ms. Halliday's house to question Stephanie face to face, she wouldn't be able to get to anyone. Over the phone interviews were never thorough, and she despised doing them, but in this case, she found it might just be necessary. It wouldn't take people long to figure out her phone number and start avoiding her calls. It always happened, and there wasn't a thing she could do about it legally. Wait for the snow to melt, road conditions to improve, and drive out to their houses personally. That was the only answer. Which is what she preferred anyway.

As she walked back into her room, she eyed the table, then the window, then her phone. Half-past four. She turned on her heel and went to the little vestibule between the closet and the bathroom and put on a pot of the hotel's complimentary coffee. The stuff was strong enough to walk across the room and slap someone, but that was good. Just what she needed.

CHAPTER EIGHTEEN

T HE NEXT DAY, THE ROADS WEREN'T ANY BETTER. AVA COULDN'T GET
to where she wanted and needed to go. At seven in the morning, she
was pacing the floor of her hotel room like a caged animal. So many
things swirled through her mind that had nothing to do with her current
case that she couldn't hold her concentration on it for more than a couple
of minutes at a time.

At eight, she called Robert Mitchell and left another message for him
to call her. At five after, she called Elsie Halliday and got the answering
machine. She walked to the window and looked out at the thick covering
of snow everywhere. The roadway was no longer distinguishable from the
rest of the landscape. If it weren't for the electric lines and poles alongside
the road, she would have lost track of it at every point where the land on
the sides was flat.

The cars in the parking lot looked mired in with snow reaching the
bottoms of their doors, and there were no fresh tracks in or out of the front

that she could see. No cars had come or gone since the commotion of the wreck the night before, and the tracks from that incident were covered.

The snow had slowed some, but not nearly enough for her to be out driving along the mountainous roads safely. She huffed and turned back to her evidence tables. What could she constructively do with her time before the snowplows cleared the roads?

"I could be in South Africa trailing my mother in the heat instead of being stuck here, mired in the snow of the Kentucky hills. That's what I *could* be doing," she grumbled as she pulled out a chair.

She looked through the files again, checked her list of interviewees again, and scanned the photos for the hundredth time without finding anything new. No connections. The crimes had happened in the same house. That was the only tenuous connection evident.

Xavier had access to surveillance footage on which he thought he might have seen Molly. Neither he nor Dean had not called Ava back about it, which meant either they weren't finished rendering and analyzing it, or they hadn't even gotten to it yet.

I know Molly. I know the way she moves, walks, holds herself, even the tilt of her head. I know everything about her. If I could just see that footage, she thought, slumping back in her seat.

She dialed Dean at nine. She didn't know what other cases he'd be working, or whether he'd be doing anything with his cousin, but it was worth a shot. The phone rang and rang with no answer. She hesitated for a moment, wondering if it was worth the attempt to try to sweet-talk Xavier into giving her more information. Not that she was entirely sure that sweet-talking would even have an effect on him.

"Xavier," he said without inflection the moment he picked up the phone.

"Xavier, hi. It's—"

"Ava, I know. Caller ID. What do you need, Ava?"

"Well, I called to ask if you had found out anything on that footage yet. I was going to make small talk, but..." she trailed off.

"I'm not good at that. I haven't found out anything yet. Eric was too busy to check on it himself so we are waiting until the results come in."

Ava smiled. That was bad news for Molly's case, but it was good news for her. If the lab hadn't yet touched the file, she had a chance to get at it without drawing much attention. "You know, Xavier, if I could see that footage, I could tell you whether Molly's on it or not. If not, you could maybe direct your energies in another direction instead of waiting around for that to be rendered."

He gave his signature dry, short chuckle. "Now you're saying your perception is better than that of the machines that were designed to do what humans could not. Otherwise, the machines would never have been necessary."

"That's exactly what I'm saying, Xavier. I grew up with Molly. A machine can't read her body language the way I can. I don't need a super-machine-enhanced image to know whether it's her or not."

There was a very long silence from his end. Ava held her breath, hoping he was getting ready to cave and send her a copy. It wasn't the most likely scenario, though. Most likely, he was sitting there with the phone pressed to his ear, his gears grinding as he tried to process what she'd said. She could imagine smoke rolling out his ears as he made his very best effort to comprehend the logic of what she'd said. Grinning, she waited a few more seconds.

"Xavier? You still with me?" she asked.

"Yes. I'm still here. That's why the phone line didn't go dead and you didn't start hearing that annoying beeping."

Coming from anyone else, she would have thought they were being sarcastic. Coming from Xavier, she had no such thoughts. He was just being Xavier.

"So can I see the footage? It's in your hands. I can't sleep at night for thinking about it. By the time the footage goes through the lab, if that was Molly, she'll be long gone from Germany, and the search will have to start all over again. We might as well all start looking at it."

Even though the other end of the line was silent, she could almost hear his impressed nod. "Good point. But I'll need to ask Dean. He's the one who actually has it."

"Where's Dean now? I called him and he didn't pick up."

"He's on a case right now. I'll send him a message and see what he says."

It wasn't much, but it was the best she would get.

"I appreciate that, Xavier. You're a good friend."

If the statement meant anything to him, he didn't show it. "I know. Keep your phone on. I don't think it's much anyway. Doesn't make sense for the ring to keep her in the Ukraine or Germany when there's much better profit elsewhere, like the island."

"Xavier, what have you found out? What do you mean? I thought you were certain this lead was solid."

"I am certain. I just don't think any of those girls are still there. They were probably taken elsewhere so they would earn more money for the ring."

"Do you mean by selling them, or renting them out like they did on the island? And where do you think they would take them for this better profit?"

"Keep your phone on." He hung up.

Ava, shocked, took the phone from her ear. "All right, Xavier. Thanks, friend. I really appreciate it, and I owe you one," she said, even though he had already hung up.

Another hour passed before Xavier texted her to say Dean had sent him the file so he could send it to her. Moments later, the file came through. She transferred it to the laptop and backed it up to a flash drive within a couple of minutes. Her stomach fluttered as she opened the file and pulled up the full-screen function.

She pushed away from the table and viewed the screen from a few feet away. She wanted to simply watch it through, take in the whole of the scenery, before trying to home in and analyze it.

The footage was grainier than anything she'd ever seen. The quality was terrible, but if she didn't try to focus too hard on one thing, she got a generalized idea of the layout, what kind of neighborhood it probably was, and how the crowd moved.

There were about a dozen women who were herded around by three large, armed men. The men were dressed for winter weather in heavy leather coats and jackets, gloves, hats, but the girls were in strappy tank tops and skimpy shorts, none of which looked like they fit properly. Their clothes were either too large or too small. Most of them seemed to have bare feet from the way they moved.

Though she wanted badly to move closer and squint at each individual

138

woman, she held her place, knowing it was important to be as objective as possible before moving in for the details.

A cab pulled into frame, and a couple stepped out. They were also dressed warmly and seemed confident as they strode toward one of the armed men. Their heads were high and shoulders were straight. No hint of submissiveness or fear. They had to be veterans in the skin trade. The woman smiled broadly, and even on the grainy video, Ava could see she was strikingly pretty, and her cohort just as handsome. They were tall and had slim, athletic builds.

The ill-clad women huddled close to each other with their arms crossed over their chests. Ava knew it was to soak up each other's body heat. They were probably fiercely cold. There wasn't a straight set of shoulders or a head held high in that group. They kept their faces toward the ground or each other, and every one of them had slumped shoulders as they pressed close to those nearest them. Some kept shifting their weight to stand on one foot and lift the other off the cold pavement.

They were definitely barefoot. It was a way of controlling the group. Take their clothes and shoes, and they won't run far in the icy cold. All they could think about was getting warm and dry. Most likely, they hadn't been fed in a day or two, either.

Ava saw money exchange hands between the smiling woman and the armed man. The man nodded to the other two, and they brandished their weapons at the huddled group of weak, freezing, terrified women until the last one was pushed through the doorway of the building. The footage ended.

Ava's stomach had gone from fluttering to knotted. She was angry at those men and that nicely dressed, handsome couple. So angry that she wished she could get her hands on them.

Moving close to the table, she pulled the laptop to her and replayed the video at half-speed with the editing controls pulled up onscreen.

The next hour she spent doing some rendering and analyzing of her own on that footage. By the time she had finished, the picture was much clearer and she could make out the faces of the couple, though when she zoomed on them, they pixeled out. The same went for the group of women. Only three of them had shoes on their feet, if you called flip-flops shoes.

The woman Xavier had been unsure about, Ava was also unsure about.

She couldn't believe that she was unable to definitively point to the figure on the screen and identify her as Molly, or as just another poor woman caught up in a nightmare.

Focusing solely on that woman, she watched the footage over and over and over. If she was Molly, there were no Molly movements other than the slight tilt of her head when she was being yelled at by the armed men. From the side, she had a similar profile as that of Molly, but Ava couldn't make a positive ID as she had hoped.

If it was Molly on the video, she had endured years of pure hell. That had taken a toll on her. Her gait had changed. So had her posture, her silhouette, and everything—even her hair. The woman's hair was lank and dark and frizzy around the edges.

But still, the way she tilted her head and looked to the shouting man reminded Ava so much of her friend that it tugged at her heart.

In the end, it didn't matter if she *felt* that it was Molly or not. It only mattered if she could make a positive identification, and she could not.

CHAPTER NINETEEN

A
T TEN, AVA WENT TO THE WINDOW AGAIN. THE SNOWPLOWS HAD come through but had only taken off the layers of snow, leaving the glistening thick sheet of ice on the road. It was still too risky to take her car out, especially on these rural roads. She decided to call Sal and see if they could brainstorm the Hidden Cove cases. Sal had digital access to most every file and photo that Ava had lying on the tables.

"I hear the whole region's snow-locked today. Are you snowed in at the hotel?" Sal asked.

"I am. It sucks, too. I'm going stir crazy just sitting here. None of my interviewees are answering or returning my calls, and there's thick ice everywhere the snowplows have touched. I've not seen any traffic at all, and none of the vehicles in the parking lot have moved since last night. I called to see if you wanted to brainstorm over the phone for a while. Are you free?"

"Actually, I'm in the office here working on another case. I'll be free later. Probably around six this evening, if you want to do it then."

Ava was disheartened but tried to keep it to herself. "Maybe. I don't know what I'll be doing by then. If the roads clear and this damnable snow stops, I'll be stopping by the office and then going to talk to Elsie Halliday and Robert Mitchell again."

"Be careful about going out at dark. You've seen how quick the weather can turn rabid around here. You'll be snowed in at one of their houses if that happens."

"I definitely don't want that, but I *have* to talk to them ASAP. Especially to Stephanie. They just keep ignoring my calls and it makes me mad."

"Welcome to the backwoods," Sal said with a chuckle.

They said goodbye and disconnected.

Ava glared out the window. She was a federal agent. Being sidelined because of bad weather seemed like a low blow, but one she couldn't do much about.

She decided her first order of business would be getting something to eat. Realizing it was already going on eleven, she marveled that her stomach had only just begun to grumble at the injustice. There was no way she was going to get anywhere driving, that was obvious. She also did not have a kitchenette in her room, so she couldn't cook there, besides, she had no food in the room. She had planned on eating out for her meals.

She approached the receptionist downstairs, who couldn't have been more than eighteen or nineteen. "Hi, I was wondering, do you happen to have a kitchen here? Vending machines, anything?"

The young woman nodded. "There's a little room around the corner with vending machines. There's not much of a selection, though. It's just chips and candy bars and sodas. Way over-priced ones at that."

"I guess that will have to do. I can't go out in this." She nodded toward the parking lot.

The receptionist shook her head. "I've been here since last night, and it looks like I'll be staying another night if they don't get it cleared some more. I know a guy who has a four-wheel-drive with chains on the tires. He might go by and pick something up for you. I wouldn't mind having something myself, actually." She pulled out her cell phone and started scrolling through her contacts list.

Ava wanted to stop her and tell her it was okay, no need to do that, but she also was very hungry, and it wouldn't hurt to have someone tell her what the roads were like away from the hotel. For all she knew, this could be the worst spot in the whole town. The town might be clear enough to drive.

The girl covered the phone. "What do you want him to get for you? Something from the diner, fast food, grocery haul?"

"What are you getting?"

"Pizza," she laughed.

Ava nodded with a bright grin. "All right. I'll call and order three large pizzas. One for you, one for me, and one for the delivery driver. I'll pay for all of them over the phone. Tell him to ask for the James order."

"Really?" the girl asked, her eyes sparkling. "You don't have to do that."

Ava shrugged. "It's the least I can do. I'm getting pepperoni and pine-apple. What do you want?"

The girl wrinkled her nose in disgust, her wonder suddenly gone. "Ew. Just pepperoni is fine."

She relayed the message to the man on the other end of the phone while Ava called the pizza joint and placed the order. "He said it would take him about thirty minutes to pick it up and get here. Apparently, the roads aren't as bad in town as they are here, otherwise it would take him at least an hour."

"That's good to know. Can you just call my room when the order gets here?" Ava had no doubt she would see the truck coming into the lot, but she wanted a smooth segue to get her out of the lobby and back to her room. She didn't have time to chit-chat with the receptionist. Maybe it was just that she didn't want to. She wasn't in a very sociable mood.

The Prague incident had taken hold of her once again, and she wanted to get back to the room so she could compare those files with the files she had on the island case. There could be some hidden gem between the two that would give her at least a hint as to where Molly and the others had been taken.

Prague had happened so many years ago, that in one sense, it seemed like another life to Ava. In another sense, though, it was as if she were still in that dark, damp, dank basement room being yelled at in a foreign lan-guage, still floundering in the darkness for answers that she couldn't grasp.

The pizza came and Ava gave the guy who looked to be all of nine-teen or twenty a forty-dollar tip. His face brightened, and then he had looked suspiciously at her.

"I didn't just do something illegal, did I?" he asked in all seriousness.

Ava laughed, unable to stop it before it burst forth. "No. I promise. I'm an agent for the FBI, I can't do anything illegal, or have you do it, without losing my job and my freedom." She waggled the box of pizza at him. "Sorry, but you delivered only pizzas. How are the roads beyond my little frozen wonderland?"

He shrugged. "Good if you have a front-wheel-drive or a four-wheel-drive like I have. Might be a little slippery in spots, but not bad as this," he gestured at the parking lot.

"What about the other little mountain roads? They look like this, too?"

"Some of them do. Which one you need to drive on, and I'll tell you." He hitched his jeans and took a stance that said he was playing the role of someone very important.

"Pleasant Hill, or out toward Pine Oaks. Either one," she said.

"Pleasant Hill is definitely closed. The closer you get to Pine Oaks, the deeper the ice is on the roads. Because of the heavy tree cover on both sides of the road, it don't get enough sunshine to melt it. My bet is that road will be closed for a while. At least a few days."

"All right. Thanks again," she said, nodding her head as she turned to the stairs.

While she devoured pizza, she looked over the files and went over memories. The way the men dressed. The way they talked. Their hairstyles, voices, accents, guns, the rooms she was in… nothing gave even the slightest hint as to where the men were from, or where they might be headed.

And even then, that was six years ago. A lot could happen in six years.

She resolved that she would get out of the hotel parking lot the next day, even if she had to bundle up and walk to town. She couldn't sit in her room bouncing from the Hidden Cove cases, to the Prague incident, to the island, for even one more day.

Leaving five pieces of the pizza for later, she closed the box and set it on the dresser. She decided to call Aunt Kay and talk to her for a while, unless she was too busy. She hoped her aunt wasn't busy, as she really needed to connect with someone not from Hidden Cove, Kentucky.

CHAPTER TWENTY

K AY ANSWERED ON THE THIRD RING. "HELLO, AVA. HOW ARE YOU, sweetie?"

It was wonderful to hear Aunt Kay's sweet voice. "Oh, so much better now. I'm snowed in here and I think I'm suffering from cabin fever."

"That sounds terrible. Your uncle thought you were doing rather well last time he spoke to you. What's changed? Are you feeling unwell?"

"No. It's nothing like that. My health is fine. It's the snow and the place mostly. The snow has put a halt to my investigation and it's driving me insane," Ava said, making sure to add a bit of a laugh to emphasize that she was only joking.

"Can't do anything over the computer or phone? Is there even internet connection where you are? I heard it's way out in the mountains."

"I have connection, but you know I work mostly with hard copy. As far as the phone, I *would* do interviews via phone if I could get anyone to answer my calls."

"Doesn't take long for people to know your number even when you're from out of town. Your uncle goes through the same thing. He buys burner phones when he gets really desperate."

"Hopefully, I won't have to worry about it by tomorrow. There's supposed to be a break in the weather and I'll be able to get back on the roads. But we'll see. Uncle Ray said you were getting ready to head out to another charity function soon." She didn't really pose it as a question but knew Kay would happily fill her in on what was up with the foundation. It was her favorite subject any time.

"I am," Kay cleared her throat and then went silent.

Ava waited, expecting more. When it wasn't forthcoming, she scowled, wondering what was wrong. "Aunt Kay?"

"Yes, dear?"

"The function?"

"Yes. What about it?" Her voice had tightened a notch or two, and she had clammed up. Totally out of character for Kay.

"Aren't you worried about attending another so soon after the last, less than relaxing one?" Ava sat on the edge of the bed, pressing the phone tighter to her ear as if she could make herself hear every minute sound. As if that would somehow give her an insight into what Kay was doing on the other end of the line. She certainly wasn't giving up much information.

"No, I'm not. Should I be, sweetie? The last one was a fluke. We all know that. Won't happen again. We've already made great strides to root out the people responsible for those criminal acts."

"Well, I'm worried about you going, and it wasn't just a fluke. It was a pre-planned murderous plot carried out by some very dangerous people. We all know that to be the fact of the matter."

She didn't want her aunt to be able to delude herself into believing the world was mostly good and people were mostly kind and caring. As an agent, Ava had witnessed firsthand exactly how wrong that perception was.

There was a long sigh and then the sound of Kay smacking her lips, a thing she did when exasperated or severely stressed. "Okay. It was terrible. We've been over that, but I can't just sit around and wither away while the foundation goes down the drain, either."

"All right. See, that's progress. At least you're admitting that it does bother you. At least now I know that you understand there is danger there.

Why don't you postpone the function? Just for a little while. Give your nerves time to settle, you know."

"No, I don't know, sweetheart. I can't postpone the function. The foundation needs it badly, especially in times like these. That's where a lot of our extra funding comes from. Every penny we take in from these events is used to do that tiny bit extra for the people we help. It allows for that extra pair of shoes, the new tires on the single mother's car. The single mother who fell on hard times, whose husband or boyfriend was abusing her and her children, forcing her to leave under cover of night with nothing but the clothes on her back and her kids at her sides just to survive. Or the young girl's extra month of counseling after she's saved from the hands of a trafficking ring. You know how desperately important that is. I can't postpone, and I won't."

Yes, Ava knew the importance of the work, but Kay wasn't the only person working to keep the Avilion Foundation running as it did. She worked in tandem with a group of like-minded people who were capable of spearheading the functions in her stead.

"What good does it all come to if you end up hurt, or worse?" Ava asked.

Another silence stretched between them. Then the sigh and lip-smack. "Ava, I love you like a daughter. You know that, I hope."

"I do. And I love you like a second mother. That's why I worry about you so much with all this happening so recently. This was a huge international network that used Avilion as a front. They lost exorbitant amounts of potential and real profits. If they blame you or the foundation in any way, you could really be endangering yourself by having another one so soon. They might see it as you taunting them."

"Stop, Ava. I mean it. You wouldn't stop working for the Bureau just because it's dangerous, would you?"

Ava chuckled. "No way."

"All right. I feel the same way. Would you quit your job because a bad guy shot at you, or even grazed you with a bullet?"

"Nope," Ava replied automatically.

"And, pray tell, why would you not quit even if you suffered such a wound?"

"Because I'm working to stop as many of the bad guys as possible before they hurt more people. I'm working toward an ideal. The scum needs to be cleaned up, and that's my job. I do this so that good citizens can go about their lives with less worry."

"You mean that you just can't let the bad guys win no matter what it costs you, right?"

Ava didn't like the tone or the direction the conversation had turned toward, but she was getting the message loud and clear. "Something like that, yeah."

"That's why I simply cannot postpone. It would be tantamount to letting the criminals win. If I hide away, trembling in fear, they win and the whole purpose of my charity is defeated."

She had a point there. Ava finally relented. "Well, if I can't talk you out of going, and I know I can't, at least take some extra precautions. Please. For me."

"That is completely doable, and thanks to Uncle Ray, is already in progress as much as possible. Besides, he'll be close by during the event. I'll be okay. I promise. And, I'll keep my eyes and ears open for anything suspicious."

"You mean Uncle Ray won't be *at* the function? He'll be working again?" Ava tensed. She had hoped her uncle would be able to attend. She had thought Kay was going to do what she could to hold the events at times when it was most likely he *could* attend.

"Oh, shush. You know how the life of an agent is. You can't schedule anything, and if you try, you're always disappointed with the results. Now, I'm telling you to stop making a fuss over me. I'll be fine. You shouldn't be worrying so much about me with all you have to worry about already."

Kay was right about not ever being able to schedule anything. Doctor and dentist appointments sometimes took months to finally get to, and she was sure the receptionists dreaded making her appointments because she had to reschedule so often. Kay was also right about Ava having a lot to worry about. Her missing mother, first and foremost, and her father.

"All right. I'll shush, as you said, but I will not stop worrying. I'll never stop worrying, Aunt Kay."

"I know you won't, but I was hoping to ease your mind a little bit, anyway. Have you had any news about your mother?"

"No. The Bureau is still working on several leads that I think might trail back to why she went missing, though. They still won't let me in on the case, of course."

"And Uncle Ray isn't much help in that department, either. They're keeping him pretty far out of that investigation, too. I'm sure your mother will be okay, though. She's strong-willed and wily. You had to get it from somewhere, you know." Kay chuckled, but the sound was hollow, humorless.

"If I hear anything, I'll let you two know immediately."

"Is your father doing well? Does he need anything? I could stop by, or send Ray if you need us to check on him. I know phone calls are good, but there's nothing like having a set of eyes actually on someone you love."

"No, that's fine, but thank you. I can tell by talking to him how he's doing and if he's fibbing about eating or not. So far, I think he's done commendably well under the circumstances."

They spoke for a few more minutes, and then Ava said she had to go. The sound of ice plows had drawn her attention, and she had watched two go up the road, throwing plumes of ice and slush to the side. A few minutes later, they had gone down the other side of the road. The pavement was black underneath, and there was no sheen from a covering of ice.

Ava thought that black pavement was about the prettiest thing she'd seen all day. It meant she would definitely be back on the road the next day.

CHAPTER TWENTY-ONE

T HE NEXT DAY, WITH THE ROAD CLEARED IN FRONT OF THE HOTEL, Ava watched from her window as two men with snow blowers and shovels cleared a path to the road. At first, she thought they would just work from their vehicles outward, leaving everyone else's vehicles blanketed and banked in, but they didn't. After clearing their interconnecting path, they moved slowly, clearing most of the lot.

It was time to get back to being Agent James, and she couldn't wait another minute. Stuck-in-her-hotel-room Ava wasn't nice, she wasn't easy to deal with. Agent James walked out confidently and got into her car. The parking lot had been cleared, but there was still a lot of coverage on the macadam. Someone, she guessed one of the men, had thrown ice-melting salt and what looked like cat litter on the remaining layer of slush.

It took about three minutes longer than forever for her car to actually blow heat from its vents. By then, she was beyond shivering and wishing to be out of the shade of the building so the windshield could magnify the heat of the sun and maybe thaw her out before she got to her destination.

She found out in a hurry that just because the roads through town were clear and drivable, did not mean the back roads or mountain roads were the same. In some places, she skidded dangerously close to the edge or to a deep ditch, and she would hold her breath, grip the wheel, and continue on like a pro. She handled the nasty road conditions like a veteran, she thought. Of course, the guy behind her in the old 1970s truck might not have had the same opinion. She barely saw him shift to the side and never once saw him get heart-poundingly, dangerously close to the edge. But still, she thought she had done a good job.

Anyway, she had finally reached Robert Mitchell's house. He had meticulously cleaned his driveway and parking area. The walkway, steps, and the entirety of the porch were also clean enough to make one wonder if the snowfall had somehow missed them completely. The yard and shrubs were blanketed in several inches of heavy, wet snow. Tree branches drooped and power lines sagged under its weight.

As she made her way toward the door, she was thankful that Mitchell had been so dedicated to clearing a path. If she had stepped in the yard, she would have sunk nearly to her knees in the snow.

She knocked on the front door. There was a light on in the hallway and in the living room. She could see clearly through the partially closed blinds. There was no movement inside, though. She cupped her hands around her eyes, pressed to the glass, and peered in, trying to see into the farthest reaches of the dark spaces and corners. But she saw nothing.

"Mr. Mitchell," she called, knocking on the door again. In the cold, each time she rapped the door, her knuckles ached. The cold had seeped into her very bones. "Mr. Mitchell, I know you're in there. Your vehicle is out here and I see lights on. Please answer the door. I need to talk to you."

She knocked louder, grimacing at the ache in her fingers as she did so. She took a look toward the snow, noting that there were no tracks—human or animal. No one had left the property on foot, and someone had recently cleared the snow and salted the pathway. If it had been done the night before, there would be splotches of snow because it had fallen until morning.

She turned the other direction to scan the border between this house and the Jakobson house. The hedges held undisturbed blankets of snow. She turned her attention back to the window in the door and caught movement, as if Robert had slipped from the living room toward the back of the house. He wouldn't be trying to run out of the house to avoid her, but he might have been just slipping toward a more comfortable room. One she couldn't see into if she moved by windows. His bedroom would have been the best location if that were the case. It was on the second floor.

"Mr. Mitchell, I just saw you in there. Stop trying to avoid me. This will only take ten minutes of your time." She waited another long minute and heard nothing. "All right, Mr. Mitchell. I guess for peace of mind, since you've not answered or returned any of my calls, and now I can't get you to the door knowing you're in there, I'm worried for your welfare. I can call the local PD and have them come do a welfare check, or I can call emergency services because I just caught a glimpse of movement and heard a thump. That could have been you falling down and hitting your head, or—"

The door flung wide and banged the inside wall. "Ain't no need to cause a scene! I'm right here. Damn shame a man can't have a peaceful day in his own house without being harassed over a five-year-old case that he knows nothing more about than what he already told you!" As he spoke, his voice rose in volume. The color in his cheeks rose in tandem with his voice, from pale tan to bright red.

"There you are, Robert. May I come inside, or would you prefer standing out here?" She smiled at him.

"Well, I ain't standing out here with that wind blowin' off an iceberg and right across me." Angrily he stepped back and motioned her inside.

"Thank you, sir. You know I really was beginning to worry if you were okay or not. That was no joke."

Scoffing, he rolled his eyes and yanked a chair from the table. "Whatever, lady. Ask your questions and be gone. I got stuff to do today."

"Oh, I thought you wanted a peaceful day at home, but never mind that. Whatever. It is your day to do with as you please." She nudged the chair out with her foot. "Thought you wanted to sit in the living room, or at least softer chairs next time, because these were too hard and hurt your back."

"Yeah, and I told you to call before you came back and I would make those arrangements."

"Well, I did call. I did. But if you're okay with the chairs, if you're comfortable, they're fine with me. I just didn't want them hurting you like you said they did last time, is all." She made a show of getting out her notepad and pen and then flipping to the relevant pages.

Robert Mitchell grew more agitated by the second, it seemed. That was okay. Ava was aiming for him to be a little riled. Angry people sometimes say things they would not otherwise say. Just like drunks—they'll usually tell you the truth without a single hesitation. Little kids will, too.

Drunks, kids, angry people. Funny how those three things have something so fundamental in common, she thought.

"All right, Mr. Mitchell. I'm just here to kind of go over what we discussed last time I was here. See, I've got a little bit of a problem with some of the statements, and I thought you could help me clear things up."

"Dear God, what else? I've given my statement. Numerous times, as a matter of fact. I've been more than helpful, and I would appreciate it if you and your lackeys could get your crap together, so I don't have to keep doing this. It's ridiculous."

"I understand, sir. It's not real fun on this end, either, I assure you. But I really do need you to give me your statement just one more time. As annoying as that is for you." She smiled and tilted her head as she placed the tip of the pen against the paper, readying to scribble shorthand.

With an irritated glare, he folded his hands on the table. "The night in question I was with a friend. We were camping and hunting several hours away from here. I wasn't even here."

She scribbled longhand, nodding. She didn't rush at it either, giving him time to add something else if he felt the need. Apparently, he did not.

"Now, Mr. Mitchell. Here's where I ran into the problem. Oh, wait," she said, flipping the page. "Could I get the name of your friend? The one you were camping and hunting with."

"Alan Watkins."

"What's the name of the place you two went camping and hunting?"

"Buffalo Mountain," he said, his voice deadpan and his eyes flaring with anger.

"What's the name of the campground there?"

"There wasn't one. We pitched tents and camped in the forest, up next to the ridgeline, lady."

She shot him a look, then smiled. "It's Agent James, or Aviva, thank you." She looked back to the paper. "What did you say you were hunting?"

He huffed a sigh and crossed his arms over his big barrel chest. "Raccoons and deer. Need me to spell *raccoon* for you, too?"

"No, thanks. I got it." She beamed a grin at him. "That's two c's, right? R-a-c-c-o-o-n?"

He didn't respond, but she didn't need him to as she meticulously made a show of writing the word on the pad. "Did you two do anything else while you were there? How many nights did you stay? Did you perhaps leave the mountain to go get supplies, food, anything?"

"We fished a little in one of the creeks up there but didn't catch anything. Never do up that far. And, no, we didn't leave the mountain for supplies or whatever. We had our food and beer with us. We stayed two nights, maybe three, hell, I can't remember for sure now. That's been five years ago."

She sat straight and flipped the pages back and forth as if she were comparing the statements. She clicked her pen a few more times, eyeing him to watch in minute detail how he'd respond to her next line of questioning. Fortunately for her, his attention seemed to be on the pages.

She let out a soft "hm," as if noticing something for the first time. She flipped back and forth a couple more times and then nodded to herself. It was all a charade, of course, but all the better to keep him on the edge of his seat.

"So," she started, then flipped between the pages. "Mr. Mitchell, here is where I'm having a problem." She tapped on the piece of paper and turned it to him, still holding her fingers to mark the other pages.

He leaned a little and looked at it. "What's that?"

"It's the statement you gave last time." She flipped to another page. "And this one here. It's the one you gave five years ago." She let the pages fall flat and tapped the one she'd been writing on. "And finally, today's statement." She looked at him, letting her face fall emotionless. "They don't seem to match, and I need to know why."

"Well, I wouldn't know. Probably because someone wrote it down wrong back then."

"No, you wrote out that statement, and it's changed now."

He rubbed his chin, and for the first time, his eyes lost their fiery anger. Now he looked worried, and his face began to pale. "Whatever I wrote that first time has to be what happened. I can't recall every detail five years later. That's the whole point of the cops having me write it down so soon after it happened. Right? That would be my guess, anyway." His breathing sped up.

"Yeah, usually that's the best. Back then, though, you were pretty adamant that you were fishing on a lake three hours away."

He nodded vigorously. "Yeah. That lake is at Buffalo Mountain. You can go check it out. I ain't lying about that. Maybe that's where we fished instead of the creek. Either way, we didn't catch anything on that trip. I remember that much."

"But not whether you were there for just one night, or maybe up to three nights. And not whether you only fished, or if you hunted, too. And, wasn't it only deer hunting and camping? Oh, no, wait, now you said there was also raccoon hunting thrown in for good measure." She stood.

"Are we done?" He shot from his seat, looking relieved and a bit scared.

"For now." She waggled the notebook. "Just gotta figure this out. You know, I don't really think you're lying on purpose. I just think that if you misremembered these things, you might have misremembered other things, too. Things about the Johnsons, or the Jakobsons." She turned and walked off the porch. "I'll call again. Answer next time I ring your phone, though, okay?"

"All right." Robert Mitchell slunk back into the shadow and the door closed slowly.

Ava decided that she needed to speak to Mitchell's friend. Alan Watkins. He was present in each version of Robert's statement. Maybe he could give a clearer picture of what the two men were really doing that night.

Robert was the common denominator between the cold case and the new case. There had to be something there that was overlooked. She couldn't find it in the notes where anyone had done more than take Alan Watkins' statement. There had been no follow-up, no phone calls, nothing. They'd let the man alone because he had alibied out, just like Robert Mitchell.

Ava wouldn't give them that benefit of the doubt without first proving there was a reason to do it.

CHAPTER TWENTY-TWO

ORWARD MOTION WAS THE ONLY WAY AVA COULD SURVIVE. IF SHE focused on the cold case, she thought she would have just that. She again had hope that she could solve it, but she would have to focus all her energies on it for a while.

She headed to the office to work on the case. She slipped through the back door and managed to get all the way to her office without being seen. That was a bit of good fortune for once.

There was only one Alan Watkins in the area according to social media. She hoped it was the right one. Fortunately for her, there was a public phone number listed. After calling it and leaving a message for him to return her call, she pulled the files from the cold case, cross-referencing his name and the number she'd looked up online with the one listed in the files. The phone number was different in the file, but a quick call to that one confirmed it was a disconnected line. She hoped the address was still accurate, at least.

She felt Alan Watkins' story could break the case. If he corroborated the fishing story, she might be able to pick at it long enough for it to unravel around him like a badly woven tapestry. If the story had been true, why would Robert's story have changed at all? Back then, it would have been simple for him to call up a friend and ask to have him tell the same story. Especially a good friend. And Alan must have been a good friend. Otherwise, Robert would have used someone else to alibi him out back then.

After five years, though, stories that are made up start to change. The sharp-edged details become blurry in one's mind, and there's a bit of fetching around, shifting in one's seat, and usually fidgeting as that person tries to recall exactly what he said all those years ago.

This was definitely the kind of interview she wanted to conduct face to face.

As she thought about that, she decided to call the Halliday residence one more time before heading out there to hopefully catch Stephanie at home. The answering machine picked up. Ava left a message and thought it was great that no one was around to see her rolling her eyes and rubbing her temple with her free hand as she did so. It was more than irritating to know that people were simply avoiding her that easily and stalling her progress.

Sure, there were probably not-so-legal things taking place in a lot of lives around Hidden Cove, but that wasn't the only place such things happened. Any sort of law enforcement was eyed with suspicion or outright disdain in such places. Ava wasn't interested in who was lighting up the occasional joint and playing puff-puff-pass in the evenings, though. She was only interested in solving a cold case that should never have gone cold in the first place.

She had come to the conclusion that a high number of cold cases from smaller towns were due to all the people knowing one another. When you see the same people day after day, week after week, your kids grow up together, your parents went to church together, there's only one elementary school that everyone has attended since 1928, there's a huge chance that you will make assumptions about those people based on what you know about them from your daily lives together in Small Town, USA.

She really didn't think these assumptions were made on purpose, or to be lazy—although granted, laziness did sometimes play a part. But that didn't matter to Ava. She believed that the duty of law enforcement was to follow any lead, no matter where it went. It doesn't matter if your own sainted grandmother is a lead. You need to check it out and make sure dear old gran is as saintly as she'd have everyone believe.

Skeletons hide in many closets. Some are buried deep; others are just behind the door.

Giving the evidence boards a cursory glance, she grabbed her coat and files and ducked out the door. Once again, she walked swiftly, and with luck, she ran into no one to slow her down.

The sky had mostly cleared and the sun was bright. Blinding glints bounced off windshields as she made her way to her car. The wind still cut coldly to the bone, though, ripping through the parking lot and blasting her coat open. The maelstrom took her breath and engulfed her core, tearing her hair back from her face and neck.

Grabbing her coat, she pulled it tight against her body and shivered as she unlocked the car. The interior had gone cold while she had been in the office. With tingling, cold fingers, she started the engine. It took five solid minutes for any heat to blow through the vents, and that wasn't very warm, just warmer than the frigid temperature she was currently enduring.

Still shivering, Ava pulled onto the road. There was little traffic. The cold had kept most people indoors, she figured.

"I wonder if it's cold where Mom is," she wondered aloud. On the heels of that, Molly's face popped into her mind. Was it cold wherever Molly was? Was she chilled to the bone? Did she still harbor hope that she would be rescued, or that she could somehow escape? If not, that probably chilled her heart and soul in a way that made the Kentucky winter seem like a vacation in the Bahamas.

The road slowly changed from the country-urban setting to a more rural one as she drove and wondered about her mother and Molly, and all the lives affected by their disappearances. Even though a victim never knows, or perhaps they do, they aren't a victim alone. They are alone in what happens to them, but their loved ones—family and friends, and in many cases, even mere acquaintances that they barely know—are affected deeply by their disappearance. It matters little whether the victim is found dead or just not found at all. Many lives are always affected, changed, and sometimes ruined by the situation.

That was one reason Ava had been so determined to join the Bureau. She hated seeing what happened to the victims, but also to their families and friends. She had seen the ripple-in-a-pond effect numerous times, and wanted badly to thwart it whenever, wherever, and however she could.

The road began its steady incline and she focused more intently on it, drawing her mind away from ideas and ideals and back to the black-top. The curvy, narrowing road that would take her to the Halliday house.

She couldn't remember how long it had been since she'd passed a car going in the opposite direction. At the edge of town? She thought that was right, but her mind had been elsewhere, too, so she couldn't be sure.

Ice still clung to the edges of the road in wide strips. To keep her driver's side tires on the clear asphalt, she had to cross far over into the other lane. She slowed as much as she dared, fearing that someone might be headed toward town and hit her head-on coming around one of the steep curves.

If she slowed too much and had to scoot out of the other lane, she might spin out and not make it up the road. Worse, she might spin out and end up over the edge. In some places, the edge didn't mean a ditch, it meant a steep drop of twenty or more feet. The terrain was as unpredictable as the weather in Kentucky.

About a mile and a half from Elsie Halliday's house, Ava saw the bad spot of ice covering the entire road before she got to it. It was in a short straight-of-way. Her heart skipped and adrenaline dumped. She had to make a decision while on the move. Give it gas and try to make it through the snow and ice patch, or stop and try to turn around.

It didn't take much thought. She pressed on the accelerator and gained a little speed, aimed her car through the center, hoping it would give her enough room for slipping and sliding without going into the ditch, and gripped the wheel.

The layered catastrophe of snow-slush-ice forced her car to the right. She corrected the steering and kept on the gas. Her heart pounded, her senses sharpened, and a sense of impending triumph came over her as she neared the far side. The road was wet but clear just beyond the patch.

The front end veered toward the left-hand ditch. Ava slowly and deliberately corrected, but the car stubbornly kept to its course. The ditch became a large ravine in her mind, and she lost her nerve at the last moment.

Letting off the gas, she turned into the skid. Finally, she did the one thing she knew not to do. Her logical brain screamed for her foot to stay off the brake pedal, but some inherent urge to bring the car to a stop overruled, and she hit the brake.

Her knuckles turned white as she gripped the wheel and tried to turn steeper into the skid. The back end of the car glided over the thick sheet of ice, and she found herself facing the opposite direction.

The car still slid toward the ditch and she almost panicked.

Almost.

Her level-headedness returned and took over in an instant. She loosened her grip on the wheel, removed her foot from the brake, and put the car in neutral. The car straightened up and she steered it easily away from the ditch and let it drift under its own forward volition toward the center of the road. When she was far enough away from the ditch, she gently applied the brake, pulled the gearshift back into drive, and eased off the brake. The car ran true back to the side of the bad patch she'd originally entered it from.

Taking a deep breath, she cleared the ice and put the brake on again. She was able to pull over into a shoulder and stared into the rearview, catching her breath. Her tracks ran right to the edge of the ditch. Another few inches and she would have been stuck there, the car tipped to one side, and probably with no cell signal.

"So close," she grumbled. If only she could have made it through, it would have been just another few blocks to Elsie Halliday's house. Three steep curves past the slippery deathtrap, and she could have pulled right into the driveway.

Shaking her head, she headed back the way she'd come. There was no getting to Stephanie for a while yet. If she couldn't get in, it was very likely they couldn't get out, either. The road could have been in even worse condition farther up.

"Yeah, or it could be completely clear," she muttered, still upset at getting so close and having to turn back. Not to mention the little incident had scared her. She hadn't been that close to panicking in years. Panic wasn't usually in her nature. Something about skidding out of control, though, had raised the head of some primal instinct, or primal fear inside her, and had led her to the very edge of panic. It hadn't pushed her over it, thankfully, but it had come pretty darn close.

At least the road to the station was safe. She could think while driving back there. Her little adventure had cost her time that she really couldn't spare. Daylight hours in the winter in Kentucky were few and precious. After dark, the temperature could plummet. Another storm could plaster the entire place in a foot of snow within hours. Anything could happen.

She had to figure out her next move and act on it while there was plenty of daylight left. Which meant, she had to be done and heading back to the hotel by at least five that evening. At half-past five, the sun would set, and she didn't want to risk being out in those mountains or on an isolated stretch of road after dark.

CHAPTER TWENTY-THREE

OFFICER REDDING NEARLY KNOCKED HER DOWN AS SHE ROUNDED the corner to head into her office. He was carrying two file boxes, and the top one flew to the floor. Papers and files erupted in the hallway, fluttering down just like so much snow outside.

Ava caught her balance. The boxes had slammed into her shoulder, spinning her in one direction and Redding in the other.

"Are you all right, Ava? I mean, Agent James?"

Nodding, she ran a hand over her hair, pushing it back from her face. "I'm fine," she said, looking down at the mess. "I'm sorry." She wouldn't want the job of sorting the papers back into their correct files.

"I should be the one apologizing. It was me who came around the corner blind. You know, like nobody else ever walks here, or something." He set his box down. "Truth is, I was mad as hell. They keep treating me like I'm some kind of lackey. An errand boy who ends up doing all the crap they don't want to do themselves." He started scooping up papers and cramming them helter-skelter into the box.

She could sympathize with his feelings. She had been the low woman on the totem pole for some time after entering the Bureau. It hadn't taken her long to earn respect as an agent, though. She bent to help him pick up the papers.

"Shouldn't we at least try to get them back into order?" she asked.

He laughed and winked at her. "I think I'll take them to Records and take my time sorting through them. They'll have to get someone else to go fetch their coffee and sandwiches and whatever else they want done for them. Just drop 'em in the box."

She shot him a doubtful look, still holding a handful of papers and mostly empty file folders.

He made an X over his heart. "I promise," he said.

He nodded toward the open box, and she dropped the papers inside. "How long have you worked here?"

Shaking his head, he blew air between his lips. "Too long to still be their runner. That much is for sure."

"Shouldn't you be out there? On patrol or beat, or something of that nature?" she asked.

Chev shook his head. "Not in this weather. We only have four vehicles equipped for bad road conditions, and none of them are mine."

"But the roads aren't all bad. Town is fine."

"The roads don't have to all be bad. Patrol routes take us all over the county, not just inside city limits." He picked up the last of the papers and dropped them in the box, then crammed the now-crooked lid on it. He stood and put it on top of the other box, picked them both up again, and grinned at her. "Out here, there's three ways of doing things. The right way, the wrong way, and the chief's way. If you're here long enough, you'll learn that about him firsthand."

Ava shook her head but said nothing. She didn't work for Chief Grady. She wasn't even working *with* him. She was there representing the FBI, and to solve a case that the chief's investigators could not. It usually didn't come to it, but if it did, she would go over his head. She would never say anything like that to anyone in this small-town precinct, though. They thought little enough of her, and most of them visibly bristled when she walked into a room. Showing off her authority would only serve to drive that wedge deeper between her and them. She wasn't there to alienate anyone, but she wouldn't take any guff from them either.

In her office, she took off her coat and draped it over her chair. How long would it stay there? She guessed not long. She had never been one to stay idly in the office when she could be out there, and in forward motion, perpetually moving toward solving something.

She took up the file on Robert Mitchell and pulled the sheet with Alan Watkins' information on it. Sliding it into an empty file folder, she picked up a legal pad and put it with the papers. She called Alan's number. Voicemail. She left another message but had no intentions of waiting to hear back from him this time.

She took his file, Robert's file, and Stephanie's. Her coat hadn't even cooled to room temperature when she slid her arms back into it and headed out the door again. If Alan wouldn't call her, she would go to his house. Hopefully, the cold had persuaded him to stay at home.

With his address in her phone, she headed out. Traffic in town had picked up, and everywhere she looked there were people bundled in layers topped with heavy coats, gloves, scarves—most of them crocheted and thick—and knit caps that came down over their ears. They walked like penguins through parking lots or along sidewalks as they carefully traversed the ice and snow. The grocery store had been swarmed. There was hardly an empty parking space anywhere.

Ava grinned. Every time snow hit, it seemed, grocery shops were the hardest hit as people panic-bought enough kitchen staples and canned food to last until doomsday. She had never understood it, but she didn't have a houseful of kids, a husband, pets, or anyone else to think about during such a time. It was just her. If she happened to get snowed in and ran out of milk or eggs, it wouldn't be the end of the world. She'd just eat and drink something else. Or she'd bundle up and walk to the convenience store down the road. She did realize that these people, most of them, didn't have that option. They lived too far away to walk anywhere if the conditions were that bad.

Soon, she was on a long, straight road, following the route outlined in red toward Alan's house. It was one of the few straight roads she'd seen since coming to Hidden Cove, and she relaxed as she drove it for several miles.

As she entered Spalding County, she was impressed by the obvious difference in the way people lived there as opposed to the way they lived in Hidden Cove. No doubt, the flatter, more manageable terrain had a bit to do with it, but so did access to better-paying jobs, she was sure.

There were actual neighborhoods with houses and nicely kept, neatly fenced lots to their backs on both sides of the road. There were few trees crowding yards, no barren spots that sprouted large rocky outcroppings, no busted vehicles propped up on blocks with part of the innards lying on the ground. It was just a neater, cleaner, more open area. The kind of place Ava wouldn't mind visiting day or night.

Streetlights lined the roads. The sidewalks were narrow, clean, and free of broken chunks—not to mention all seeming freshly cleared of snow. Back in Hidden Cove, most of the sidewalks still lay under several inches of thick ice and snow. The houses all seemed to be made from bricks, or had pristine vinyl siding, unlike so many homes in the rural area of Hidden Cove.

On top of this, the mountains didn't butt up against any of the houses, overshadow them, or cast an inescapable shadow over them. More than half the backyards she could see had picnic tables and large grills. She envisioned a community of people who knew each other and were all on friendly terms. Maybe they even had community cookouts. It was a modernized version of a Norman Rockwell painting.

Alan's house, however, was not in the area that brought a smile to her face. His house was further out. She actually spotted it long before she turned onto the long gravel driveway. The man owned acres and acres of flat land. Even though there was snow covering all of it, she could make out large tracts of land that had been tilled, turned, and covered. In the spring, those tracts would sprout crops. There were huge barns and two stable houses near his massive ranch-style house.

Ava saw the fenced-in circular run where horses were broken to saddles and trained. She wondered if he trained them for shows. The place was big enough to board horses for others, have a riding school, or to be a business in which paying customers rented horses and a guide to tour parts of the state unreachable by vehicle and too vast to go on foot.

She parked to the left of the double-door front entrance and took her files in hand. With a sigh, she said a silent prayer that Alan wasn't as much of an ass as Robert Mitchell or Jack Kearns had been.

To her surprise, meeting Alan was much more pleasant. Although obviously very wealthy, Alan was down-to-Earth and quick to smile and ask her inside. He held the door until she was inside and then closed it. Stepping in front of her, he led her to a room on the right side of the long entryway.

"Mind me asking why the FBI is getting involved with a cold case way out in the boonies like this?" He offered her a seat.

Ava sat in an oversized cushion chair, her feet resting on what she thought was a faux goat-skin rug. It fit the décor of the room perfectly. She explained to him about the cold case, and her involvement, getting a feel for him as she talked and he responded.

His responses were open and seemed more honest than any others she had acquired.

Opening her files, she removed the legal pad and got a pen from her pocket. "Mr. Watkins, I just need to confirm your alibi for the night in question. You know, where you were, if you were with anyone, that sort of thing."

His demeanor was unaffected, but she thought his eyes hardened a bit and the set of his mouth was a bit firmer.

After a long pause, he nodded. "Sure. I was out with a friend."

That took Ava so off guard that she stared at him unblinking for several seconds. "Oh. Okay. Uhm, what friend was that?"

His brow furrowed as he thought. "You know, that's been a long time ago. I barely remember what I had for supper last night." He chuckled and shifted his gaze to the window behind her.

"Robert Mitchell?" she suggested.

He nodded a little, and then Ava witnessed the moment the light bulb went on behind his eyes. "That's right! He was with me. We, uh, we went out."

"Went out? As in, out to town? To a bar? Camping?" She watched him carefully and could see that he was struggling.

"I mean, yeah."

"Mr. Watkins, do you remember what you told the investigator five years ago about where you were and who you were with that night?"

"Sure. Yeah. I do."

But she could see that he didn't remember what he'd said. Not clearly, anyway. He might have recalled the gist of it, but not the details.

"And? I just need to hear it from you so I can put it in my notes. You know, a formality. That's all." She smiled when he looked up at her.

"Yeah. I was with Robert. We went out to the bar that night."

She wrote this down. "Was that the only place you went?"

"Probably not, but just to be honest, without a little help, I'm not gonna remember at all. Like I said, I barely remember what—"

"You had for supper last night. Yes, you told me that already." She eyed him and didn't see a man who was trying to deceive her. She thought he had already deceived the other investigator all those years ago, and now he simply couldn't remember the lie he'd told.

"Don't you have my statement in those files there?" He grinned, but a little tic had developed at the corner of his left eye.

She nodded. "I do. I also have Robert's statements. All of them."

His grin dropped. "All of them? How many times have you questioned him?"

"A few. That's confidential, you know." She smiled quickly and went straight-faced again just as quickly. "I need you to tell me where you two were that night. If you can't, I'll have to start a thorough investigation into your movements around that time—and just so you know, it could be quite disruptive to your present life. I mean, I'll have to come around a lot. Every day or two probably, question all your friends, your coworkers from then and now, bosses, housekeepers, girlfriends, you know the whole routine. So, it would behoove you to tell me what you do remember about that night, and about your and Robert's whereabouts."

"I have a different life now. I have a wife and a business of my own. I didn't even live here back then."

That made sense. It explained why his phone number and address were different. "Are there things that went on back then, or perhaps even now, that your wife wouldn't approve of?"

He glared at her, and then he shifted in his seat. "Ain't that always the case?"

She shrugged. "I don't know, sir. All I know is that I cannot take that into consideration if I have to dive into your past. Whatever surfaces…" She shrugged again.

"All right. I don't remember what I told the other investigator. Okay?"

She nodded. "That's a start. Do you remember where you were or who you were with?"

"Yeah. I was with Robert." He sighed and shook his head. "We did go to the bar, but we didn't go in. We sat in the parking lot for a while after dark."

"Which bar?" She was writing everything down, thrilled at the prospect of finally hearing the truth.

"Stuckey's. 'Bout an hour from here. Down 107 near the junction at the state line."

Ava looked up with a raised eyebrow. "That's quite a ways to drive just to sit in the parking lot of a bar."

"Yeah. Tell me about it." He looked at her with a sheepish grin. "The things a man will do to be with a woman he ain't supposed to be with, eh?"

"You or Robert?" She kept her face emotionless.

"Both of us," he admitted, lowering his tone and looking to the floor. "I was seeing a woman out there, but I had a steady woman here."

"Your current wife?"

He nodded. "We've been together eight years, and she thinks I've always been as faithful as I am now." He looked up at her. "I am, you know. I quit all that years ago. Saw the error of my ways and settled down. I'm happy now. *We're* happy now."

"What about Robert? Who was he seeing that he wasn't supposed to be seeing?"

He looked to the ceiling with a heavy sigh. "I suppose it don't much matter anymore. She's gone now."

"It matters to me, sir. It matters to the case, too."

He shook his head, the weight of whatever secrets he was holding clearly heavy on his shoulders. "Ellie Snodgrass. She was married to a big-time lawyer from Alabama. He moved to Kentucky, met Ellie, and they married young. Before he was big-time. By the time he was big-time, Ellie had fallen out of love with him, but not his money. Robert didn't have money but made up for it by being especially attentive. Robert loved her, and in her own way, I guess she loved him."

"What's her husband's name?"

"Herb Snodgrass. Don't go digging around his business, either. Won't do you any good, anyway." He rubbed his face with both hands.

"Why's that?"

"Because Ellie died six months ago. Car wreck. It was pretty bad, from what I hear. Her death messed Robert up something fierce. I don't know that he'll ever recover completely. She was on her way home from one of their trysts when it happened."

"Ellie is who he was meeting that night at Stuckey's?"

"Yeah. She'd traveled with her husband from over in Randall County down to Tennessee where he was going to stay for some trial he had. She didn't stay, of course, and she was going to stop by the bar and pick up Robert. They were gonna spend the weekend together. Camping up on Buffalo Mountain. I have a cabin up there that we always used for extended hunting trips, or if one of us wanted a little vacation away from everything. They were using it that weekend, though."

"I'll need that address, too."

He gave it to her, and she thanked him.

"Am I in trouble for lying back then? Robert didn't kill anybody and I knew that. I just didn't want anyone digging around and exposing him and Ellie. That husband of hers would have ruined him. Maybe even would have had him killed. Herbert's not a very good guy."

Ava didn't think any of them were acting like very good people. Not back then, anyway, but she kept her opinion to herself. "I can't promise that none of this will be brought to light. If it does, and someone decides to pursue it, that is out of my hands. I'm only interested in getting the truth and solving this case. It's serious to lie to any law enforcement during the course of an investigation, you know."

He nodded and his chin quivered. "I swear on my life that Robert and Ellie were at that cabin all weekend. There's no way he could have killed that man or made his wife disappear. You'll see what I'm talking about when you drive up there. And I know they were there because me and that other woman went up there. We ended up staying in a tent out back to have some quiet and some privacy."

"Were the two of them arguing?" She gave him a confused look.

He stared at her for a second or two, and then let out a chuckle. "No, ma'am. It wasn't arguing noises they were making. Not arguing at all."

Taking his meaning, she shot to her feet and closed her files. "All right, Mr. Watkins. Thank you for your time and for your honesty." She extended her hand. He shook it. "Even if it was five years late."

Chagrined, he nodded, stuffed his hands in his pockets, and looked at his feet. "If it's at all possible..." He looked askance at her.

"If it's possible." She headed for the door, stopped, and turned. "Oh, Mr. Watkins, just to be thorough, and to keep from dropping by unannounced, what was the name of the woman you were seeing that weekend?"

"Stacy Whitaker. She's from Spalding but lives in Combes now. Other side of the state near the Tennessee border. Leastwise that's the last I heard."

She wrote it down, closed the file again, and walked out. It was a good feeling to know that her gut instinct about Robert had been correct. He had been hiding something from her. He had been lying.

But did that make him a murderer? Far from it. But all she could do now was follow this lead where it went.

Driving back toward Hidden Cove, she plotted her next moves in the case. The long straight road was as good a place as any to do that.

CHAPTER TWENTY-FOUR

AVA SPENT THE REST OF THE DAY MAKING CALLS, TRYING TO FIND out about Ellie Snodgrass. She pulled up maps to see the roads around Stuckey's. Down 107 next to the junction meant nothing to her, as she wasn't familiar with the place. It took hours, but she finally found the newspaper articles, online news segments, and finally her death certificate.

Within an hour of finding all those things, she decided to pull up the official reports about the accident. After calling the local PD in the area where the accident took place, she also had those reports. There had been an investigation into the cause of the wreck. Although it had officially been ruled an accident, some of the investigating officers had their doubts. The brake fluid had been almost completely drained, and there was a questionable nick in the brake line that they thought might not have happened during the crash.

That information set Ava's mind in motion again. Into high gear to be exact. What if the wreck hadn't been an accident? Had Robert perhaps put that questionable nick in the line in a fit of jealousy? If Ellie had been heading home to her husband, maybe she'd been arguing with Robert, and he had done it in the middle of a rage. Ava had seen worse happen in the name of jealousy. Much worse. So it definitely wasn't out of the question.

If Ellie only died six months ago, that meant it was likely that they had been seeing each other for several years. That was a long time for a relationship of that nature. Robert being as private and living his quiet, solitary life back in the hills had probably been a bonus to Ellie. She didn't have to worry overly much about her high-profile husband finding out about them. After all, who would Robert tell other than Alan? And seeing as how Alan had a steady girlfriend, she didn't have to worry about him saying anything either. He wouldn't want word getting out and people questioning his part in the whole thing.

Ava added her notes to the proper forms and put them all in the appropriate files and folders. She closed them and sat at the desk for several minutes in complete silence, thinking about Robert Mitchell.

Her gut told her something was still very wrong with the picture. What if Robert really did have something to do with Ellie's death? What if he did kill Dustin? Had he kidnapped Katherine? Maybe Ellie found out about that and that was the reason she ended up dead.

Or what if it was the opposite? What if Katherine and Dustin had found out about Ellie and he had them killed to keep their silence? It seemed far-fetched, but it was worth considering.

Two men murdered, one woman murdered, one woman missing, another woman dead in a questionable accident. Five lives torn apart.

That was five too many incidents with Robert Mitchell as the common denominator in Ava's opinion.

If the Johnsons and the Jakobsons had lived in another area, would Ava be scrutinizing their closest neighbor so ardently?

Stacy Whitaker was next on her list. She made some calls, but everywhere she called for records seemed to be closed already.

Ava called Sal. It was time to start delegating some of the work so she could keep her forward momentum on the case.

"Hey, Sal. I need some help with the case. You should be able to get the information I need over the phone, but it'll have to be done tomorrow, I suppose. During normal business hours. I started calling too late today."

"Yeah, it's after six. Most places close down at four or five out here. What do you need?"

"All the information you can find on a Stacy Whitaker. All I know is that she lived in Spalding County five years ago and now she lives in Combes on the other side of the state. No address, no phone, nothing. She used to date Alan Watkins."

"She have something to do with our cold case?"

"I don't know. She can corroborate Alan Watkins' new statement from then, though. Or refute it. In which case, I will have to go back and talk to him again."

"I don't remember her name in any of the statements I read through."

"No. You wouldn't because it wasn't in them. Mr. Watkins has changed his statement. It no longer matches any of the statements given by his good friend Robert Mitchell."

"The neighbor. Right. It could be bad for him, for both of them really, if they lied."

"Well, they did. They weren't out hunting or fishing that weekend. They were out carousing with women."

"This sounds like a big development. Got the details?"

"Robert's long-time girlfriend was a married woman. Unfortunately, she died six months ago in an auto accident. Alan's girlfriend was more like a side dish. He had a steady girlfriend and was seeing Stacy on the side. He ended up marrying the steady girlfriend and is now more worried about her finding out than any charges that might be filed against him for lying to the police."

Sal chuckled dryly. "Sounds about right. Par for the course in my experience. You said Mitchell's girlfriend died, huh? What was her name and details?"

"Ellie Snodgrass. She did die. I already checked out that lead. From what I found out, it was just as Alan said. But there was doubt about it being an accident. They were never sure if her brake line was cut, or if the damage they saw happened during the wreck. There were at least two people who stated they thought it had been *nicked* on purpose before the wreck."

"As in not cut completely?"

"Yes. Just enough that the fluid leaked out as she drove back home to her husband."

Sal clicked a pen. The sound was loud over the phone. Ava knew she was thinking, analyzing, and would likely come to the same conclusion she had.

"You think it might have been done by our Mr. Mitchell? A fit of jealousy, or after an argument?"

"I don't know, but I was wondering about it."

"Yeah. It seems a lot of people within Mr. Mitchell's reach either end up dead or missing. Is it just coincidence, or is he a really dangerous man hiding behind the façade of a quiet single man who likes his privacy?"

"If Stacy corroborates Alan's story, I will be less inclined to peg Robert as a serial killer, but there will always be that question in the back of my mind. As you said, too many people met a bad end and he was the common denominator."

"I'll do what I can. I'll start first thing in the morning and give you an update tomorrow evening. Sooner, if I can."

"Thank you, Sal."

They ended the call and Ava looked to the evidence board. She had more to add to the section where Robert Mitchell had been placed. She stood and walked to the board, picked up a marker, and started adding Alan's account of their whereabouts in straight, neat, small writing.

She had no doubt that by the time she had finished with the cold case, there would be precious little white space left on that board.

As she was leaving for the day, Detective Hopson met her at the back door.

"Hello again, Agent James. Are you surviving the rabid rampages of Mother Nature here in the hill country?" He pushed the door open, stepped out in front of her, and held it for her to come out, too.

"Thanks," she said, sidestepping him and giving him a wary glance. He hadn't been so considerate and nice since she'd been there, and she didn't know why he was suddenly being so, unless he had ulterior motives. "I can't say I'll miss it when I'm gone."

He laughed and pulled his long coat tighter. "Making much progress raking over old ground?"

She side-glanced him again. "I'm sorry. What?"

"The cold case," he snipped, shaking his head as if she were the dumbest person he'd met all day.

"Oh, yes and no." She wouldn't give him the pleasure of saying either way.

"That's like saying winning the lottery is good and bad, or Granny's apple pie was good and bad. Are you pregnant?" he said. Then mimicking a woman's voice, he answered, "Well, yes and no, honey." He shook his head again. "That's what's wrong with your generation, and I'm afraid it'll only get worse in the one that your generation raises. Be solid and give direct answers. Stop pussy-footing around and being so damn delicate with everything."

His cheeks had gone red, and Ava thought the chill in the air had nothing to do with it. He was a walking stroke or heart attack just looking for somewhere to happen. The man's temper alone would probably be enough to do the trick, but add on all those extra pounds around his middle, and it was a recipe for disaster.

Instead of waffling and giving him a direct answer, she grinned at him. "Every generation says the same crap about the younger one. It's been that way forever."

Veering away from her and toward his car, he huffed. "When you're my age, you'll be bitching about the younger generation, too. Then you'll see how true all your gripes about them are."

He opened his car door and flopped inside, closing it harder than was necessary. Ava supposed it was the equivalent of a toddler having a tantrum, only he had outgrown throwing himself on the ground and kicking and screaming. Giving him another cursory glance and seeing that he was muttering to himself as he started his car, she got into her own.

"Not so sure he outgrew it," she remarked as she turned the key in the ignition.

From one interaction to the next, she never knew if she would be dealing with Tolerable Detective Hopson or Detestable Detective Hopson.

CHAPTER TWENTY-FIVE

THE NEXT MORNING, AVA WOKE EARLY AND HEADED OUT TO GRAB A light breakfast. She had the suspect list with her as she ate and looked over it again and again.

Jack Kearns was not off her radar. Something about the man bothered her, other than his lack of manners. He had reason to kill Dustin Johnson. But if he had been the perpetrator, what had he done with Katherine? Kidnapping seemed unlikely. He had been at a hotel in Florida with his family. He wouldn't have had time to dispose of her body along the way, and if he had taken her alive, where could he have stashed her? Why would he have done it? There was never a ransom to her family or friends. And Ava thought it was highly unlikely that he had taken her back to Florida with him.

A thought hit her that chilled her worse than the winter weather. Not that she hadn't thought of it before, that's why Asher Patterson and Jack's names had remained so high on her list. This time, her mind jumped to all kinds of ties with human trafficking rings. Finding Katherine might get her a step or two closer to finding Molly. Although there were thousands of people trafficked every year in the USA alone, it was still a tight-knit community of people who actually went out and dragged victims into their grasp and took them to trade and sell.

What if he had taken Katherine back to Florida with him? What if he had connections to the trafficking ring there? It was rumored that he had ties with the Cornbread Mafia even though he lived in Kentucky, and the territories for that particular crime ring were known to be only in Tennessee and Georgia. It was a long shot, but that group could have ties with the group that took Molly.

But what if?

Any tie, no matter how tenuous, was still a tie that could be tracked. She couldn't ignore the possibility once her mind had developed it.

She quickly scribbled notes about it. She needed to talk to Asher Patterson. Maybe she could get something useful out of him although he was in prison and likely had little to lose, or gain for that matter, by remaining quiet.

She hurriedly finished her coffee, ordered one to go, and left the diner. The sun was up and bright, there were few clouds, and the wind was much calmer than it had been for days. Snow Plow trucks rumbled in the distance as they headed out to the back roads and the main roads that led into other counties.

The route to Belton should be clear enough for her to drive there. If she could speak with Asher, it would be one lead checked off her list, and more notes to add to the whiteboard.

Ava went to the station office long enough to phone Sal and let her know the day's plans and to get directions for the Belton County jail. She made another call. Belton County agreed to her visit, gave her a time, and she headed out.

Now there was a fire in her to find out all she could about Kearns' involvement with the Cornbread Mafia. If human trafficking was involved, she would see that an investigation was opened in that area, too. She harbored a special hatred for human trafficking rings and all people in cahoots with them.

The Cornbread Mafia was under constant surveillance, and often there were arrests made, hopeful leads gathered, and then the trails always went cold. The last raid she had heard about involved the arrests of over a hundred people, but none of them had turned state's evidence. None had rolled over on the higher-ups. They simply took their charges and sentences and were put away.

It was satisfying knowing that many terrible people had been removed from the streets in Tennessee alone, but Ava knew the dynamics of the ring well enough to know that within a month, there would be other people replacing those arrested. Maybe even more. It was the same in every state and every country where drug and/or human trafficking was prevalent. As far as she could tell, no place was free of such nefarious activities, but some places had less of it than others. She had often wished she had chosen somewhere other than Prague to celebrate turning eighteen.

"If wishing made it so," she whispered. A line from some old Scottish nursery rhyme drifted through her thoughts. If wishes were horses, beggars would ride. "How true."

Going through the process at Belton County Jail was longer than she thought it should have been. No doubt, if she had arrived with other agents, the thing would have taken a lot less time. She was asked the same questions several times, and the questioning officer eyed her suspiciously each time as if daring her to change her statements in the slightest.

"If you are going to let me speak with Mr. Patterson, could we just get on with it? If you refuse, I'll come back tomorrow after making a call to my superiors, and I'll talk to him then. I do have an investigation to get on with."

The man held up his hands and laughed sarcastically. "Well, just hold your horses there, little lady. We have to go through this every time someone gets an unscheduled visitor. Doesn't matter whether it's family, a lawyer, or an agent from the FBI. Wouldn't want anyone watching and listening to accuse me of not doing my job." He raised his eyebrows and pointed toward the overhead camera.

"Don't refer to me as *little lady* again. It could be construed by anyone watching and listening," Ava looked directly up at the camera, and continued, "as a form of sexual harassment." She looked back to the officer.

The officer set his jaw and stood up to his full height. Without a word, he opened the door and waited for her to go through. He led her to an interview room where Patterson had already been seated at the end of a long metal table. One of his wrists was handcuffed to a bar on top of the table.

"Thank you, Officer. I'll call when I'm done."

"You have ten minutes. Sorry, them's the rules around here. Anything more and you will have to go make that phone call and return tomorrow." He smirked and stepped out, closing the door behind him.

Ava nodded to Patterson as she sat. "Asher Patterson, I presume."

"Otherwise, I'd still be out in the gym enjoying my few minutes of free time, wouldn't I?"

His bald head shone under the fluorescents. He bunched his face into a mask of disdain and his eyes sunk into deep shadows, giving him a rather gaunt look.

"I'm sorry to interrupt your free time, Mr. Patterson." She was not. He was a bad man who had a rap sheet as long as her arm. Her motto had always been, *if you play, you pay*, and Mr. Patterson was currently in the paying phase of that saying. Again. "I came today to talk to you about someone I think you might know rather well. He's linked to a case I'm working."

"What's in it for me, if I do know this man?" He leaned his arms on the table and laced his fingers together as a predatory grin stretched across his face.

"Well, we can get to that after you tell me if you even know him or not." She smiled and laced her own fingers together. For the moment, they looked like two very civilized people having a conversation, but she felt as if she were in a Mexican standoff.

"No," he said, shaking his head. "We can get to that now, or you'll never know if I know your guy or not."

Without posturing anymore, she nodded. "Jack Kearns."

Asher's eyes widened. It was only a fraction, but it was enough to signal to Ava that the name was indeed familiar to him. His fingers, which had been laced tightly, fell lax for a second, and his mouth twitched just a tiny bit at the left corner. Then he was looking at the table, toward the two-way mirror, then to the door behind Ava, and finally to her.

"What the hell you come in here asking me about a Jack Kearns for? Who sent you?" His voice went low and he practically hissed the words at her. His brow furrowed and his mouth pressed into a deep frown as he waited.

Ava stared at him levelly, taking in all the minutiae of his reactions. "So, you do know him." She started writing on her paper.

"Hey, stop writing that down," he said in that hissing low voice.

She didn't respond, just kept scribbling. She was only writing down the directions to the jail, but he didn't know that.

"Hey!" He slapped the table with both hands.

Ava looked up sharply at him. "What, Mr. Patterson?"

"Don't be taking stupid notes like a high school kid in the classroom. Just don't. I don't want your visit connecting me to anything or anyone after you leave here."

"Are you afraid of Jack Kearns?" She made sure to enunciate the name loud and clear.

Making a big show of blowing that idea off, he flopped back in his seat as far as the handcuffs would allow and put his left ankle on his right knee. A super-macho stance. At least Ava was sure he thought so.

"All right. Tell me about him, then. How do you know him?" She poised the pen over the paper.

"Huh-uh. You put that pen down, and we might talk. I said no notes. Shit like that is too easy to drop, too easy for others to see." He looked around again as if paranoid that someone was going to overhear him.

"Mr. Patterson, you're in jail because you've done some really bad things. Why do you keep looking around like that? You know we're being watched and listened to. Just talk to me about Jack Kearns."

Rolling his eyes, he moved to lean forward over the table again. "Stop with the name-throwing, too. Just call him *he* or *him*. Trust me, I'll know who you're talking about. And, I'm in here for petty crap mostly. Not the big stuff like your guy is into."

"You call drug running, distribution, selling, and manufacturing *petty crap*?" The disbelief rang through in her words. It was truly unbelievable what some people thought of as petty, mostly harmless crimes.

He nodded. "In comparison, yes, I do. I never said I would win a Mr. Nice Guy of the Year award."

"In comparison to what and who?"

"Your guy, for one. If I were to say he's in the CM, would you have a clue what that meant?" He kept his voice so low that she had to really concentrate and watch the movement of his mouth to make out his words.

"I'm not sure. I don't think it means anything to me," she replied, thinking she was getting ready to hear a double-dose of BS.

"Just remember it because a lot of your uppity, wealthy people out there, the ones everybody thinks so highly of, are in it."

Then it hit her. The Cornbread Mafia. Their eyes met, and Patterson smiled and nodded at her.

"There went the light. I thought you might figure it out."

"You're sure about that?" Of course, he could be lying. Making things up just to pass the time and have some entertainment. It would be hard to prove, but even harder to disprove his story, she supposed.

"I know that he only answers to one man, and that man answers to no one at all."

That meant Jack Kearns was far higher up on the chain than she was expecting. He worked directly with the leader of the Cornbread Mafia. That explained the huge house and all the property and the items in the house that she would never, ever be able to afford, no matter how much she worked or saved.

"I thought that was only in two states a bit more southern than Kentucky."

"Well, there you would be dead wrong. It's an ever-expanding empire, and it flattens anyone who gets in the way."

"How do you know all this?" Maybe he would give her some detail that she could use to find out whether he was telling the truth about it all.

"What's in it for me?"

He had hooked her, now it was time to go in for the kill. She had to give it to him, he had played her like a cheap fiddle. She was in no position to offer him anything.

After a moment of hemming and hawing, she shrugged. "I'm in no position to offer anything. It's not like I can just snap my fingers and get you out early. I can't even promise more time in the gym. I have to get authorization and wait on paperwork from my superiors for anything of that nature. That would mean disclosing all this information to them that you are so ardently trying to keep me from writing down. My hands are tied here. But I would greatly appreciate it, and you would be doing something honest and right for a change, if you could just give me a name or tell me how you know all this."

"If you're asking for the name that I think you're asking for, forget it. I just called him The Nameless. Suits him. I never saw him. Never even heard his voice. Only heard his name once, and that was by total accident. Not someone you want to know too much about, and anything you do know, you definitely don't tell."

Ringleaders of organizations like these were ruthless, soulless people in her experience. She understood his refusal to give the name, but he had given her something just as important. Asher Patterson was involved with that particular ring. Probably a low man, a street-troller, but still worked for them. He definitely knew enough to know Jack and the leader worked together. From that, she surmised that the two might even be friends, or at least on friendly terms.

"Is there anything else you would like to divulge before I leave?"

"Not unless you want to use your womanly charms to try and get me a cell by myself, or maybe a shorter sentence. The warden is an old horn-dog, you know. He might be persuadable by such a young—"

Ava stood and snatched her tablet and pen from the table. "Guard!" She moved to the door. "Guard! I'm all done in here."

The door across the room opened and two heavily muscled uniform officers removed Asher from the room while he was still saying as many sexist things as he could think of.

Leaving Belton County Jail felt like heaven. The place was dank, dark, chilly, and felt like misery when she had entered. A simple visit to such a place would have been enough to deter her from a life of crime; she couldn't understand why so many people became repeat offenders such as Asher. One stint should suffice and make people never want to return.

CHAPTER TWENTY-SIX

A
VA DIDN'T STOP BY THE STATION ON HER WAY BACK. SHE WENT
straight to Robert Mitchell's house again. She had called him a total of
eleven times since they'd last spoken, and he hadn't bothered returning
a call. While the weather was decent, she would drop in and ask him a
few questions.

In Robert's driveway, she spent the better part of five minutes re-ex-
amining her intended course of questions. At first, she had thought to
go in guns blazing. Not literally, but by telling him immediately that she
knew his statements had all been lies and start accusing him of a number
of things in the cold case.

On the drive, however, she had come to think that wasn't the wisest
course to take with him. And although she was armed, it might still not
be the safest course seeing as how she was at his house alone again. The
place was pretty well isolated, and no matter what happened short of a
bomb detonating, the closest neighbors wouldn't hear a thing. Everybody
was still holed up inside their homes out that far. The rural side of town

was nothing like the town side. The temperature was much colder and the snow was much thicker. The only cleared places were the roads and a couple of driveways.

And, of course, Robert's drive, walkway, and porch. She wondered as she sat there if that was to keep from tracking the mess inside, reduce the risk of falling, or to keep anyone from knowing when he'd been in and out of his house.

She shook those thoughts out of her head, instead deciding on questions she would ask him. He wouldn't like it, but then again, he hadn't liked her last round of questioning, either.

Robert was standing on the other side of the door, watching her through the window when she walked onto the porch. The sight of him standing there shrouded mostly in darkness, the hard set of his glaring eyes, and the grim set of his face shocked and startled her when she looked up.

As soon as they made eye contact, he stepped forward and opened the door. "Well, well, well. Agent James. What are you doing lurking in my driveway on such a horrendous day?"

She waited a moment for her eyes to adjust to the dimness before moving farther inside. "Well, you never returned any of my calls or messages. Again. So I was out and thought I'd drop by and see if you were home."

"Looks like you got lucky," he said, motioning for her to enter the living room.

Her gut tightened and the fine hairs on her neck and arms stood up as she stepped into the room. The vibe in there was off, but she couldn't discern the reason. A quick scan showed no sign of weapons, and her keen sense of hearing didn't perceive any movements that would alert her to another person's presence. For some reason, she still had the unrelenting urge to remain standing until whatever was causing that tingling warning sensation was resolved.

Robert sat heavily on a short, stout-looking sofa on the opposite side of the room, leaving her standing with her back to the doorway. There was a small sofa near her left leg.

Maybe it's because my back is to the doorway, she thought. Then a more sinister voice offered, *or maybe he's a psycho serial killer and your Spidey senses are tingling because he plans on adding you to his collection.*

Barely keeping herself from shuddering, she turned and looked around the room again. "You have a lovely home, Mr. Mitchell," she started, vying for a better view of the kitchen and hallway beyond.

"Thanks. You can sit and we'll get started. Soonest begun, soonest done, my gran always said."

His smile didn't reach his eyes. In fact, it didn't even affect his face enough to bunch up the wrinkles at the corners of his eyes. His calm and quiet demeanor didn't fit his personality. And none of it made Ava any more comfortable.

Finally, out of excuses for standing and looking around, she had to make a choice. Either sit down and ask her questions, act like a real agent, or leave. If she left, she thought she might well never get to ask her questions. The answers she needed might be lost forever.

She perched on the edge of the middle cushion, wishing to be sitting in the hard kitchen chairs again. They would be easier to get up from if anything did happen. But she wasn't in the kitchen. She was in the claustrophobic, poorly lit, oddly-laid-out living room with a huge man whom she suspected might be a cold-blooded murderer.

Getting hold of her nerves, she laid the file on the sofa and held the notepad on her knee. Her mouth was dry as dust, and she couldn't get out her first question. She found herself listening intently for any sounds other than the ticking of clocks and Robert's noisome breathing.

There was nothing.

That only added to her sense of unease.

Maybe that's the cause of it, she thought. Whose house is so quiet?

Every time she had been there, it had been the same weird silence. She thought if her home was so quiet, it would make her crazy. But Robert didn't seem to notice. She almost wished he had a radio playing somewhere just to break that silence.

"Well, what did you dig up that brought you all the way out here in this weather? I know you weren't just *in the neighborhood* and decided to drop by."

"Never said I was. I was already out in this weather." She wanted to launch right into the *you're lying* spiel, but her unease held her back. That, or good sense. "I just wanted to ask you some more questions about the Johnsons."

"Dear Lord in heaven. I already told you everything I know about them." Even that was said in a voice that was much too light and airy to be his natural voice and reaction. There was a hint of a chuckle in his words and on his face.

Something is definitely not right, she thought, her instincts bristling. *He's enjoying this, or he's enjoying some aspect of it.*

"Mr. Mitchell, Katherine was a good-looking woman, wasn't she? I've seen pictures and all, but as a man, would you say she was good-looking?"

"Yeah. Any man with eyes could see that much, and if I said otherwise, I'd be lying."

"She was a good woman, too. Right? As far as taking care of her husband, her home, things like that."

Squinting at her, Robert nodded. "Again, yeah. Everybody knew that."

So, he's interested in telling me anything as long as he thought everybody *knew that already,* she thought as she tapped the paper with the pen. "Mr. Johnson, though..." she purposefully let her words trail off hoping he would finish the sentence.

"Nah. He wasn't very good-looking, in my opinion. But what do I know? I'm a man, too, so I don't know what women think of as good-looking. I can tell you, it's not always what they show on TV or in magazines. A lot of women don't care for that kind of handsome looks."

"What do they prefer? Those women."

"A man who's not so vain. A man with some meat on his bones, some substance to him other than looking good in a picture." He shifted to sit straighter.

The set of his face suggested that he was talking about himself.

"How did you think Mr. Johnson treated his wife? Just your opinion."

"Why would you ask me that? Shouldn't you be asking their respective family members?"

She shook her head. "Their answers might be biased. I've found that most of the time, the family thinks the significant other never treats their son or daughter as well as they should. It's bloodline bias. Happens a lot. It can really skew an investigation. I want an unbiased opinion."

He scrutinized her for several seconds. "Maybe you should ask some of her friends. Or his. They would know better than me."

"See, there's where I run into a problem. It seems they had very few friends, and the ones I can find… well, it would be about the same as with the families. His friends are going to say she treated him sub-par, and her friends are all going to say he treated her badly."

"Well, he didn't treat her like a princess," he muttered, then looked at her as if he'd said more than he planned.

"She waited on him hand and foot, didn't she?" It was time to play the understanding buddy. "Probably yelled at her and demanded she do things he could've done himself, too." She huffed, rolled her eyes, and nodded. "Seen that about a thousand times, too." She paused to look directly at him with a faint smile. "You could have treated her better. A lot better."

"Damn straight, I could have." Again, that look made it seem as though he'd said more than he intended. "Are we about done here? I was just leaving."

"She snubbed your advances, didn't she, Mr. Mitchell?" Ava slid the pad to the sofa with the files and put the pen into her pocket. Under her coat, the reassuring lump of her gun gave her a bit of courage and comfort.

Robert's eyes turned fiery. "Agent James, I think you've yet again worn out your welcome. It's time for you to scoot on down the road and find someone else to harass."

"Where were you the night of the murder and disappearance?"

"I already told you." His voice went cold and dropped half an octave as he leaned forward to put his elbows on his knees.

Ava was again seeing just how large Robert Mitchell was. Plenty big enough to have carried a struggling Katherine Johnson out of the house, manhandle her to wherever he wanted her, and incapacitate her.

"No, see, what you told me turned out to be lies. Your statement to the previous detective was a lie, the statements you gave me were lies. All of them. I think the only true things you have told me so far are the ones you told me today. And I think Katherine Johnson refused your advances, hurt your manly pride, and you didn't like it. Not a bit."

"You're crazy," he replied, but his eyes said something else.

"What did you do with her, Mr. Mitchell? After you shot her husband, what did you do with Katherine?"

Robert shot to his feet. His leg hit the coffee table, scooting it toward her.

Ava was on her feet with her hand on the butt of her gun, her heart thundering, adrenaline coursing.

He pointed toward the front door. "Get out, now!" he thundered, managing to tower over her even from the other side of the table. "Leave and don't come back without a warrant."

"You want this settled once and for all? You want me to leave you alone from here on out?"

"Damn skippy. I want to be left alone about all of this. You are disrupting my entire life with your crazy, half-cocked ideas. I don't have time for this."

"Then why did you lie about where you were?"

"I didn't," he said, dropping his arm and deflating a bit.

"Mr. Mitchell, I checked your story. You were seeing Ellie Snodgrass. It didn't help my opinion of you that she died in a car wreck and that there were suspicions about it not being an accident. Can't you see where I'm coming from?"

His whole demeanor seemed to go limp at once, and he flopped back onto the couch, defeated. "I was seeing her, yes. I loved her. Still do. No matter what you think, I'd never hurt that woman." He nodded toward the neighbor's house. "Or that one."

Calming her tone, Ava perched on the edge of the sofa cushion again. "Mr. Mitchell, did you hurt Ellie? Did you damage the brake line on her car?"

"No. That's plain stupid to even suggest. We were in love, but she didn't want to give up the money her old man was raining down on her all the time. She couldn't help being worried about money. Look at me. Not like I'm some loaded lawyer. But in our way, we were madly in love. Her husband was just a minor obstacle. She would've left him soon. I'm sure of it."

"So, you're not the type of man to hurt a woman. That's good to know. What about Katherine, now? Did you do something to her?"

"Jesus, no." Exhaling deeply, he sounded exasperated but tired.

That was good. Ava had counted on wearing him down mentally. "If you really had nothing to do with her disappearance, let me have a look around. I can write it up in the report that you willingly let me search the premises. It'll only look good on you; help clear your name for good."

She stood and waited for his answer. She felt sure he would agree. All he wanted was to be done with the whole thing. If he was truly innocent, there would be nothing to worry about.

He shook his head. "No. I want you to leave."

"If I leave, I have to report your lies. That's going to look really bad on you, Mr. Mitchell. I'm trying to help you out. I know you never wanted your years-long affair with Ellie getting out, but if I have to leave, rest assured that it will definitely get out."

Looking incredulous, he leaned forward again. "Are you serious? You're *blackmailing* me?"

"No, no, no, Mr. Mitchell. It's not blackmail. Just the facts. I'm bound by the law to report your lies. There will be more questions. You'll have to come back to the station and go through the whole thing all over again, only under much more scrutiny than before. Could be a real mess for you. But if you let me have a look around, and I find nothing, what would be the point in me reporting all that?"

After a very long silence, he grinned at her. "You just showed your hand, and you're holding nothing, Agent James. You can't get a warrant without sufficient evidence. So, apparently, you don't have any evidence, and there's nothing you can do. So, now that you've been so rude and threatened me, I'll ask you again to get out of my house. Come back when you have that warrant, and I'll happily let you search all you want. Until then," he stood and walked past her into the hallway and to the door, which he opened. "Goodbye, Agent James. Better luck next time."

Ava left, hiding the sheer frustration on her face. She had been out-maneuvered by a man she had underestimated, and it made her furious. Firstly, at herself for the rookie mistake. Secondly, at Robert Mitchell for being so dang smug about it. He'd bested her, and he would wallow in that triumph far longer than she cared to think about.

As for his untruthful statements, she would head to the office and start drawing up the reports immediately.

CHAPTER TWENTY-SEVEN

Just before lunch the next day, Ava's uncle Ray showed up at the Hidden Cove station. He stuck his head through the doorway and grinned. "Hey, Ava. Long time, no see."

Ava rushed over and hugged him. Happy for the distraction, but happier to see him. It had indeed been a long time. "What are you doing here?" Ava showed him in.

"I was heading home from my last assignment and thought I'd stop and see if you wanted to grab lunch." He looked over her shoulder toward the covered evidence boards. "Got it covered?"

"Yeah. I have to if I get anything else done. This morning, it's been paperwork. If I leave it uncovered, I obsess."

He laughed. "Must run in the family. So, are you caught up enough to take lunch with your old uncle?"

Glancing at her desk, she covered the reports she'd been working on and nodded. "I sure am. Let's go."

They got into Ray's SUV and he started the engine. "It's a pretty day, but it's a bit brisk. I should have worn a thicker jacket."

Ava, bundled in her thick coat, nodded. "This is a literal heatwave compared to the last few days. The only thing colder than the weather is the cold shoulder I get from most everybody here."

"They'll warm up to you eventually. Just give it some time. They'll figure out you're not the bad guy."

"I hope I'm not here that long." Ava thought she would solve the case and be moving on within a couple of weeks. At least, that was the hope that kept her going even when she seemed to hit a brick wall with every turn in the case. "Speaking of being here, how long are you in town for?"

"Just until tomorrow evening. I told Kay I'd meet her back home tomorrow night. She's going to be away until then, too."

Sighing, Ava shook her head. "So, she is determined to be out traveling for the Avilion Foundation in this messy weather and without you, no matter how dangerous it is."

"Pretty much. You know how she is. Stubborn enough to fit right in with this family." He laughed. "Where are we heading to eat?"

It was Ava's turn to laugh. "Well, I hadn't really thought about it. In a town like this, we'll have to go to Calhoun's Country Kitchen. The food is good."

"All right. Sounds like my kind of place. Just give me directions."

Ava knew that any place serving burgers or fried chicken would meet Uncle Ray's standards. He liked just about any kind of food, and truth be told, if she let him, he would drive right to the nearest fast-food joint and order at the drive-thru.

They made it to the restaurant, and Ray parked near the big side window. Ava thought it must run in the family to always park where the vehicle would always be plainly visible, too.

Looking around, he smiled. "This is pretty nice. The setting is gorgeous."

"Yeah, it's nice all right. The inside is a bit dated, but it's super clean and all the staff are friendly."

"You ready?" He got out, not waiting for a reply.

Ava chuckled and joined him, figuring he must be hungry. Probably hadn't eaten anything until then. She knew that was just part of working for the Bureau. Sometimes they ate on almost normal schedules, but for most of their time, they just grabbed a bite here and there only to keep their stomachs from growling too loudly.

They sat in a booth at the window directly in front of the SUV. After looking over the menu for five minutes, they both ended up ordering burgers. After the server walked away, they both laughed.

"One of the pitfalls of being in the Bureau is that you get so used to grabbing quick food that you can't sit down and actually order a meal anymore," he said.

"Burgers are so versatile," she replied with a laugh. "Hot, cold, sitting in the restaurant, or eating behind the wheel while you're driving. Nothing beats a burger," she added, grinning.

It was good to have someone to talk to who understood her life and her career choice. Since being in Hidden Cove, she'd felt completely isolated, totally different than anyone else, the perpetual outsider.

"Have you heard any more on your mother's case? Are they keeping you up to date on their progress?"

"The Bureau's completely locked me out. But I have a friend who's a PI who's been following some leads. There hasn't been anything new in a while, though. She's like a ghost. Poof! No trace." She shook her head.

"Hey, that's not necessarily a bad thing. You know that, right?"

She looked at him unblinkingly. No, she didn't know that, she wanted to say. It was a terrible thing when it was her own mother who was untraceable. It left Ava with terribly vivid ideas about what could have happened to her, or what might be happening to her still.

"Seriously, Ava. It's a good thing. If the FBI can't find her, that means that whoever the bad guys are, they probably can't find her either."

"Probably. See, there's where I have a problem with the whole thing. They *probably* can't find her, but that doesn't mean they *haven't*."

"Wherever she is, I'm sure she's there of her own volition. She chose to go off-grid, off the radar, and she's doing it because she considers the outcome to be more important than what happens now. While she's missing."

"But what could be so important that you have the entire world looking for you on purpose?" That was a question she never had a suitable answer for. "What could possibly make her willingly leave me and Dad behind without warning? She had to know how much we'd worry."

Ray nodded solemnly. "I'm sure she weighed the decision. She probably labored over it for a while. We don't even know how long she'd been planning this. It could've been years. I don't see anyone disappearing so completely without great, detailed planning."

Ava hadn't considered that angle, but she gave it a moment's thought and decided he was right. Had her mother been acting differently over the last few years? Had there been times when she'd done something that seemed a bit out of character? It was something to think about, for sure. She nodded. Ray was right. But if she'd been planning it for a long time, that meant she had also been following some lead or another that no one else knew about, or that no one else had considered important. Also something to think about. And look into.

She decided to change the subject. "How much does Aunt Kay really think she'll bring in from this one function? I know she won't consider extra precautions and extra security because I've already talked to her. She said you were going to be close by, but I'm not sure I believe that, either."

He chuckled and shook his head. "She thinks the amount will be substantial. She's taking into consideration not just the donations from that night, but the potential new supporters that will sign up for the long haul once they really emphasize the way they're rebuilding the foundation."

Ava raised her eyebrows. "And are you going to be close by? Truth."

He looked out the window with an enigmatic grin. "You shouldn't worry so much about everybody else, Ava. You've got enough on your plate as it is. She'll be okay. I'll see to it. I've talked to private security, and she won't even know about them until it's too late to make a fuss."

"So you're not going to be there." Ava had thought as much after speaking to Kay. It had just been something in the way her aunt had assured her Ray would be nearby.

"Tell me about this case you're working. You know, the one you've got the sheets over at the office. That's a sweet little office, by the way. I wouldn't have been surprised to find you languishing in the storage closet in the basement without even a window. Single bulb dangling from a cord," he moved his hand back and forth, imitating the swinging bulb, and laughed.

"It's a step or two above that, I guess, but it's not much room to work

198

in. It's claustrophobic even with the window, but without one, I would likely have been working solely out of my hotel room."

Their food arrived and they ate, making small talk for a while. Ava was glad. She didn't really want to admit to Ray how much trouble she was having with the cold case, and eating gave her enough time to formulate a more palatable story to tell him.

"So, about the cold case?" he asked, taking his coffee from the server.

"It's coming along, actually. I uncovered a few new leads, and I'm following them, and boy-oh-boy, it is a twisted little path for sure." She chuckled, hoping it made it sound as if she were making good headway.

"New leads? As in plural?"

She nodded.

"How many?" He set his coffee down and crossed his arms, leaning back into the cushioned back of the booth seat.

"Well, I haven't finished with my interviews, but so far I have two good ones." She couldn't help but shift in her seat under his steady gaze.

"How many interviews do you have left to conduct, and is anyone going with you to do them?"

Crap, she thought. She sat forward. "Okay, I have quite a few interviews still, and I can't get any cooperation from anyone, and no, no one is going with me to do the interviews. Most of the people I need to talk to either won't answer their phones or don't have a phone. When I go to their houses, they aren't home. And this weather," she threw both hands up toward the window, "isn't making it easy for me to even get to their houses when I think they might be there. Because I'm *re*-interviewing them, I can't just order them to come to the station. They've already done that, done their parts in the eyes of the law, so I can't make them come to me." She shrugged and took up her own coffee. She figured she was going to need about a five-gallon bucket of the stuff just to get her through the rest of the day.

"To say the least, you're stressing over this. Sounds to me like you're getting pretty frustrated."

What would he say if she told him about her latest interview with Robert Mitchell? For sure, he would lecture her. It had been a mistake to do what she'd done since she'd gone to his isolated house alone, and no one had known where exactly she was at that time.

She simply nodded.

"Tell you what. I can stop by your office in the morning and have a look. If you want. Sometimes, a fresh set of eyes can do wonders for a case."

As if she weren't feeling enough like a failure, letting her uncle help really added some heft to that idea. But she needed a nudge in the right direction. She had little choice if she hoped to solve the case. She supposed that if she did recruit help, who better to get it from than her own uncle? He wouldn't belittle her over it, wouldn't hold it over her head. He would just help if he could, and that would be between them.

"Are you sure?" she asked.

"Positive. I'm here to help if I can. No promises, but I'll look over it. Sometimes, it's like getting snowblind. You've looked at it so long and so hard that it all starts to look the same. The details kind of disappear."

She nodded. "Exactly! I was afraid I was just being a miserable failure."

He laughed and then drained his coffee. "Not at all. You're probably not eating right, and I daresay not sleeping much, either. That contributes to the effect because sleep deprivation does terrible things to your cognition after a while."

She nodded, grinning sheepishly. Still feeling a little like a failure for accepting his proffered help, she also felt some genuine relief that he had not judged her or her approach to the case.

Things were looking up again as they left the restaurant. Hope renewed, Ava went back to her office and uncovered the evidence boards and jumped into the case once again with enthusiasm.

CHAPTER TWENTY-EIGHT

A T EIGHT IN THE MORNING, RAY STOPPED BY AVA'S OFFICE WITH A pair of steaming coffees. He was smiling when he entered, and she reciprocated. She had been up late thinking over her decision to let him help and trying to sort out as much of the case as she could before he got there. She wanted to be nothing less than prepared when he came to visit.

"You sure know how to start a day off right," she said, taking the giant cup of coffee. "Where'd you get these, anyway?"

"Convenience store at the other end of town, just past the McDonald's." He grinned and lifted his Styrofoam cup in a toast. "To the case," he said.

They toasted, and Ava laughed. To the case, indeed, she thought.

"You've got the covers off the boards. That's a good sign," he noted as he moved closer to them. "Want to give me a little background, or do I need to go in without it and see what stands out to me?"

"I'll give you the story." And she did. It was a long one, though. Much longer than it had been when she took the case on. Much had been added to it since then, and she told him about the connections she saw between the old and the new cases. While she talked, he looked over the pictures and the written information several times, then he moved to the files on the table below the boards.

After she had finished, he turned to her and nodded. "Come over here a minute."

He had no doubt found something terribly screwed up with her technique, or something monumentally simple she had overlooked. With a mounting sense of dread, she walked to stand beside him, her hands clasped behind her back.

With one finger, he lifted the topmost photo of the basement. "You've placed these pictures a bit higher than the others. You've doubled them. I'm guessing this one is from the cold case files, and this one on top is the one you took when you examined the house."

She nodded.

"Placing them higher, and in the center where the two boards meet tells me that you think these pictures are very important." He dropped the top picture back into place. "Maybe they're central to both cases. That's what your setup suggests to me."

"You're right. I do think the basement is key."

He took a pair of glasses from his shirt pocket and slid them on. Leaning in, he looked at the basement photos for a long time. "Okay. Tell me why." He took off the glasses and replaced them in his shirt pocket. "Why does that concrete basement floor seem so important to you?"

She pointed to the newer picture, placing her finger just under the barely visible pieces of vinyl flooring at the far corner. "See that?"

He glanced at it and nodded. "Looks like pieces of vinyl flooring that were torn off when the bigger piece was removed."

"Something isn't right about that flooring to me. The Jakobsons weren't very wealthy, and that flooring was pretty pricey. Doesn't make sense why they would go to the expense and the trouble to put it down, and then rip it right back up again. It had literally been down for almost no time."

"Are you certain the Jakobsons put it down?"

"It was installed while they owned the house, yes."

He shook his head. "Did the Jakobsons physically go down there and lay that vinyl, or did someone else?"

"I can't prove it, but I think Mr. Jakobson did it by himself."

"There's your lead. Find out who put that vinyl down. I'm betting it really wasn't Mr. Jakobson. From the files and notes, he seems like he would have been more comfortable hiring that work done. Making the purchase doesn't mean he did the actual work. Don't forget that in all these cases, the hired help are usually The Invisibles. Housekeepers, gardeners, pool cleaners, landscapers, carpenters, electricians, plumbers…" He held his hands out to the sides and made his eyes big. "That's a lot of people who had access to the Jakobsons' home, and therefore, to them. Maybe there's a motive there. Now, how does that tie in with your cold case?"

"Because ripping out the flooring put the basement right back the way it was before, and the Jakobson's were living until that happened. Someone wanted that basement to remain the same, but that wouldn't be a reason to murder them."

"Not to you or me, it wouldn't. But who would have wanted the place to stay the same as it had always been?"

Wracking her brain, Ava came up with nothing. "I don't know."

"My guess is, whoever ripped up that flooring. Look for building permits, renovations, addition permits, anything of the like that would leave a record, or that they had a record of. That's your lead. Your gut was leading you in the right direction, I'm sure. Even if Mr. Jakobson put down the flooring, you need to know who was in there afterward that might have wanted to rip it out again. Then you need to find out why. That's a start."

She nodded again, relieved that he also thought the two cases might have been related somehow. If he didn't, he also didn't berate her for thinking so, and he definitely didn't tell her there was no way they were related.

Redding knocked on the door and held up a stack of mail. He motioned that it was for her. Ava waved for him to come in.

"This was left with the other mail. It's for you." He handed her only one envelope instead of the whole stack she had thought he meant.

She looked at the postmark. Las Vegas, Nevada. She looked to Uncle Ray. "I don't know anyone out there. It's been forwarded from the post office box back home."

He shrugged. "Don't look at me. I don't either. I don't think so, anyway. Did you request forwarding?"

"Only for the mail that gets delivered to that P.O. box. It's where all work communication goes." She hadn't had much in the past year, but it was always a good idea to have it go to a more secure location. In her mind, it was.

She carefully tore across the short edge of the large manila mailer and pulled the smaller, personal-sized envelope from inside. Scrawled across the front, in her mother's handwriting, was Ava's name, and her post office box address from back home. Ava's legs felt like rubber, and she had to sit.

Ray rushed to her side. "You okay? You're pale as milk."

She held up the envelope for him to see, and he blanched white.

"Your mother's handwriting," he said in a faint voice. He sat on the edge of the desk. "You shouldn't open it. Bag it and call it in to the Bureau. They'll need to examine it for trace evidence, and you don't want your DNA and prints all over it."

Redding came by the still-open door and peeked in. Seeing Ava in the seat, pale and looking shocked, he stepped in. "Agent James?"

Ava looked up at him. "Get me an evidence bag." She looked at the two envelopes and shook her head. "Get me two."

His gaze flitted from the envelopes to Ava, and then he was gone, trotting away to get the bags.

Ava was numb. She couldn't take her eyes off the small envelope. She wanted to open it and see what her mother had written. Was it proof that she was still alive and well? Or was it something she'd been forced to write? Probably not, she thought. It had a traceable P.O. box on it. She wouldn't have given that up. How long ago had it been written? The date on the outer envelope was a week old, but whatever was in the smaller one might have been written any time between the day she disappeared and a week ago.

After bagging both envelopes and carefully sealing them up, she placed the call.

CHAPTER TWENTY-NINE

IT TOOK OVER AN HOUR FOR AN AGENT TO ARRIVE, AND WHEN SHE did, Ava was shocked that Sal Rossi was the one in charge of inspecting the envelopes. Ava had intentionally *not* told her about her mother or Molly because she didn't want everyone around her looking at her as if she were handicapped by these things.

Sal looked at Ava with pity as she took gloves from her examination kit and pointed to the evidence bags. "I'm sorry, Ava. I had no idea until an hour ago." She took the bags from Ava. "I really need everyone out while I examine these."

"Come on. Let's go find a vending machine in this place," Ray told her, putting an arm around Ava's shoulders and leading her out of the room.

In the breakroom, Ray scanned the snack options, making faces at most of them. He turned to her. "You want to go grab a pizza or something? I saw two pizza joints on the way into town."

Ava shook her head. "I don't want to leave the station until Sal's finished with the letter. I want to hold it in my hands. Read the words. I need to do that."

Ray pulled out a chair and sat. "Listen, kiddo. I know this is tough, but you can't rush the processing. You know it will take hours. Another agent is on his way here to help her, but it will still take forever. That's just how it is, and you can't sit here and make yourself sick while you're waiting."

She crossed her arms and sat still. She wouldn't, *couldn't* leave until she had seen the letter. Food was the furthest thing from her mind. "If it was Aunt Kay, what would you do?"

He opened his mouth to give a knee-jerk response, then closed it again. After a moment, he shook his head. "I can't say, Ava. That hypothetical situation and this very real one are two different things entirely."

She nodded and scoffed. "Exactly what I thought you'd say. What about if it was Grandma?"

"I might not be in your shoes, and I might not be able to tell you how I'd react if I was, but I am here for you. I'm your uncle, and I'm supposed to look after you. That's what family does, you know?"

That knocked the fire out of her. She had been angry and had wanted to argue with him, with anyone, really, but his words had hit home. That's what family does. *Yes, it is*, she thought, wishing her mother were there to comfort her.

"Do you want me to go find out what it says? I can probably do that much."

"Not unless I can hold the letter and look at it. I have to be able to see it to make sure it's really her. I would be able to tell if she was writing in a hurry, under duress, in the dark, or a number of other things that an agent who knows nothing about her will be able to tell."

He nodded. "Then it's best if we wait until they've completely processed it. They can't even make copies until that's done. The environment has to be mostly stable to keep from degrading any trace evidence on the paper. It's tedious work."

"I know. I've seen it done before." She huffed and threw herself forward, covering her face as she put her elbows on the table.

Walking to the vending machine, he grunted. "You know, if you won't agree to pizza, we'll have to just ingest a couple of these gut grenades and hope for the best." He tapped the glass on the sandwich machine and grimaced. "Do you really want to spend the rest of the day in the bathroom?"

Despite her worry, she chuckled and shook her head. "Not at all."

"Talk about keeping your mind off your worries for a while. Phew. I think that would do it." He sat again and took out his phone. "I'll call and see if they deliver. You think I should splurge for the officers here, or do they like pizza?"

Ava shrugged. "Not a clue. They aren't *that* friendly with me, remember?"

Twirling his phone between thumb and middle finger, he looked around for a few minutes. When he looked back to Ava, he stood. "Come on, kiddo. We're breezing out for a while. No need to sit here for God knows how long, tying our guts in knots. It won't do a bit of good, and might do a lot of bad." He held out his hand to her. When she made no definitive move to get up, he shook his head. "Nope. I'm not taking no for an answer. Don't make me carry you out of here. Think how embarrassing that would be." He grinned and offered his hand again.

"You know, I love you, but sometimes you're impossible to deal with." She stood and slapped his hand away, grinning.

"I thought that was a requirement in this family."

They went to the nicer of the two pizza places and spent two hours eating pizza and talking about the cold case, Kay's foundation, and Ray's last case, which had been full of danger and excitement as usual. They talked about anything and everything except Ava's mother and Molly. She knew he was being careful to steer the conversation away from those topics in a bid to keep her from dwelling on it so much, but it didn't do much good. She could worry at the pizza place just as enthusiastically as she could have back at the station.

"You're still worrying, Ava. Get it off your mind for a while. Let the old brain rest a bit. I'm telling you, it's for your benefit. Stop fretting."

"What can I say? I'm an expert at multi-tasking. Besides, I thought worrying endlessly was also a requirement to be part of this family."

"It's been a long time since I told you this, but you, Aviva James, are a class-A brat."

"And who made me that way?" She pointed at him. "Between you and Dad and Mom, how could I be any other way?" She slid out of her chair. "Now, this brat is ready to go back to the station. Surely, Sal will be done by the time we get back."

Before they reached the station, Ava's phone rang. It was Sal.

"Are you finished yet? What's wrong?" It wasn't her usual way of answering the phone, but this was not a usual situation.

"I am. Nothing is wrong here. Everything went smoothly. I'll give you all the details when you get back here. Are you still at the station? Benny said he couldn't find you."

"Ray and I are heading back. We'll be there in five minutes." Ava hung up. "They're done. Said she'd give me details when I got there."

The remainder of the ride was in silence. Ava knew he had many of the same worries she had, he was just trying to be the strong one for her sake. She loved him for that, but it was unnecessary. She'd never tell him that, though. Instead, she would thank him for being there, hug him, and tell him she loved him. That was also what family did.

Sal bombarded her with information as soon as she walked through the door of the tiny office.

"Great, you're here. Okay, it definitely came from a remailer service. Practically impossible to trace, although sometimes we do get lucky, so, we'll follow that as far as we can. There are fingerprints on the smaller envelope, though I'm guessing they will belong to some generic guy either at the post office or at the remailer or even in the factory where it was made. All I can say is that they don't match your mother's prints, yours, Raymond's, or Redding's, although we did find two partial prints on the corner of the envelope that matched yours. I figure that's where you pulled it from the larger envelope. The prints are running through the system now, but it might take hours, or even days before we get a hit."

"You might not get a hit at all, either. Just depends. If the print belongs to someone who doesn't have a record, there you go. Kaput!" Ava tossed up her hands and let them fall to her sides. "May I please have the envelope and letter now? I really need to read it."

"Oh! Of course." Sal turned and picked up the evidence bag. She passed it to Ava. "The envelope and the paper are too common to trace. And nothing about the ink suggests any special type of pen was used, nothing to lead us to any specific location. I'm sorry I don't have more for you."

Holding the bag in both hands, Ava nodded. "Thank you, Sal. I just want to read this now. You understand."

Sal nodded. "I do. I'll just take my stuff and get out of your way. I'll head to the hotel. I'm staying there now. If you need me, just call."

For a minute, Ava thought Sal was going to hug her. She took a half-step back to avoid it if she did, and thanked Sal.

Uncle Raymond stood by the desk as Sal and Benny left the room. "Ava, you want me to stay or go?"

"I just need a few minutes alone with it, please. Don't leave the station, unless you just have to get going."

He shook his head. "I'll wait. It's fine. Take all the time you need. I have to make some calls anyway."

As he started to close the door, Ava yelled for him. "Don't tell anyone about the letter. Not yet. I have to figure out what I'm going to tell Dad after I read it, but I don't want the news of it getting back to him secondhand."

Ray nodded.

"Not even Aunt Kay, please. Not yet."

"You got it, kiddo."

He was gone, and she was finally alone.

Sitting at the desk, Ava took the small envelope out of the evidence bag and laid it in front of her. Her heart thudded and her hands trembled.

My Aviva,

I'm sorry about all the worry. You shouldn't fret, though. I'm following a lead, but I can't give any details. Know that I am okay. I'm using a remailer because electronic devices are no longer safe. They are too easily hacked/traced. I can't risk it. Don't know when I'll be able to write again, but I will.

Love you always,

Mom

CHAPTER THIRTY

T EARS PRICKLED AT THE BACKS OF HER EYES. NO SOONER HAD SHE felt the first prickle than they were falling down her cheeks, hot and burning against her chilled face. Little fiery streaks of pure emotional turmoil.

For a brief time, her lungs locked up, her throat constricted, and her stomach felt as if she had been hit with the end of a baseball bat. Fearing she was about to pass out, Ava fought her way back to some semblance of normalcy. After a few minutes, she was able to get hold of her emotions, put them in place, and wipe away the tears. By sheer force of will, she regained composure enough to open the door and find her uncle.

In the break room, Ray stood looking out a long skinny window at the snowy scene beyond. Ava stared at him for a moment, wondering what was going through his mind. Was he anywhere close to being emotionally wrecked by the new development? Was he anxious to read the letter, or at least learn of its contents? Was he planning what to do next in regards to Elizabeth James?

Or perhaps was he only considering the time it would take him to reach home in the clearing weather conditions? Maybe even just standing there dreading getting back out in the cold. She wasn't psychic; she had no way of knowing what was going through anyone else's head. She was doing good to keep track of what was going through her own.

"Uncle Ray?" She walked toward him with the letter held out.

He spun. "Ava, is everything okay?" He reached for the letter.

"She's alive. Or, at least, she was when she wrote this. It's really her."

He read it quickly. He sighed, betraying more relief than what he'd implied earlier. "I told you she would be fine. She's smart and tough."

"Promise you won't tell Dad anything about this. If you tell Aunt Kay, swear her to secrecy until I've had a chance to sort through this enough to even be able to tell him myself."

"You have my word, Ava. I won't tell him. I'll not even tell Kay until you let me know you got hold of Hank. Are you feeling better now?"

She nodded, took back the letter, and folded it. "Still, I have more questions than I had before. She didn't even give a hint of what she's doing. She could be following any lead anywhere in the world."

"And, as I said, I really believe she will be all right, and she'll be back as soon as she's finished following that lead. I'm telling you, this took some serious planning. She didn't just up and vanish on a whim. She's thought it out, contemplated her actions, and she knows what she's doing."

"I hope so." Ava hugged Ray. "Now, you better get on the road and start heading home. Kay will have your head on a platter if you're really late."

They said their goodbyes, and Ava went back to her office. For the next hour, officers, detectives, and even the chief came by to ask if she was okay, was everything all right, what was the big commotion about, and many other questions. She already had a form-type answer for them, and each person got exactly that reply, whether it perfectly suited what they asked or not. Eventually, the story would make its rounds, and a lot of information that she had wanted to keep private would probably leak into it. That's the way it always happened.

With the letter tucked safely in her pocket, Ava tried but failed to concentrate on the cold case. Her mind kept going back to her father.

Should she tell him about the letter? She was sure she should. He deserved to know that his wife was still alive and that she had chosen to go off-grid. But would it hurt him to know she had willingly disappeared without a word of warning?

Should she divulge that her mother was chasing a lead? That would most likely worry him. He was already out of his mind with worry for her.

The last thing she wanted was to hurt or worry her father more at this point.

She was thrilled at getting the letter, but she was also upset with the lack of details. Though, if the letter had been intercepted by the wrong people, the only thing they could have gotten would have been Ava's P.O. box address. That could have been dangerous for her and her father. Surely, her mother hadn't overlooked that detail. Then again, maybe that's the reason she hadn't sent more communications in the form of handwritten letters.

There was no proof of life, but who else could have written in Elizabeth's handwriting? Who else would have sent it? Who else would have known she always called her "my Aviva"?

She was satisfied that her mother had written the letter and that she was doing so under fairly normal circumstances. She was certain a handwriting analyst would go over the letter, but she expected only that he would confirm what she already knew.

"Why couldn't you just tell me where you are and what you're up to?" Ava whispered to the empty office.

The answer was obvious, but still, Ava wished.

Elizabeth was tough as nails when she needed to be, anyone who knew her could vouch for that. And even Uncle Ray knew she could take care of herself, but that did little to assuage the fear and the sense of doom, both of which grew daily, at the thought of her mother being out in the world somewhere that she didn't know, wasn't familiar with, and where no one knew her. Possibly where she didn't even understand the language. It would be frightening at best, and deadly at worst.

Maybe I'm more scared than she is, Ava thought. When I'm out in the field, I know I'm in danger, and I have no doubts usually that I will be able to handle whatever comes my way. Maybe Mom is the same way.

She hoped her mother wasn't out there somewhere terrified. The thought of that brought tears to her eyes again, and she had to fight harder that time to keep them at bay.

⌒

That night in the hotel room, Ava paced, carrying the letter and rereading it every few minutes. The phone was in her other hand. She hadn't called her father but was close to doing so.

A quick glance at the clock confirmed that it was after eleven. She decided it would be best to wait until the next morning to call him. If he was already asleep, she didn't want to disturb his rest. It wasn't like he got much of it these days.

At half-past-eleven, she slid under the covers and turned off the lamp. In the darkness, she tossed and turned. In the silence, every tiny sound was enormously bothersome. Even the sound of the wind rustling the branches outside annoyed her. The tiny drip from the bathroom faucet that she hadn't noticed before. The vague footsteps of people on the floor above her. And finally, the sound of her own breathing. All of it seemed like a raucous cacophony that kept her from being able to relax and fall asleep.

She sat up with an aggrieved sigh and tossed aside the covers. She grabbed the phone and punched in her father's number. He had to know about the letter. That's all there was to it. She hoped it did him more good than harm, but either way, she had no right to, and could not, keep it from him any longer.

Surprisingly, he answered on the second ring. Ava glanced at the clock. It was after midnight.

"What's wrong, Aviva?" He sounded tired and scared.

"Nothing, Dad. I'm okay. Sorry for calling so late. I expected you'd be in bed already. Are you okay?"

"It's only a little after twelve, honey. These days, that's early. What's going on?"

Ava told him about the letter. The sound of his watery sniffle broke her heart, and she wondered if she had done the right thing by telling him. Or had she been being selfish and only telling him to ease her own mind, so she could rest a bit easier?

"Did someone hack her cellphone?" he asked, still sniffling a bit and trying to be quiet about it. His voice had a foghorn quality to it.

"I don't know, Dad."

"Do you think she's still in South Africa?"

"I don't know where she's at. They haven't figured out how to trace her movements yet, and if she got rid of the cell, there's no way to track her at all. It's not like she's leaving any kind of paper trail. Just this letter, and it's probably untraceable."

"This has something to do with the murders at the gala, doesn't it?" He covered the phone and blew his nose.

Ava hated to keep telling him that she didn't know, but she had no answers for his questions. None of them. And he continued to ask them for several more minutes.

"Dad, I have all the same questions that you have. I just don't have any answers right now."

There was a long silence. "I understand, honey. I do." Another long silence. "I want to see the letter. I need to see it, Aviva."

She could totally empathize with that. The same feeling had overwhelmed her until she got the letter in her hands and saw it with her own eyes. "I can get a copy for you. I'll send it as soon as I can today."

"Why can't you just send me a fax copy right now, or better yet, take a picture of it with your phone and send it to me?"

"That's probably not a good idea. Other people could see it, and we have no way of knowing what's being monitored and what's not. If I knew where Mom was, the country, at least, I might feel safer doing that, but for now, I'll send it Priority."

He finally gave up and agreed.

They said goodnight and disconnected.

Ava didn't feel as relieved as she had hoped she would after telling him everything, but she was at least tired enough to sleep.

That was one step in the right direction.

CHAPTER THIRTY-ONE

A MORE THOROUGH SEARCH OF THE PAPER RECORDS IN THE Johnson case revealed that there had been renovations done to the house. There was a brief description that included work to be done in the basement and the attic. The attic had to have a new window and a new access ladder that was up to code. The basement was just generalized as 'renovation work'.

A quick online search showed that there had also been an addition permit for the property. The hand-drawn diagram looked like one a fourth grader could have drawn. The best Ava could make of it was that there was a small building added in the backyard. She had seen a small shed there during her visits, though she had not done as thorough of a search in or around it as she had the house. But a ten-by-ten outbuilding didn't leave much room for hiding anything. Considering that one had been empty after searches from both sets of investigators, she doubted it was of any significance to the case, but she made a note to search it with a fine-toothed comb. It was her job to do a more thorough search, to make sure nothing had been missed.

There were no names associated with the renovations or the addition except Dustin and Katherine Johnson's. The contractor who actually did the work remained a mystery.

The records from the new case showed no renovation work at all, no permits for anything other than a fence that was never installed. Again, there was no name in the files indicating who was going to install the fence.

The fence was supposed to run the perimeter of the property. At six feet high, it was meant to ensure a modicum of privacy.

Ava wondered about this. Why did the Jakobsons feel that they needed privacy? And from whom? Their only neighbor within sight was Robert Mitchell.

He had not mentioned anything about his neighbors that indicated he even knew about the planned fence. Had he known? If so, how did he feel about a privacy fence between his property and that of the neighbors? Did he have some kind of history with the house or property that could have triggered him to commit the new murders only to prevent the fence from being installed?

It was a long shot, but Ava wasn't discarding the idea. People had murdered for much less. Murderers often inserted themselves into the active investigations. Some kept mementos from the murders to keep so they could relive the incident for a number of screwed-up reasons. It wasn't an impossible idea that Robert had murdered Dustin, kidnapped Katherine, and then, when something went wrong, killed her. Maybe having a clear view of the house reminded him of Katherine. Especially if he could see into any one of the windows where she might have been visible daily. For instance, the kitchen window, or a bedroom or bathroom window where he had an unobstructed view of her.

Ava still hadn't cleared the thought that some man had become obsessed with her, and that obsession led to the heinous act that had taken place. The thought that Robert might have been that very man wouldn't leave her head, either.

"What do we covet?" she asked aloud. "Things we see every day," she answered herself.

Robert would have seen Katherine every day. She was truly a beautiful woman, and Ava had no doubt many men were attracted to her. But Robert lived alone, was practically a hermit. He rarely went anywhere other than to work. He would have been able to feed his obsession, and with little social interactivity, that could have turned into a fantasy in which he could be with Katherine. Maybe he thought the only thing standing between them was Dustin, Katherine's partially disabled husband who yelled at her and treated her worse than she deserved. That's what Robert had said.

Combine that with his years-long affair with Ellie Snodgrass, and his friendship with Alan Watkins, he certainly didn't seem to mind the idea of running around with multiple women. Maybe his obsession with Katherine was the idea of having a girlfriend a little closer to home.

"Or, maybe he had a hero complex, a savior complex when it came to Katherine, and he thought he was saving her from Dustin when he shot him. Then, when Katherine didn't see it as being saved, he had to kill her, too."

There was a big problem with that theory, though. Where was she? If he did kill her, where was her body?

"Maybe that's why he didn't want me snooping around his house," she said, tapping her fingernail against her tooth as she looked at the pictures on the board again.

There was a good chance that Robert might know who the Johnsons had contracted to do the renovations to their house. He most likely saw the contractor, or contractors, coming and going. And it was likely that the Johnsons would have mentioned the renovations during normal conversations with Robert. As he'd said, sometimes, they had a beer on the porch together. The occasional, casual get-together, but nothing special.

In her opinion, he knew too much about them and their lives for just the 'occasional beer on the porch' routine. Being the only two houses in that area, she would bet that they all knew each other quite well.

It stood to reason that he would have some kind of helpful information about the contractor.

Katherine's family might have known, also. Another person who might have had knowledge about the renovations was Dustin's brother, Greg Johnson.

If any of them had the information she needed, that meant one less trip to Robert's house to talk to him. In one way, she thought that was very good. In another, though, she wanted to go back and talk to him again. Not that she wanted to upset him or disrupt his life, but she wanted to be able to look around. Now she could look for anything that looked as if it might have belonged to a woman; anything that would not fit with his lifelong bachelor style of decorating.

The forms lay on her desk that she had filled out about his misleading statement to the original investigators. She hadn't yet filed them, nor reported his misdeed. Even with that, she wouldn't have enough to get a search warrant, and if she filed it, she would instantly go on his bad list, and he would never talk to her again. Not about anything useful, anyway.

She half-expected all the men involved with that first investigation to laugh it off anyway. They were a bunch of good ol' boys who would still think he was completely innocent. All he was doing was seeing a married woman and trying to cover both their asses so her husband wouldn't find out about them. That sort of thing goes on all the time. But more than that, in a town as small as Hidden Cove, everybody knew everybody else, and that sense of familiarity came with blinders. No one there thought Robert Mitchell, the quiet man who never missed a day of work and never caused any trouble, could possibly be involved with something as horrible as murder.

Thinking over the situation for another half-hour, Ava decided it would be best for the case if she first talked to the families. They would be more willing to give her the information, and it would be quicker for the progression toward resolution.

Dustin's older brother, Greg answered on the second ring. He sounded tired.

Ava told him who she was and what she needed.

"I can ask around if that's what you need, but Dustin never said anything about who was going to do the work for him."

"But you did know he had planned on renovating the basement, adding the building, and having the work done in the attic?"

"Yeah. Everybody knew. At least, everybody in the family because we were all happy for him and Katherine. They had their first home together, the financial stability to fix it up the way they wanted, and hopefully, they'd be starting a family soon." He inhaled deeply. "That's what we were all hoping for, anyway. Including Dustin and Katherine. Has there been a new lead? I mean, why didn't these questions get asked before now?"

Just as Uncle Ray had said. Service workers are mostly invisible, and often overlooked by local police. "It's just my way of covering all bases. There's been nothing new yet. If there's a change in status, though, I'll personally let you know. And there's no need to ask around about the contractor unless you think someone for sure knows who it was. I'm going to be doing a lot of asking around myself."

She repeated the same process with Katherine's parents after hanging up with Greg.

Cybil Ray, like the rest of the family, knew her daughter and son-in-law planned on doing renovations, but wasn't sure who the contractor was.

Her husband Tom took the phone, and Ava heard papers rustling on his end. "Agent James?"

"Yes, sir?"

"I have a name here, and I think it's the name of the company Dustin hired. Katherine or Dustin must have mentioned the name at some point because it stuck out to me when you asked about the contractor. I can't be certain that they actually hired them. Renos by JD is the name. Some friends either used or recommended them. There's another name here, also. Jubal Reiser. A lot of people in the area have used Jubal's company over the years."

Ava wrote down the names. She had neither of them in any of the files. She was sure she would have recalled them if she had seen or heard them. "What's the name of Jubal Reiser's company?"

"It's Jubal Reiser Residential Construction. Everybody just calls it Jubal Reiser's, though."

"Thank you very much, Mr. Ray. This will help out. If I find out anything new, I will personally let you and your wife know."

They hung up, and Ava looked at the names. As the neighbor,

Robert Mitchell would have seen whoever was doing renovations for the Johnsons. It would have been nearly impossible not to notice when there were only two houses up there.

I guess my old friend Robert will just have to deal with yet another visit from me, she thought. "Two birds, one stone, sort of," she mumbled as she tucked the paper in her pocket. There would be no need for the notepad. All she needed was a name, and most likely it would be one of the two on the paper.

CHAPTER THIRTY-TWO

THE DRIVE WAS EASIER THAN IT HAD BEEN IN DAYS. THE WEATHER seemed to be warming up, and Ava didn't have to run the heater on full blast as she drove to Robert's house once again.

This time, he was waiting for her. He came to the door with a deep scowl and a stormy expression. As he opened the door, he seemed larger somehow, more intimidating, and Ava was instantly uneasy.

"Let me guess, you want to come in again." He stepped aside and motioned. "Well, by all means, Miss Agent Lady, come on." The expression he wore was the polar opposite of his words and actions, which she knew were grandiose to the point of sarcasm.

She shook her head. "No. Actually, I just wanted to ask you about renovations. Construction laborers and companies in the area." Suddenly, she didn't want to needle him. In fact, she wanted to be away from him, and she regretted not calling Sal to join her. Since she was now staying at the hotel, it would have been simple, but sometimes, the simple things get overlooked.

Something clicked in her mind; a light came on.

Service workers are overlooked. They are invisible. Your eye just slides right over the simple things. All of those thoughts ran through her head as she blinked mutely at Robert. Her gears were grinding, but she didn't know which direction they were headed.

"Well, spit it out already. What about them? After all, that's what I'm here for—to be your font of information." He stood with his arms crossed, feet wide, and his belly peeking out from under the bottom of his pocketed T-shirt. His eyes carried a plain and obvious disdain for her. He was angry at the world and ready to fight.

"Do you know who did the renovations for the Johnsons? They had work done to the basement and the attic, I believe."

Seemingly caught off guard, Robert's expression changed to confusion. He shook his head as if trying to clear it. "Beg your pardon?"

"The Johnsons. Who did their renos? Do you know?" She repeated.

After several moments of floundering, he shook his head again. "I'm not sure, but I think it might have been one of Jubal Reiser's guys. He had a lot of men working for him back then, and sometimes they brought in their own help and paid their wages in cash from their earnings. I can't remember the guy's name, but I'm pretty sure he was Jubal's. Why?"

It was her turn to shake her head. She couldn't tell him why. Unless she wanted him to think she was onto another lead and off his trail. The thought crossed her mind, but she didn't pursue it. That was a move for later, if anything panned out with the contractor.

"So, you don't think it was Renos by JD?"

"No. His men were more… how do I put this? They were… more professional, I guess is how I see them. The Johnsons were okay on money when they moved in, but I would say they didn't have the kind of money it would take to hire JD's company. They're expensive. I used Jubal years ago for a whole kitchen reno. I know his is quality work, but the men are less professional. Like, they don't have fancy work shirts with their names on 'em, and jackets, and matching pants. You know what I mean?"

She nodded. "Yeah, I know what you mean." She looked to the house in question and then back to Robert. "Did you ever see the man? I mean, could you identify him?"

Immediately, he shook his head. "No, that's been five years ago, and the only time I ever saw him, it was just a glimpse as he was going in and out."

"I thought you saw him well enough to know he worked for Jubal Reiser, though." She squinted at him. Was he playing her?

"I saw his *truck* well enough to say that. Him? I only caught glimpses. It's not like I invited myself over to their place just so I could see who was working for them. I told you, we weren't that close. Why would I even care who was there?" His cheeks reddened and the scowl returned.

She held up her hands and nodded. "You're right. That was a bit presumptuous, I guess. Thanks for the help." She turned to go.

"That was really it?" He chuckled disbelievingly.

Stopping on the top step, she turned back to him. "Yes, Mr. Mitchell. That was it. Believe it or not, I'm not the bad guy here. I'm only trying to solve a case and give two families some sort of closure about their children."

That sobered him and his gaze dropped. He looked up at her and nodded with a twitch of the lips that she supposed was a chagrined smile, then he closed the door.

As she got into her car, Ava dialed Sal's number.

"Hi, Sal. You busy today?"

"Well, I was going to the spa and then out to eat at that fancy French restaurant I like so much, but if you need me, I can put all that on hold. If I must," she said as if it were the truth.

"I really appreciate that. Maybe after work, you could show me the spa. I could use a little R&R, too."

Sal chuckled. "Okay, enough of that fantasy. What do you need, Ava?"

"I need to track down some construction and renovation companies. Would you go with me? We might need to split up and go talk to some of the past employees. It would go quicker if you could help do that."

"Oh, God! Yes, please. I've been in this room too long already."

"You just got here yesterday," Ava said.

"Yeah. I've been in this room doing a whole bunch of nothing for almost twenty-four hours. Where do you want me to meet you, and when?"

The sound of Sal putting on a jacket made Ava grin. "Calhoun's. Thirty minutes. We'll go over the case so I can catch you up while we grab something to eat."

"I'll be there."

Ava drove to the restaurant with a renewed pep in her step. Now that Sal was within easy reach, maybe the case would move along quicker. She could delegate work to her temporary partner. Ava had never been great at that sort of thing, but she knew if she ever wanted to advance in the Bureau, she would have to learn.

That could have been another reason behind Fullerton's decision to send her out on cold cases. She hadn't thought about that aspect of it. Every case was a case, and it was serious, but it was also a learning experience. There was always a lesson to be learned—from tiny and hard-to-recognize lessons to large and hard-to-miss lessons.

Why hadn't she thought about that before jumping to conclusions that Fullerton thought she was unfit for any other work? Because she was hardwired to lean toward self-doubt. Something else she would have to work on.

As she pulled into the restaurant's parking lot, she also made a mental note to try tracking down Frank Lauter again. She also needed to go by Ms. Halliday's house and see if Stephanie was home, since the road there had surely cleared. Stephanie had given an alibi for Frank for the night of the murder, but again, Ava had to check the box beside his name, and beside Stephanie's name, so she could say that she went over every detail of the case. And Frank had done construction work for the Johnsons. It was altogether possible that he had been the one who did the basement and the attic and built the outbuilding. She wouldn't know for sure until she could either eliminate him from the list by finding that someone else did the work, or because she confirmed that he had done it.

So many twists and turns. So many things to set in motion before she could actually move this along.

She turned off the engine and went inside to join Sal. It would be a working lunch, but Ava didn't know much of any other kind of lunch. She doubted that Sal did either.

CHAPTER THIRTY-THREE

A VA AND SAL LEFT THE RESTAURANT AND HEADED TO THE ADDRESS they had found for Jubal Reiser Residential Construction Company. An online search had struck out, and though there was the occasional review here or there, she couldn't find one in the last decade. Fortunately, the building was still listed on the map. It was located only a short ten-minute drive from Calhoun's.

It seemed to Ava that almost everything was located within about a thirty-minute range from the police station, which sat almost at the center of Hidden Cove. Harlan was small, but in comparison to Hidden Cove, it was practically a metropolis. She supposed a lot of places that she thought were small were large in comparison to the small Kentucky community.

Jubal's was a cinderblock building with little in the way of decoration. It seemed nothing had been done to the place to make it look like a top-of-the-line, sleek, professional business. It was just a plain building, painted white probably decades ago, and was now dirty, faded, and looked almost abandoned.

Sal stood by her car. "Doesn't look like much, does it?"

"No. Looks like it might be closed down. The size doesn't scream big business to me, either. I thought he had a lot of men working for him."

Sal lifted her eyebrows and shook her head. "Maybe a long time ago. If five men were considered a lot. Couldn't have been many more than that in here at one time. There's just not room enough for them and their tools."

On the property were four large structures besides the 'office'. Only one of those structures could have been called a building. It had corrugated metal walls and roof. A roll-up type door took up most of the front side. The other structures were covered with the same type of industrial roofing but were open. Ava thought these must have been used for lumber and wood storage.

A ten-foot-tall chain-link fence surrounded the property. The only building they could approach was the office.

Ava peered through the filthy windows, noting that the place had indeed been used as the office. A row of lockers spanned the far wall. File cabinets and a monstrous metal desk took up the left-side wall. Just under the window she and Sal looked through sat a long table with an ancient coffee maker, a toppled stack of Styrofoam cups, and a few scattered plastic spoons.

Cobwebs draped over every surface and looked like gossamer blankets over the items on the table.

Sal whistled low. "I think you struck out on this lead. This place hasn't been used in *years*. Look at all those cobwebs." She backed away from the window and scanned the adjacent properties.

Ava did the same. "Maybe they'll know where Jubal is." She pointed to a neat, two-story cedar house across a small branch to the right of the little defunct office.

Sal shrugged. "Possibility. My bet is Mr. Reiser is either dead or long gone from here."

"Worth a try," Ava shrugged, heading toward the footbridge.

An elderly man with a cane answered the door. "I help you ladies?" he asked, eyeing both women with watery blue eyes.

His shock of white hair blew in the light breeze, reminding Ava of the cobwebs in the little building. He looked ancient and his skin was deeply lined with wrinkles, but his large hands still looked strong. At one time, he had been a strong man. Time and hard labor had bent him and worn him down.

Ava introduced herself and Sal as FBI agents. "I was wondering if I could ask you a few questions about someone who might have worked for you in the past."

He nodded once, never altering his expression. "Come on in. It's cold out there. I hate winter nowadays." He motioned for them to follow him into a room immediately to the right. "Used to love it. That's a young man's prerogative. Cold don't hurt when you're young. Now I mostly hibernate and hope it goes away soon. Of course, springtime ain't much better with all its rain and wind. Hurts the old bones, and ain't no friend to the joints."

He groaned loudly as he settled into a sofa chair. "You ladies sit where you like. I have to sit here. This chair is easy on my back and I don't have to wrestle my way out of it when I stand up again." He grinned and the wrinkles deepened to crevices as his skin bunched.

"Thank you, Mr. Reiser." Ava and Sal sat on the opposite side of the room facing him.

"Just Jubal, please." He put the cane between his knees and rested his hands on its top. "What questions do you have for me?"

"I don't know if you recall a case that was in the news a few years ago. The Johnsons? Dustin and Katherine?"

Sal leaned forward. "Out on Pleasant Hill Road. Near the top. Young couple. Hadn't been married long."

Jubal's brow furrowed and his silver-white eyebrows nearly touched in the center. "Yeah. The man was shot in the house and the woman disappeared. This have something to do with that?" His voice rose as if he had thought that was old business and had been finished.

Ava nodded. "I need to know who did the renovations in their basement and attic. I was told the man who did them might have been one of yours. Do you remember if he was?"

"Lord have mercy, no, he wasn't one of mine. I've only had three full-time employees since I retired. That happened long before the Johnson case ever came about."

Ava looked at Sal. Sal shrugged. It was just enough of a movement for Ava to discern, but it said, *Look at him. He's ancient. What did you expect?*

Ava nodded. "When did you retire?"

"It's been nigh on nine years now. Last time I was even out that way was to do a full kitchen reno for Robert Mitchell. He was their neighbor. That was my last job, actually. It proved to me what my doctor had been telling me for years—I was too damn old to be doing that stuff anymore. It took ten days longer than it should've, and it took me over a month to recuperate. I've walked with a cane ever since. Can't trust my back or my knees anymore. They go out on me without warning and dump me on the floor, or on the ground. They have no shame and no mercy."

He raised one finger to point at them. "Enjoy your youth, ladies, but don't abuse your bodies. Take care of yourselves. If I had known I was going to live this long, I would have taken a lot better care of myself when I was young." He chuckled and nodded.

Ava grinned; Sal laughed. "I heard my daddy say almost that exact same thing when he was only in his late forties. He worked construction. Industrial metal construction," Sal said.

Jubal nodded. "It's hard work. No one wants to do it much anymore. Wood, metal, residential, industrial." He shook his head. "I lucked out when I got my guys. They practically run the business themselves. I don't have to do much more than make sure they get paid and keep the files."

"Do you happen to know any other laborers who might've taken on that job?" Sal asked, leaning her elbows on her knees and smiling as if she were having a conversation with her grandpa.

She seemed so comfortable talking to the man that Ava envied her. Perhaps it was her years of experience. Or, maybe it was because she was from a rural Kentucky town herself and she just knew how to talk with other Kentuckians.

"There were a few men who worked alone in town. You know, not for any company or anything, just themselves. I can't remember names offhand, but I have files somewhere over there in the office because I tried to hire 'em one year. I think there were three or four. I dogged a couple of them relentlessly because they were good and I was trying my damnedest to expand my business." He scoffed. "Still had big dreams of becoming a millionaire back then. Thought I still had enough left in me to sit back and run it all from here even though I couldn't do the work myself anymore. Even old men with tons of experience can still be dreamers to the point of stupidity. Anyway, they all refused. Wanted to remain freelance for whatever reasons, and I gave up eventually. But I may still have all their names in the files. I could get you a list together by tomorrow."

"Thank you. That would help us a great deal," Sal told him, glancing at Ava as if to ask if she wanted anything else from the man.

"Mr. Reiser, uh, *Jubal*, what did you think of Robert Mitchell?"

He shrugged. "Nice enough fella. He was pretty quiet and stayed out of my way, let me do my work, which a lot of people can't seem to do. Paid me on time. Never complained. I always pegged him as a bit of a dreamer, but I can't fault a man for that, now, can I?" He chuckled again.

Ava and Sal thanked him. Ava handed him a card with her name and contact information on it. "If you don't mind, whenever you get that list together, just get hold of me and I'll come back and get it."

"I can give it to you over the phone. Quicker and easier. Trust me, when you're my age, you'll wish you had done a lot more to save time and effort."

He insisted on seeing them to the door. "I'm old, but I ain't completely broke-down, yet. When I get too broke-down to see women to the door, as is only proper, they can just stick me in one of those old folks' homes and leave me."

Ava thanked him again as they left.

"We going anywhere else today?" Sal asked at the cars.

"I was going to, but I think I should wait on the list. It'll cut down on a lot of useless running hopefully. Besides, I think I have a phone call that I really need to make. It'll take a while, so I think I'll use my evening to do that, and I'll call you in the morning."

"How about we just meet at the station around seven or eight? That way we'll both be up and at 'em by the time Jubal calls with the list."

"You think he'll call that early?" Ava unlocked her car, chuckling.

"The older they are in the rural areas of the world, the earlier they start their days. Trust me, he'll call early." Sal opened her door. "See you in the morning bright and early."

"Hey, do you want to ride with me, then? I don't mind." Ava thought she might enjoy the company on the short ride.

Sal seemed to think about it for a moment, and then an icy gust of wind blasted across the small parking area, and both women gasped. Ava suddenly wished she had worn her thick coat. She should've known better than to trust that the weather would remain semi-warm for long.

"I'll take my car in case we need to split up and go to different locations," Sal said, smiling as she pulled her door shut. She waved at Ava and started the engine.

Ava nodded, gave her a thumbs-up, and turned the key in the ignition. She couldn't get the heater running quick enough.

Ava stopped by the station long enough to lock up her office, and then she went to the hotel. Dean, Molly, and the trafficking ring had been on her mind more and more as the day had worn on. She needed to call him, hear his voice tell her that there had been nothing new so she could clear it from her mind for another day or two. That seemed to be the best she could hope for these days.

CHAPTER THIRTY-FOUR

DEAN PICKED UP ON THE FIRST RING WHEN AVA CALLED LATE THAT afternoon. She was grateful to be talking to him, and not just about the case, but her thoughts were swirling too much to think about anything else.

"It's good to hear from you. How are things going?"

"They're going. That's about all I can say. It's tough with Mom still gone."

"I'm sure it is. Keep your chin up, though. You know all of us have your back, right? We're keeping all our ears to the ground on your mother's case, and we're still working on Molly's case. I promise to keep you in the loop with any new leads that show up."

"I really appreciate that, Dean," she replied. She wasn't exactly sure what had blossomed between them—she refused to call it a crush—but his voice calmed her down. For a moment, she closed her eyes and imagined that she was right there in Harlan, and that they were just next door in Xavier's bizarre house of wonders, not miles and miles away.

"When are you going to be finished with your case? Do you know yet?" he asked once he put the phone on speaker.

"Oh, I have no idea when I'll be finished. As soon as I can be done. That's all I can say at this point."

"Oh. Must be a really hard case if you don't have any idea how long it'll take."

"Eh. I think the weather has some bearing on it. It's hard to investigate like I need to when it's ten-below hell-no cold and there's snow and ice everywhere."

"I don't think that's a legitimate temperature," chimed in Xavier from the background. "Snow and ice shouldn't make such a difference. You can walk everywhere in Hidden Cove that you would need to go. I looked it up on the computer. It's a small town."

Ava chuckled and shook her head. "*Town* is small, Xavier. The rural areas are where I need to be, though, and they're not that close and not easy to walk to." She cleared her throat. "That's not really what I called to talk about, though."

"I know. You want to know about Molly and your mom," he replied bluntly.

"Way to put a point on it, Xavier," Dean commented.

"I mean, he is right," Ava told him. "Do you have any news about Molly's case?"

"Not new. Just all the things you already know," Dean replied. "Are you planning anything for New Year's?"

Ava hadn't really thought about New Year's celebrations. With her mother missing, Molly's case being so close to her conscious thoughts all the time, and now the cold case, she had simply lost track of time. She didn't want to leave her dad alone on New Year's, though. Even if there was no huge celebration, she would go to be with him and say goodbye to the old year and hello to the new one.

"I don't have solid plans, but I will spend the time with my father. How about you?"

"We might watch the ball drop on television. Emma and Sam are going to some actress's birthday party for that movie they're making," he said.

"A movie?" she raised an eyebrow.

"Yeah, I think it's some made-for-TV thing. About Lakyn Monroe, that influencer who was working on Xavier's case. Emma's been consulting on set about it. She's... not very happy with the results."

"I can't imagine why," Ava said, which made Dean chortle in response. "Hardcore, no-nonsense Emma Griffin on the set of a motion picture? That's something I'd like to see."

"It's definitely something," Dean agreed.

"Well, tell everybody hello for me," she said. "And Happy Holidays." She missed the team but was simultaneously glad to be in a position where she could start to make her own way. It was a good move for her, even if it meant having to work cold cases. Seeing every case as a learning experience had helped her feel better about the whole situation.

"I will. Happy Holidays, in case I don't see you before then."

She ended the call and took a minute to lay back on the pillow. Hearing the warmth and laughter of her friends really put into perspective her own feelings of isolation.

Barely ten minutes passed before her phone started vibrating again. She looked down at it with a frown, wondering why Dean would call her back so quickly.

"Hey," she started.

This time his voice was much more intent. "Ava?"

"Yes, it's me."

"I just got word from one of my contacts. There's new information about the trafficking case."

Ava's heart raced and she sat straight up in the bed. She gripped the phone tight and held her breath. Had they identified the woman on the footage? Had they tracked down any of the men or the couple who'd been seen blatantly buying young women?

Had Molly been found?

Dean cleared his throat. "Seven women, who were abducted from Prague five-and-a-half years ago, were recovered in Morocco three years ago. They were recovered by local law enforcement, and we're just now learning about it. None of them are Molly."

Ava's heart fell. She was, of course, happy that those women had been rescued, but she had hoped Molly would be among them. "Have they all been positively identified?"

"Yes. They're going through interviews with the Bureau now. I can't make any outreach until well after that time, but I'll try. If they're willing to talk, that is." Papers rustled and he was quiet for a moment. "I'm sorry. That's all I have. I know it's not what you hoped."

Having her hopes dashed repeatedly was becoming the norm, and Ava just wanted off the phone. "Thanks. I guess I'll talk to you later, Dean. Have a good one."

"I know you, Ava. You'll call me soon enough for updates. Fingers crossed I'll have something better next time."

Ava chuckled, glad that his humor was able to break through her emotional state. "You're right. There's no guessing to it. I'll talk to you later. See you."

"Oh, and Ava?"

"Yeah?"

"I'm sorry."

"Don't worry about it," she said. "Later."

"Bye."

For the second time, she hung up and laid back down, though this time frustration crept in instead of wistfulness.

Instead of thinking about how let down she was, Ava decided to get lost in the case again. She dialed Elsie Halliday's number. She fully expected to get the old-time answering machine yet again and was pleasantly surprised when the woman answered.

"Ms. Halliday?" Was her mind playing tricks? Was it really still the recorded message, and she was just so desperate for something to go right for a change that she was hearing a human voice?

"Yes? This is Agent James, right?"

Smiling despite the news from Dean, Ava stood up. Suddenly, she was full of energy again. "Yes, Ms. Halliday. This is Aviva James. I was calling to ask if your daughter is there. I really would like to talk to her."

"She's not. She went on vacation to the beach. She called me two days ago. I've been meaning to call you and let you know, but with me taking care of Remmie, it's easy to forget stuff until it's really too late to call."

Of course she was on vacation. What broke waitress would stay at home during the winter? Especially when there was a beach she could lounge on? "Why didn't she take her son?" Ava asked before she could stop herself.

"He didn't want to go." Ms. Halliday lowered her voice. "He don't like the man who was taking her. Said he'd rather build snowmen and stay here with me."

"Oh, so someone *took* her on vacation." That explained a lot, Ava supposed.

"I guess he's her new boyfriend, even though she says he ain't."

"Does she have a phone where I can call her and set up a meeting time for when she gets back?"

"Stephanie should be back in two days. You can come talk to her then. I have to go now. Goodbye, Agent James." She hung up the phone.

Ava eyed her own phone as if it might be a dangerous animal. What was it with everyone either ignoring her calls completely or just hanging up on her?

She marked the date for two days later when Stephanie was supposed to return, and then went to the hotel. She was tired and chilled, and all she wanted was to be comfortable and find some answers to something, anything.

She picked up a newspaper on her way to her room. After her shower, she sat on the bed working on all the little puzzles in the paper.

At least I have these answers, she thought. *I don't have to wait until tomorrow or two days from now, or whenever.*

Later, she called her father and told him she would be home on New Year's Eve so they could do something together. It seemed to please him that he would not be going to an office party, or avoiding it and getting those pitiful stares from coworkers.

Ava hoped the new year would bring good things.

CHAPTER THIRTY-FIVE

A T SIX-FIFTY THE NEXT MORNING, JUST AS THE SUN WAS BARELY peeking over the horizon, Ava and Sal walked into the station and headed for the office. They had just taken off their coats and Ava had started a pot of coffee when her phone rang.

"Agent James? This is Jubal. We talked yesterday."

"Yes, sir, Mr. Reiser. Is everything okay?"

"Just Jubal, if you please, ma'am. Yes, I just called about that list of names. I have it. You know the Jakobsons who just recently bought the house were looking for someone to help finish the work in the basement. They called me, but my client list was too full. My boys were all scheduled up for a few months. The Jakobsons didn't want to be put on the waiting list. Said they didn't like to schedule that far down the road, and they wanted it finished soon."

"Do you know who might have done the job for them?" Ava took her seat and grabbed a pen, ready to write down any names he might give.

"Maybe one of the men on this list I got for you. They're all still local and still working."

"Should I come get the list?"

He laughed. "No, ma'am. I can read it to you. Just four names."

"All right. I'm ready anytime." She gave Sal a thumbs-up.

"Anders Miller. Frank Lauter. Charlie Halbert. Matthew Schultz. That's it. I tried to hire them all and none of them would even think about working for a company. Course, I reckon I understand why. Mostly, anyway."

"Why's that, Jubal?"

"Well, if they can do work for cash money, they don't turn it in for tax purposes, you know. If they work for someone like me, they get paid by the hour, taxes are taken out, and they pay their Medicare taxes and such, then they just get a regular paycheck. Lotta guys don't like that. They'd rather work for cash under the table. Me? I was always too afraid of being caught." He chuckled.

Ava listened with half an ear as she looked over the list. She drew a star by Frank Lauter and tapped it when Sal looked.

"That's okay, Jubal. If you think of any more men who worked for cash back then, would you care to give me another call?"

"I don't mind at all, but I won't think of any more men. Not like there's an over-abundance of construction workers 'round these parts."

"All right, but if you do," she said, smiling at Sal.

"I'll call the prettiest FBI agent I've ever met."

Several snarky comebacks crossed Ava's mind, but she rejected them all. He was being friendly and in his down-home way, he was complimenting her. "Thank you again for your help, Jubal. You have a good day."

"More than welcome. Bye now."

"Goodbye," she said, hitting the button to disconnect.

Sal was going through the paper files and had already pulled everything they had on Frank Lauter.

"You think he's the one?"

Ava shook her head. "I don't know, but I still haven't been able to track him down to re-interview him. His ex-girlfriend who confirmed his alibi is being awfully evasive, too. I got hold of her mother last night and she said Stephanie was on vacation at the beach with some guy and would be back in two days. Wouldn't give me a phone number, the guy's name, the beach they were at, nothing."

Sal looked at the papers in her hand and then at the board. "Is this all we know about Frank Lauter?" She flapped the papers as she stared at the pictures of the house.

"For now, but I plan to change that." Ava took the papers and flipped through them. "Today, if I can." She pulled the paper that had his address and phone number and put the others back on the desk.

Sal looked at the paper. "He's still local. Want to go drop in on him?"

"Normally, I would call first, but the way my luck has been going with that, I think we should just drive over there. Not that it's been much better in that department."

"Worth a shot," Sal shrugged.

It took them nearly half an hour to get to Frank's house. It was in just as bad disrepair as it had been when she'd come every day three days in a row. There was a fresh layer of snow over everything, but it was like he hadn't even lifted a finger to bring in any of the tools or random debris.

Ava gave silent thanks for the covered porch. They made their way trying to step in the shallowest points of snow where it looked as though someone else had made several trips to and from the porch. One of the chains on the suspended porch swing had broken and one end of the swing touched the floor. Beside the broken swing sat an old wooden rocker that looked as if it might fall through if anyone dared sit on it.

"Thought this guy was a career handyman," Sal commented, raising her eyebrows and shaking her head.

"You know what they say; career housekeepers usually have the untidiest houses, mechanics' cars are always beaters that barely run, and apparently handymen's houses are in the worst need of repairs."

Sal rolled her eyes. "Something like that, I guess. Or he just doesn't give a crap about his own place. You know I'm thinking drunk, druggie, something along those lines, right?"

Ava nodded. "Crossed my mind, too. No mention of it in the records, though." She tried the doorbell first, already knowing there would be no sound from inside the house. She chuckled dryly and knocked loudly.

After several seconds, she knocked again, and called out to Mr. Lauter, announcing who she was. The whole scene felt like deja-vu.

Sal shook her head. "If he's in there and he is on drugs, he'll never come out now."

Ava scowled. "It's safer to announce who we are rather than spook someone who might already be paranoid."

Sal looked around pointedly at the landscape. "Not out here. Not always."

That shook Ava. Rural ways were unusual, she knew, and she was aware that it could pose more potential dangers, but she hadn't let it sink completely in that they were basically in the wilderness, in the middle of nowhere. They didn't know the land the same way locals would know it. If anything happened, sure the perpetrators would eventually be caught, but if drugs were involved, they likely wouldn't be looking that far into the future. They were definitely people who lived in the moment.

"Well, we can't make those kinds of assumptions about Mr. Lauter. We've never even met the man. Maybe he works long hours and it's difficult to find enough free time to do anything here."

Ava knocked again. "I don't think he's home." She pulled out her cell and the notepad where she'd written his number.

"If he's in there, he won't answer," Sal said, crossing her arms.

"No, but if his phone rings, we'll know if he is in there," Ava said without looking at her.

There was no sound of ringing from the house, and Lauter didn't answer. Ava didn't leave a message.

"He's not here," Ava said, heading for the steps. "Yet again. Let's go see if we can track down where he might be working."

Sal followed, and they left. Ava was glad to be leaving the place. The vibe was off somehow, and it made her edgy. Trying to pass it off as being due to Sal's warning comments, and her own over-thinking about the setting, she drove away, watching the house shrink in the rearview, knowing she would have to go back to it before the investigation was finished.

CHAPTER THIRTY-SIX

AFTER AVA AND SAL FINISHED AT THE OFFICE, THEY GRABBED AN early dinner at Calhoun's. Ava had grown to appreciate the down-home style of cooking, and she liked the friendly atmosphere of the place. Sal was good company, too. Having her around made Ava feel a bit less isolated and alone. It seemed that everyone at the station did their dead-level best to avoid her at all costs.

After dinner, Ava pulled her coat tightly around her and huddled inside it against the brisk wind that had kicked up. The sun was nearly set, and the Kentucky landscape slipped toward darkness fast.

"You heading back to the hotel?" Sal asked.

Ava looked around a moment and then shook her head. "I think I'm going to go by Lauter's place again and see if he's home yet."

Sal stopped and looked at Ava solemnly. "I should go with you. That's not a place you want to go alone."

After a slight hesitation, Ava nodded. "You're right. If you would rather go back to the hotel, though, I understand. It's been a long day."

The mountain of paperwork they had sifted through and the forms they'd filled out had been exhausting. She would have rather been out chasing down bad guys on foot through the desert than sitting at a desk staring at papers and a computer screen all day.

"Are you joking?" Sal laughed and hit the lock button on her key fob. She thumped the passenger side door of Ava's car. "Let's roll. I'm ready for some physical action. I detest being tied to a desk all day. Trust me, I get enough of that at my office back home."

They went to Lauter's house again. This time, an old long-bed, green and white, Chevy truck was parked with its nose toward the Cavalier in the garage. Only the living room had a light burning, and it looked dim.

Ava parked facing the porch with her lights on bright so they could see if anyone was outside before they got out.

"I don't see any movement. Just the living room light on," Sal noted as she scanned the side of the house that still lay in darkness.

"They don't believe in streetlights out here, do they?"

"Not in the rural parts," Sal said matter-of-factly.

Ava turned off the engine and opened her door. Sal opened hers and got out, but stood looking around for a few seconds. With the headlights no longer burning, the darkness seemed palpable. After her eyes adjusted to the dark, Ava moved toward the porch wondering why no one had come to see what the bright lights shining in the window were about.

With Sal beside her, Ava knocked on the door. Both women listened for sounds from within. Only the television playing the local news. She knocked louder.

Heavy footfalls grew more distinct as someone came to the door. Ava bristled.

The door opened slowly. All that stood between Ava and the tall, pale, scruffy man was the storm door.

"I help you?" His gaze constantly shifted from Ava to Sal and back.

Ava reached for her badge. The man stepped back and grabbed the doorknob as if to shut the door on them. She saw the panic in his face and held out a hand.

"Mr. Lauter? My name is Agent James. This is Agent Rossi. We're with the FBI." She flipped her badge over to show him, and his panicked expression turned to complete bewilderment. "We'd like to talk to you for a minute if you don't mind."

He didn't move to open the storm door. "What's this about?" Absently, he shifted from foot to foot and rubbed at the week-old scruff on his cheeks and chin.

The muscles in his forearm flexed and relaxed with the slight movement of his fingers and hand. He had broad, blunt hands. The hands of a carpenter.

"It's about a murder-disappearance that happened about five years ago. The Johnsons over on Pleasant Hill Drive? We are just re-interviewing everyone from that case; trying to clear it up and give the families of the victims some closure. You did some renovation work for them, didn't you?"

He eyed her suspiciously. "I'm a handyman. That's kinda how I make my living. Yeah, I did some work for 'em. And I already talked to the police about all this back then."

Sal stepped closer. "Mr. Lauter, we don't mean to impose, but could we just take five minutes of your time? I promise we'll make it as short as possible."

He hesitated a few more seconds before finally opening the storm door. "Come on in. It's too cold to stand here with the door open. It's lettin' out all my heat."

The smell of kerosene was strong inside the house, and Ava immediately spotted the heater sitting in the middle of the living room floor between the television and the couch. That and the television were the only lights on, though. Ava looked up at the ceiling for light fixtures, and Mr. Lauter leaned to the side to look behind them.

He pointed. "Light switch is right there. I can't reach it, but you can. Just flip it up."

Sal flipped it and a bright, bare bulb came to life overhead.

"You want to sit somewhere?" Mr. Lauter turned to the living room. Reaching inside the wide doorway, he flipped on a light. "There's light in here, too," he said in a mildly sarcastic tone as he strode into the room, leaving the women to follow. Or not.

Ava looked to Sal, who seemed a little on edge, but not put off by Lauter's actions. They joined him and sat on the couch across from him.

"I had an alibi for that night. I already told the police." He leaned back in his seat. "I knew nothing then, and after all these years, I still don't."

Ava nodded. "Yes, all that's in the records we have. What were you doing at their house?"

"I did a basement renovation for them. You know, new couple, their first house, they had big dreams of everything being perfect, so they wanted even the basement to be livable. I guess they had no plans to raise gardens and put away their own vegetables, because they wanted to be able to use the basement like another living room, or something."

"And you were able to do that for them?"

"Mostly."

"What do you mean *mostly*?" Sal asked.

"I mean that when they saw how expensive the sheetrock and lumber and ceiling tiles were gonna be, they wanted me to fix the basement in stages. I told them I could get most of the lumber on my account down at the lumber yard, and they could keep a running bill and pay me as his paychecks came in, but they didn't want to do that. Then..." his gaze shifted from Sal to Ava and back. "Then *that* happened."

"Did you put vinyl flooring in the basement for them?"

"Nope," he said, shifting in his seat.

"Did you happen to work for the Jakobsons after they moved in?"

"No. I didn't know them. Terrible what happened." He shook his head and glanced at the newscast.

Lauter had relaxed, but Ava still saw signs of tension in his posture and in his face. They were small, but present nonetheless. Like the fine sheen of moisture on his brow, the little tic at the outer corner of his right eye, and the way his fingers constantly gripped and let go of the fabric on the arm of his chair.

They talked for five more minutes and Ava could not see any sign that he was anything other than he claimed. He had been the Johnsons' handyman who had been working on their basement at the time. Nothing more.

Back in the car, Sal blew out a sigh of relief. "Can't say I miss the smell of kerosene. We used to have two of those heaters when I was growing up. You're always too hot or too cold with them. There's no middle ground, it seems. And everything you own ends up smelling slightly oily by the time winter's over."

"What did you think about him?" Ava asked as she drove away.

"I'm not really sure. He seemed to be telling the truth, but it felt like he was hiding something. Maybe just nervous because the FBI was sitting in his living room, though."

Ava nodded. That's what she had thought, too.

By the time they reached Calhoun's, the restaurant was closing for the evening. Sal went to her car, and Ava drove on to the hotel to put a few notes down that would go in the case file the next day.

CHAPTER THIRTY-SEVEN

AFTER GOING THROUGH THE LIST FROM JUBAL, AVA AND SAL MADE new files for Anders Miller and Matthew Schultz. Their stories seemed legitimate, and Ava thought they would be cleared as soon as she could check out their stories. Both men had been working in an upscale suburban neighborhood on the outskirts of Bowling Green during the murder. Work had been slow in the immediate area, and the two had teamed up to make more money. Anders had even hired a couple of young guys there who were looking to make a few bucks.

Charlie Halbert, Ava knew, was the man who had been driving the Jeep Cherokee the night of the wreck outside her hotel. She also knew he had a penchant for drinking and hitting the bars. Redding had told her that.

Halbert was still in the hospital when Ava and Sal found him. He was able to talk to them enough to say that he had been remodeling his parents' home during the time of the Johnson murder-disappearance. He remembered because the news broke while he was there, and his mother had brought it up at dinner that night.

Although Ava didn't care for the family-as-alibi situations, she knew in places as small as Hidden Cove, families were close.

Ava and Sal compared notes in the car in the parking lot of the small county hospital.

"I need to find out who put that flooring down and who took it up," Ava said. "I think the two cases are connected. I can't get it out of my head. I know Hopson said he was working the Jakobson case, but I want to talk to someone and find out if they know anything about that basement flooring."

Sal nodded. "Okay, but if Hopson hears you're out talking to his interviewees, you know he'll throw a fit about it."

Ava shrugged with a grin. "He'll just have to be mad. He blows a fuse over anything and everything anyway. Might as well make it worthwhile."

"I like the way you think, Agent James," Sal chuckled.

"If Derrick Jakobson bought the vinyl, I think there's a good chance that he asked someone to help him put it down, or at least move it around. That stuff isn't light. Especially not a large piece of it."

Sal snapped her fingers. "Brother? Best friend? Father?"

"I'm thinking brother." Ava went through the short list of names she had finagled from Hopson, and from her own quick check on the intranet at the station. "Henry Jakobson." She pointed to the name. "Can you get the address while I drive?"

"Already on it," Sal said as she tapped information into her phone.

They ended up at a small brick house in a nice, quiet, tree-lined neighborhood. They weren't rich people, but they were living easier than the most rural residents Ava had seen. Henry's neighborhood looked like a place where the residents lived comfortably. Perhaps still from paycheck to paycheck like so much of the national population, but she bet their paychecks came with more money on them than their rural counterparts' checks did.

After inviting them in, Henry offered them something to drink, nothing alcoholic, just water, coffee, or tea, which seemed to be standard fare.

"No thanks, Mr. Jakobson." Ava and Sal sat at the dining table. The room was bright because of all the windows and the glass French doors that let out onto the side patio.

"I talked to Detective Hopson, has something else come up in the case?" He sat.

"No. We just wanted to ask about the renovations your brother and his wife were doing to the house."

"He never got to them." Henry's eyes welled with tears and he stood up. "Damn shame that somebody did that to them," he said as he walked to the patio doors. "It's not right. They never hurt anybody, and their future was looking so good for them. They'd had a rough few years, but they'd really pulled it together." He wiped discreetly at his eyes.

"I'm sorry to have to ask you about all this, maybe we should come back—"

"No. It's all right. Whatever it takes to help catch the bastard who killed them." He strode back to the table and sat again. "What did you need to know about the renovations?"

In cold cases, the people involved usually aren't as emotional. Years go by, wearing off the rough edges of their sorrow and grief. They go numb. But with newer cases, emotions are raw. That was the part Ava disliked most about her job.

"Do you know who put the vinyl flooring in the basement?" Ava asked him.

"I helped Derrick put it down. They didn't have a lot of money, and they wanted to do everything they could before hiring anyone."

"Were they planning other renos?"

"Yeah. For one, they wanted to finish out the basement. I think Krystal had her heart set on remodeling the kitchen and little JJ's bedroom, too." His voice cracked at the mention of the little girl, and Ava had to force herself not to think about the baby who would grow up never really knowing her parents. "We're applying for custody of her. Me and my wife. She'll never know how great her parents were. They were so happy when they had her. That was the extra push they needed to get their lives heading in the right direction."

Ava gave him a moment before continuing. "Do you know who they were going to hire?"

He shook his head. "They had only contacted a few people but hadn't made a decision yet. They called Renos by JD and set up an appointment for someone there to give them estimates. Charlie Halbert. He's a local guy. Frank somebody, who's also local, and one more, but I can't remember the name. If I think of it, I'll call you."

Sal wrote down the names. "Do you know if any of those men ever went to the house?"

He shook his head. "Derrick didn't say anything about it last time we talked on the phone. That was just two days before..." he trailed off, his words stopping as his breath hitched.

"Do you know who took up the vinyl in the basement?" Sal tapped her pen on the paper.

"No. We put it down, and I wouldn't think Derrick would have taken it back up for any reason. It was too hard to put down and too expensive to tear out like that. Maybe the cops did it for some reason."

His bewildered expression was easier to look at than his ragged grief.

"Mr. Jakobson, thank you for talking to us. I'm sorry we've bothered you, but we've got all we need now. If you need anything, feel free to call." Ava handed him a card with her contact information.

The women were quiet as they headed out of the neighborhood. Ava supposed Sal was lost in her own thoughts about the case. It was good to let one's mind roam at will for short bursts. Many times, in Ava's experience, that was when insight came and inspiration hit.

"You know that if Derrick and Henry didn't take up that flooring, that only leaves the killer. No one else was there. Henry talked to his brother two days before the murders. If he had been planning on re-doing the floor, he would have mentioned it to Henry."

"But why would the killer take the time to rip it out?" Sal let her hands thump on her lap. "It might be nothing in the end. We might be wasting our time and energy even thinking about it."

Ava put the car in park at the station. "But it *feels* like something, doesn't it?"

Sal nodded. "Unfortunately, it feels like a headache getting ready to start up."

They went inside.

CHAPTER THIRTY-EIGHT

For about the thousandth time, Ava stood in front of the evidence board staring at the pictures of the victims. She took the basement photos down and put them back up side by side.

Where had the killer taken Katherine Johnson five years ago? Why did the murderer in the Jakobson case take up the vinyl flooring?

Was Katherine still alive? Could she have had something to do with Dustin's death?

Nothing Ava had dug up suggested that.

Sal walked over and stood beside Ava. "You seeing something I don't?"

"I don't know," Ava sighed, not taking her eyes from the photos.

"Talk to me. Maybe we can bounce it off each other and figure it out."

"Where's Katherine Johnson?" Ava put her finger under the woman's picture.

"No one knows. No evidence she was murdered. No evidence she struggled with anyone. No body ever recovered."

"Why did the Jakobsons' killer rip up that flooring?" Ava moved to put her finger under the basement photos.

"I think we're the only ones who even took note of the vinyl, so there's nothing in the files about it."

Ava leaned close, willing the pictures to give up their secrets. After several seconds, she groaned and put her hands over her eyes and leaned her head back in frustration. "I feel like it's right here in front of me."

She looked back to the board and snatched the basement pictures off it. She walked to the window to examine them in the bright light. "Right here," she muttered.

"Ever heard of overthinking it? Trying too hard?" Sal sauntered over to her with a smile in an attempt to cheer her up.

"Yes, but that's not what I'm doing. I feel it in my bones. The answer is right under my nose. I just have to find it." She brushed past Sal and started to hang up the pictures again. That's when she saw it. A lighter part of the concrete. She held the picture in the light again.

"What is it?" Sal leaned close to see what had gotten Ava's attention.

"Right here. Do you see that lighter patch of concrete?"

"Yes. It's probably just the way the crappy lighting was hitting the floor." Sal moved away.

A terrible thought occurred to Ava, and a cold chill gripped her body. "What if Katherine never left that house?"

Sal turned to her. "What? Like she's been living in the attic or in the walls like in some horror movie? The crazy woman with the wild hair and scary white face." Sal chuckled, but it was humorless.

"No." Ava pointed to the picture. "What if she's there?"

Sal's eyes widened. "*Under* that concrete? As in, someone killed her and *buried* her there?"

Ava nodded. "That's exactly what I mean. Why's that patch lighter than the rest? It looks newer to me. Frank Lauter is the one who did the basement renovation. That was five years ago."

"You think Lauter's the killer?" Sal took the picture to analyze it.

"I'm thinking it's either him or Robert Mitchell. Either one of them had means and opportunity. In both cases, too."

"But what was the motive?" Sal squinted at the photo. "We need to go look at that again. You can't really see that clearly in the picture."

Ava drove to the house on Pleasant Hill Road in record time. Both agents went straight to the basement. This time, they trained their flashlight beams on the concrete.

"That part isn't much lighter, but it does look quite a bit rougher. As if he didn't take time to make sure it was smoothed down like the rest of it." Sal squatted and motioned for Ava to feel the difference.

"It looks weathered and aged. It's not something the Jakobsons had done."

Sal agreed. "Are we going to ask for it to be torn out?"

"It's still part of the active investigation; we won't get permission unless we have more proof." Ava stood and eyed the patch. It wasn't square or rectangle, it was more of a messy circle. Like the kind a kid would draw when they were first learning shapes.

"Are we thinking the same guy killed the Jakobsons and the Johnsons?"

"I am." Ava turned to face Sal. "What if, five years ago, the killer buried Katherine right here, poured concrete over her, and left Dustin to be found only because he was running out of time?"

"But where's the evidence that Katherine was killed? None of her blood was found anywhere. Didn't even seem to be a struggle."

"Maybe he had time to clean up. Maybe he strangled or smothered her. She wasn't very big. A strong man like Lauter or Mitchell could have controlled her easily."

Sal shook her head. "I don't know. I still think there would've been some evidence. I don't know about Robert, but Frank Lauter..." she scoffed. "I don't think he'd be able to clean up that well. It's not like he's criminal mastermind material."

Ava mulled it over. Robert Mitchell didn't seem to be a mastermind, either. But he was shady. She couldn't rule him completely out. Especially knowing how easily he had lied to the police and the investigators. And he had gotten his friend to lie for him, too. He had to be persuasive, evasive, and a bit of a sociopath to pull off a stunt like that without giving something away.

"I know Robert Mitchell lied about where he was and what he was doing that night. His friend lied for him, too. But he doesn't seem like the type that could clean up a murder scene, either. Though, it's not impossible for someone to clean it up enough to fool the police."

"Okay, why would the Johnsons' killer wait five years for another couple to move in here, and then kill them, too?" Sal looked up the stairs.

The beginnings of a headache made Ava's eyes ache. She sighed. "I don't know." She looked at the floor again. The more she looked, the more she imagined Katherine Johnson lying under there, tossed in like so much refuse and covered in concrete. Her blood boiled. What gave anyone the right to take another's life? Why did anyone think they could toss a human away like trash and get away with it?

"Stephanie Halliday should be home today. I'm going to talk to her. If anyone can blow Lauter's alibi, it's her." Ava headed upstairs, angry at getting so close to answers, yet being so far away from them at the same time.

Sal followed. "I thought her alibi for him was rock-solid."

They got into the car. "Yeah, but I've found that a lot of decisions out here are made because everyone knows everyone else. No one wants to think their family, friend, fellow church-goer, or their neighbor is a cold-blooded murderer."

"I can't argue with that. That's just life in small towns." Sal buckled her seatbelt. "By all means, then, let's go talk to Stephanie."

CHAPTER THIRTY-NINE

STEPHANIE WAS STANDING ON THE FRONT PORCH, WRAPPED IN A blanket and smoking a cigarette when Ava and Sal pulled into the driveway.

"That her?" Sal asked.

"I think so. Haven't met her yet." Ava quickly parked and got out. "Stephanie Halliday?" She asked, moving toward the porch.

"Who wants to know?" The woman flipped her cigarette to the yard.

Ava held up her badge. "Agent James. This is Agent Rossi. I already spoke to your mother. She said you'd be back today."

Her expression soured. "Yeah. She told me. You want to come in?"

"Sure," Ava said, following her inside.

"Remington is watching cartoons. Let's talk in the kitchen. I don't want him to hear what I have to say to you."

In the kitchen, Ava asked in a low voice, "What is it that you have to say to us, Miss Halliday?"

"You want to know about Frank's alibi five years ago, don't you?"

Ava nodded.

"I can tell you right now, I'm taking back what I told them back then. I lied. I know that can probably get me in trouble, but I've lived with this ever since then. I've been looking over my shoulder every day and every night. I'm sick of it, and I can't take it anymore."

Sal pulled out a chair. "Here, Stephanie. Sit down and tell us what happened."

Stephanie let the blanket slide off her shoulders and draped it over the back of her chair as she sat. "I woke up that night and Frank wasn't in the bed. I heard noises, but I thought he was just in the kitchen getting something to eat or drink because he has insomnia. Diagnosed with it when he was a teenager, but refused to take the medicine for it. Doctors said there wasn't nothing else to do for him if he refused to take it, so he just suffered with it. Truth told, so did I, because when he was up roaming around at night, he usually woke me up being so damn noisy." She picked up a pack of cigarettes, opened them, and laid them back down.

"Did you get up to check if it was him making the noise?" Ava asked.

"No. I fell back asleep because I figured it was him like it always was. When I woke up the next morning, though, he was right there in bed beside me, snoring away." She fingered the pack of smokes again. "I was trying hard to make our relationship work, you know?"

Ava and Sal nodded in unison.

"Well, I told the cops back then that Frank was with me all night that night. I didn't tell them about the picture of the woman in Frank's closet, though. That happened before the cops got around to interviewing us. I was mostly just jealous when I found it, you see? Then I saw that couple's picture on the television before Frank got home that evening. It was the same woman. Or at least I think it was. If it wasn't, she was that Johnson woman's sister."

"This picture was in Frank's closet?" Ava asked.

"Yeah. Folded in half in the pocket of his jeans. They were laying on the floor, and I was straightening up. I felt something in the pocket, so I took it out and looked. I was so mad at him. I thought he was fooling around on me. Then I saw the news, and she looked so much like the Johnson woman. I knew he had been working at their house, and it scared me a little, but not nearly enough. I should've come clean when the cops talked to us."

"I don't understand. Did you confront Frank about the picture?" Sal asked.

"Damn straight, I did. I threw it at him and screamed and accused. I was scared and furious. I had worked so hard to make it work between me and him. He said he wanted to have a family with me, but then I found some other woman's picture hidden in his pocket." She shook her head.

Her eyes were angry, and there wasn't a tear in sight. She'd had a long time to think about the situation, and if there'd been hurt feelings before, she seemed to be over them.

"Then why didn't you tell the cops when they came around asking questions?" Sal asked, leaning in close to keep her voice low.

"Because I was stupid. I thought there was still hope for us, you know? I didn't want to get him implicated in something crazy and mess everything up for us. You have to understand that I was crazy over him. Literally, I was stupid and blind in love. I should have run as soon as I realized how much like that woman the picture looked. But that was my Frank, my life, my family."

"What happened to the picture?" Ava asked, hoping Stephanie had kept it.

"He supposedly threw it out the night we argued about it. He might still have it, for all I know. I'm not with him and trying to make our little family work anymore, and I've had years to think about everything that happened back then. To be honest, I am afraid he might have done something to that couple." She leaned forward and whispered. "And, if he did, it had something to do with Katherine Johnson. The more I've thought about it, the more I'm sure it was her."

"Would you officially swear to the information you just gave us?" Ava asked.

She held up her right hand. "Swear to God Almighty, himself."

"I guess you wouldn't mind taking a lie detector test and giving a new statement. Just to make it official?" Sal asked.

"It's time for all this to be finished. I'll do whatever I need to do."

Ava stood and handed Stephanie her card. "Thank you for telling us this. I'll be getting in contact with you soon. You'll need to give another statement, just procedural stuff really."

Stephanie nodded, took the card, and picked up her smokes.

Ava and Sal left, and Ava was sure Stephanie would be on the porch again, smoking in the cold, wondering if she really did do the right thing.

CHAPTER FORTY

MMEDIATELY UPON REACHING THE STATION, AVA CALLED FULLERTON to report the new findings.

"I'd like to request that the basement floor be taken up, sir. I really think that's where Katherine is."

"I'll make a call and get back to you. Be ready to move when I call. You'll have to be there in case anything is found."

Ninety minutes later, Fullerton called back. Ava and Sal drove back to Pleasant Hill Road. Two uniformed officers from the station were there, and a man was in the basement preparing to remove the patch of concrete. Ava pointed it out, and he got started.

Ava stood halfway up the steps, too energized to go outside where the uniforms were. Sal paced the kitchen for a few minutes, and then joined Ava.

"Hey! Somebody better come look at this," the man called up half an hour later.

Ava raced down the stairs and to his side. She peered down at the bare earth where the concrete had been. The corner of a tarp stuck up through the dirt, and the shape of a head was visible underneath where the concrete had pulled the dirt out with it.

It was hard to see with so much concrete dust, but it was unmistakable.

"I ain't touching that. Am I done here?" The man had backed to the stairs.

"Hold on. You don't need to touch anything. Hand me that shovel, Sal," Ava held her hand out as she looked at the shape under the tarp.

Using the shovel, she removed enough dirt to see that the concrete had been removed from the entire body, and then she told the man to speak with the officers before leaving.

Sal called in the forensics team. After they arrived, they were meticulous but fast about their duties. The body was that of a woman matching Katherine Johnson's description. A handgun had been placed in a bag with a woman's panties, shorts, and shirt. The bag had been placed with the body inside the tarp. The fingerprints were still intact on the gun.

Ava felt as if the world was spinning. Everything was dreamlike. It was her first official case in charge of an investigation, and she had followed her gut. Her instincts had been right so far, now she just had to wait for the tests to all come back.

It only took a few days. They seemed like the longest days of her life as she waited. When the reports came in, she and Sal read them together.

Katherine Johnson had been sexually assaulted. During the assault, she had been strangled to death. There was DNA under her fingernails, but it had degraded too badly for it to be used in identifying her attacker.

Ava read the fingerprint analysis report, and her heart raced, her adrenaline pumped. "Do you see that?" She pointed to the name.

"Frank Lauter, Ava, you were right," she said with a big grin. "What do you say we go catch a bad guy?"

Four uniforms followed Ava and Sal to Frank's house. The warrant for his arrest had taken all of thirty minutes to get signed. Everything was moving fast. Almost too fast to be processed. This was the part of her job that Ava liked. When it was all boiling down to the end and the blood was racing through her veins, her muscles thrummed with adrenaline, and the bad guy was getting ready to go down.

Frank was at his truck when they pulled in. As soon as the two cop cars were in sight, he bolted toward the woods behind his house.

"We got a runner!" Sal yelled to the cops as they filed out of the cars.

Ava was already on the move, and the sounds of her backup were fading as she ran after Frank.

In the woods, the sun hadn't melted away all the snow. It crunched underfoot as she ran. Frank was in her sights. His nondescript khaki coat stood out like a sore thumb against the pristine white snow. She kept her eyes laser-focused on him, trusting her body to keep her upright.

He dodged and zagged behind trees, over bushes, around rocky outcroppings. The man ran like a deer, surefooted and fast, trying to avoid capture. Ava's breath puffed out in great white clouds. All she could think about was how he had hurt Katherine and then buried her in the basement of her own house after murdering her husband. She had surely known the love of her life was dead. Just as surely, she had probably seen and felt her own end coming. What terror had she felt? What pain?

All of it at the hands of this horrible man.

The thought pushed her legs faster. She let her emotion consume her, let it spur her onward. Her lungs burned, and she felt the burning exhaustion coming on, sped up by the icy cold conditions. Fighting through that first spate of exhaustion would lead to what everyone called a runner's high, and in that state, she always felt as if she were gliding instead of running, and she could keep it up indefinitely.

Suddenly, Frank dropped out of sight. She assumed he had tripped and fallen, but as she flew toward the spot where he'd gone down, she didn't see him. Instead, she saw a drop-off. She grabbed for a tree and tried to stop, but it was too little, too late.

Her feet hit the icy patch and went over the embankment, sending her straight back onto her shoulders to roll head over heels twice. She managed to position herself in a horizontal position mid-tumble and began rolling down, bouncing off rocks, roots, and small trees as she sped toward the bottom of the ravine.

She caught glimpses of Frank as he moved away from her. Coming to a stop, she pushed up onto her knees and hands. The world spun uncontrollably for a five-count, and then she pushed to her feet. Her right cheek burned and her right shoulder didn't move exactly right.

But she didn't have time to waste checking over her injuries. Frank was getting away. Or, at least, he was trying. He hopped and hobbled. His left leg looked badly injured. A dark part of Ava hoped it was broken.

"Frank, stop!" she shouted.

He did not. She hadn't expected him to. Her body started pumping along like that of a prime athlete again, and she ran, quickly covering the distance between them. She didn't slow down as she neared him, though. Instead, she threw herself full-speed into his side and back, knocking him to the ground with a heavy thud.

The whoof-sound he made as she knocked the air out of him was somehow satisfying. She tumbled to the ground with him, but recovered and was back on her feet a second after going down.

"Frank Lauter, I have a warrant for—"

He kicked out and caught her left knee. She crumpled to the ground and threw her hands up just in time to block the next kick aimed at her face. She twisted his ankle and pressed her weight against it, a move that would break it if he struggled too hard.

He rolled with it and screamed as he used his injured leg to kick her off him. As she vaulted toward him again, she saw blood spatters on the snow. He turned away from her and scrambled to his feet. When he turned, he had a short, stout stick with a wickedly jagged end.

"What are you going to do with that, Frank? My partner and four uniforms are headed this way right now. You really think you can kill me and outrun them? You're losing blood, Frank. Give it up."

"I might not get away, but if I go down, I'm taking you down with me," he growled through gritted teeth as he jabbed the stick toward her face.

She moved deftly out of reach. "I have a warrant for your arrest, Frank. You murdered a woman and her husband."

He lunged forward, vocalizing a half-scream, half-growl as he tried to jab her in the face with the stick again. She judged his reach and moved back a half-step. As he lunged again, she twisted to the side and slapped the stick. It was solid. Possibly deadly, if he landed a blow to the right area.

"You killed her husband and then raped and murdered her, Frank." Ava dodged again, but the business end of that stick grazed her neck, drawing a thin trickle of blood.

He grinned. "Think you're tough, don't you? Women like you need to be taught a lesson." He swung and Ava jumped back to avoid being hit.

Backing up several steps, she looked for an area clear enough to take him down with minimal injury to herself. He was determined to hurt or kill her before the others reached them.

As she was backing up, he ran the few steps toward her, holding the stick out as if to plunge it into her right arm. She moved in the other direction, but he anticipated her. He swung out with his fist and caught her in the side of the head.

The force of the blow silenced the world; an explosion of blinding white in her left eye left the scene without depth. He was coming at her again as she regained her balance.

Uncle Ray's training took over, and she faced Frank. Maybe he thought she was stunned, maybe he thought he'd won, but she knew he was wrong.

He drew the stick back and aimed for her throat. Everything happened in slow motion. She waited until it was nearly too late to move, then she twisted to the side, grabbed the stick in her left hand, kept turning toward him until it was coming out of his grip, and then she elbowed him in the throat with her right arm.

As her spin slowed, she caught her balance. Frank grabbed his throat and fell to his knees. She tossed the stick away and pushed him facedown to the ground. He choked and coughed. Putting her knee in his low back, she leaned forward and put her elbow on the back of his head.

"Frank Lauter, I have a warrant for your arrest in the murder of

Dustin Johnson and the rape and murder of Katherine Johnson." She read him his rights as she pressed the side of his face into the snow.

The uniforms ran to the scene, huffing loudly. Ava moved off him and sat on a stump while they cuffed him.

"You okay?" Sal asked.

Ava nodded, slowly catching her breath. "Better since we collared that bastard," she huffed, nodding toward Frank. She grimaced as all her injuries sent pain signals. She put her hand to her neck and felt the sticky blood there.

"You are going to be feeling this day for a while," Sal said. "Can you walk?"

"Yes."

Sal helped her to the car. The ambulance came only moments after she sat down. The adrenaline faded, and she began shaking. She went to the hospital without arguing.

CHAPTER FORTY-ONE

HE NEXT DAY, AVA WAS RELEASED FROM THE HOSPITAL. FORTUNATELY, all her injuries were minor. Just a few scrapes and bruises. She was most worried about her shoulder, but the doctor assured her that it would be fine after a few days' rest. Sal drove her to the hotel.

"They searched Frank's house and found a necklace that belonged to Katherine Johnson. It was hanging from his bedpost. You'll never guess what they found under the shed this morning."

Ava shook her head. On his bedpost. A souvenir from a rape-murder hanging on his bedpost all those years. Assessing her own injuries, she decided it was well worth it to get a man like Frank Lauter off the streets.

"What was in the shed?" Ava only hoped it wasn't a body.

"The gun used in the Jakobson double homicide. Well, they have to wait for all the tests to come back to prove it, but ballistics finished with it this morning, and they said it's the same gun."

"So, he did kill the Jakobsons. Did he ever give a reason for any of this?"

"Swears he was in love with Katherine and didn't want the Jakobsons covering her up, disrespecting her and her house by re-doing the whole basement. Mrs. Jakobson was hell-bent on doing it, though. His words, after Detective Hopson accused him of being a pathetic, heartless bastard who wasn't worth the bullet to kill him."

Ava's eyes widened. "Wow, Hopson had a temper tantrum on the right person this time, at least."

At the hotel, Ava hugged Sal. "Thank you for everything. It's been great working with you."

"Any time. You know my number."

Ava smiled and handed Sal a card. "And there's mine, just so you have it on hand. Call me whenever."

Sal laughed and put the card in her pocket, nodding. "Do you have plans for New Year's?"

"I'm going home to be with my dad."

Ava packed that day. It took her until that evening to get all the files and photos from the tables packed up into boxes. As she stacked them on the table and put her suitcase up there, someone knocked on the door.

"Who is it?" she called.

"Redding."

She opened the door. Redding grinned at her. "I thought you'd be leaving ASAP. Can't say I blame you, though."

She moved so he could come inside.

He shook his head. "You look like you were in a car wreck. You're going to be sore for a while."

"So I've been told."

He held out an envelope awkwardly. "This is from some of us at the station. Just to say we appreciate what you did and hope you get to feeling better. I thought you would be in the hospital longer, and I went there to give it to you. The nurse told me you left."

"Thank you, Chev." She took the card. It was a standard Get Well card with a handwritten *Thanks for all you did* note inside. There were seven signatures on the left side and four on the right. One of which, she noted, belonged to Detective Hopson.

Redding talked for only a few minutes, and then he left. Ava watched

AVA JAMES AND THE FORGOTTEN BONES

as he went to his car. Her breath fogged the glass of the window and she drew her name in the condensation.

She turned and walked to the table, put her suitcase and the boxes on the small baggage cart, and rolled them out of the room. She was happy to be leaving, and happier that she had solved the cases.

It was time to go home. There was a New Year to celebrate with her father.

EPILOGUE

UNKNOWN

THE CITY BELOW WAS NEVER QUIET, NEVER STILL. HE HATED IT HERE. He wished he was back in his comfort zone. It was hot where he was; even in the nighttime, the heat was nearly unbearable.

But he had a job to do. And he *always* completed his jobs.

The mark had been on the move for weeks, and now, all of a sudden, she had stalled out in this godforsaken city. He had mistakenly thought the constant swell and rush of people on the streets below would make it simpler to get close to her, but it had not.

She was practically a ghost in a crowd, moving swiftly and gracefully in and out and around the pedestrians; ducking into alleys, doorways, winding her way through the streets as if she knew them well. As if they were her hometown.

He knew better than that, though.

She was as much a foreigner here as he was.

All he had to do was find out where she was staying, what her business was in the city, and where she kept going every night. He had the answers to exactly none of those questions even after two weeks of trying to pin down her lodgings. The best he had come up with was a general zone where she passed through every day, but from a different direction every time. Soon, though, she would have to start repeating her in-route, and that's when he would be able to back-trace her path.

He was a patient man. He had time. But he did wish to be back in Russia where the temperatures were more to his liking.

He made a mental note to never migrate south of the equator on a permanent basis.

He leaned against the wall by the window. Even the bare bricks he leaned against were warmer than was comfortable, and sweat rolled down his face and neck. His contact here had set him up in a terrible location with no way to cool the room except a wobbling ceiling fan and a metal electric fan that was probably a throwback from World War II.

High-end prostitutes, the ones that preferred being called *escorts*, and worked for madams who were worth bundles of money, frequented the hotel across the road. The clientele there were all multi-millionaires. Some were businessmen, others had inherited their wealth—they were what some called old money.

Every one of them who entered the hotel across the way was into illegal business, though. None of them were altruistic. None of them cared for the world at large, except that it was a place to satiate their aberrant desires.

The alley to his left was the demarcation line between the rich playboys' side of the city, and the dirty, gritty, hard side of the city, where a man or woman would just as soon stab a man in the eye as to walk on by him.

That was the side that drew his attention at the moment. There was movement at the far end, where there were no lights and rusted, over-filled dumpsters.

It was the mark. She was making her way via the alley. She'd never done that before.

He didn't have to see her clearly to know it was her. She had a certain characteristic to her movements, a swift stealth that was absent in the residents and local alley rats who usually rolled up in the alley for some secret drug deal or to scavenge through the dumpsters for food.

Putting the lens to his eye, he squinted in her direction.

The world was thrown into a green wash. Definition was rendered brilliantly where there had been nothing but dark shapes and deep shadows before.

The woman was still nearly a hundred feet away, and he stood a full story above her, looking down.

As she neared, his trigger finger itched to go to work, but he had to keep himself in check a little longer. The boss wanted to know what she was up to before his job could be concluded.

The bill of her baseball cap kept her face covered just enough that he could never get a clear look at it, but that would all change. She would get comfortable. Brave. Arrogant. She would make a mistake.

And that was when he would be there to swoop in and take the opportunity.

But for now, he watched.

And waited.

AUTHOR'S NOTE

Dear Reader,

Thank you for reading book 2 in the Ava James FBI Mystery series. I hope you come to love and support our young agent Ava James like you have loved and supported Emma Griffin.

If you can please leave me a review for this book, I would appreciate that enormously. Your reviews allow me to get the validation I need to keep going as an indie author. Just a moment of your time is all that is needed to ensure Ava James' series can continue.
Ava and the team are counting on you!

Yours,
A.J. Rivers

P.S. If for some reason you didn't like this book or found typos or other errors, please let me know personally. I do my best to read and respond to every email at mailto:aj@riversthrillers.com

ALSO BY
A.J. RIVERS

* Also available in audio

Made in United States
North Haven, CT
16 February 2023

32680794R00167